WINTER HARVEST

WINTER HARVEST

CORALIE HUGHES JENSEN

FIVE STAR
A part of Gale, Cengage Learning

GALE
CENGAGE Learning

Detroit • New York • San Francisco • New Haven, Conn • Waterville, Maine • London

GALE
CENGAGE Learning·

LIBRARY OF CONGRESS CATALOGING-IN-PUBLICATION DATA

Jensen, Coralie Hughes.
  Winter harvest / Coralie Hughes Jensen. — 1st ed.
    p. cm.
  ISBN-13: 978-1-59414-889-7
  ISBN-10: 1-59414-889-9
  1. Shakers—Fiction. 2. British—Massachusetts—Fiction. 3. Massachusetts—History—1775–1865—Fiction. I. Title.
PS3610.E5626W56 2010
813'.6—dc22   2010009033

First Edition. First Printing: July 2010.
Published in 2010 in conjunction with Tekno Books.

Printed in the United States of America
1 2 3 4 5 6 7 14 13 12 11 10

For Bruce, my loving husband, and best friend, and Hannah, my dog.

ACKNOWLEDGMENTS

My first exposure to the Shaker way of life came when I first moved to New England and visited the Canterbury Shaker Village in Canterbury, New Hampshire. I would like to thank the tour guides who took the time to answer my often difficult questions.

My appreciation to Hancock Shaker Village Inc., an educational organization that has faithfully kept its Shaker history museum and preserved its buildings and grounds in a state that allows one to experience Shaker ingenuity and simplicity. I would also like to thank the tour guides who patiently answered all my questions about living in a commune nearly two centuries ago, and the gift store, where I bought books on the history of the Shakers. I studied each book closely, in order to better understand the intentions of the ministry and the ambience of their simple life.

Thank you, Old Sturbridge Village in Sturbridge, Massachusetts for allowing me to immerse myself in the country life of New England up to 1840. From this outdoor museum, I was able to glimpse many of the little details I used in *Winter Harvest*.

I would like to thank Alison Gaede, my sister, who said this book was her favorite of all that I have written, and of course, my husband, who eagerly accompanied me on my trips to serve as my memory both by listening and by taking photographs.

1. LUCY

"It was a moonless night. The darkness was so heavy it tumbled down over the grassy field. The pond, a black syrupy molasses, swallowed the speckled starlight. Mary usually liked her walks, the clatter of late autumn keeping her company—the persistent whirr of crickets, the crackle of dried leaves underfoot, and the swoosh of wind through the straggly branches. But this night was hushed, the cloak of shadows muffling all sounds. Mary didn't even hear the approach. She felt it, the ground shuddering restlessly, like a spasm that sends concentric ripples through water—a signal that launched dread in the pit of Mary's stomach," Elizabeth whispered, her face contorted by the flicker of flames from the hearth.

We young girls sat cross-legged in front of her. Our mouths agape, we wrenched our skirts and twisted our fingers. Charity closed her eyes in an effort to stop the flow of words from reaching her brain. Molly's mouth gaped so wide, you would have thought it would be stuck open forever. But I did not move. I could not move. My ankles and wrists were frozen in place. A scream hovered just below my vocal chords, thrusting upward, but my throat was constricted and unable to release any sound at all. My chest throbbed in anticipation as I waited for the climax.

"Mary could feel the hot breath on her neck before she heard him," Elizabeth continued. "She smelled it too—burnt flesh and dung. Her skin prickled, but not enough to make her move, to step away, or, God forbid, to run. And when he touched her, she closed her eyes, trying not to look at his tortured visage, knowing who he was by the stories that preceded him. He caressed her arm, ripping her sleeve and leaving a track of blood to her elbow, his long nails having become claws so he could survive in the forest. Then he grabbed her waist and pulled her to face him."

The screams began to escape from the mouths of Elizabeth's young audience who had already scattered like leaves in the wind, hiding behind chairs or tables but unable to escape because Elizabeth had locked the doors. I still sat cross-legged before her, trying to act stoic but unable to move or even close my eyes to the ugly scene I knew Elizabeth was about to reveal.

"Mary pushed him away. She poked at his eyes, but the skin of his eyelids came loose in her hands. He clung to her, trying to get her to kiss him, but when she twisted to pull back, his grip slipped, his talon-like nails running along the front of her torso. Blood and insides oozed from her wound. He grasped at her neck to turn her toward him once again, but she wrenched away—too hard, slitting her throat on his claws. As her knees buckled from loss of blood, she slid from his arms, feeling the repulsive hirsute skin against hers. Suddenly, he *howled*, piercing her eardrums. He thrust the swooning body above his head in triumph before flinging Mary into the pond, the thud producing numerous wavelets along the shore."

"Did they find her?" Molly asked.

"Not at first. She'd lost too much blood and couldn't swim. Finally the pond must have released her, I guess, because her grave's in the forest."

"Where?" asked Charity.

"In that small cemetery at the end of the path. Haven't you seen the assemblage of headstones there?"

"No," we all said in unison.

10

"I'll have to show you. We can take a walk there while the weather's still good. The Community's built on what were once three different farms. The one out in back of the pond here belonged to the Fieldings. Mary Fielding was the daughter. The headstones are for that family."

"How old was she?"

"She was sixteen or seventeen, I think—and a devout follower of our mother, Ann Lee, as were her parents. Mother Ann was scouting the area, looking for recruits for her church. John and Mariah Fielding would house Mother Ann when she traveled from New York, and she'd perform meetings right there in the farmhouse."

"What happened to them?"

"Before our church, the United Society of Believers, was established here, the locals persecuted families who helped Mother Ann. First, the hairy man murdered Mary. A few years later, the authorities dragged Mr. and Mrs. Fielding to the city jail to try them for treason. This was a new country, and people were still fearful British spies hung around, trying to bring down our fledgling government. Mother Ann was British, so people must have thought the Fieldings were her agents. Anyway, they never went to trial. The jail burned down with them still in it. Someone claimed the hairy man did it. With them dead too, no one cared enough to seek revenge for Mary's death. In their will, the Fieldings bequeathed the farm to Mother Ann, but I don't think they really left," Elizabeth said, dropping her voice. "Someone's out there protecting those headstones. Someone we can't see in the dark."

"Did they catch him?" I asked, my voice squeaking like a trapped mouse.

"No. They looked for him for years and years and even tried to ambush him. Unfortunately, he always escaped capture."

"But he'd be dead by now, Lizzy," said Charity. "He'd be too old."

"You'd think so," said Elizabeth, her face still animated. "But some of us have seen him walking around on late autumn evenings—like tonight."

"No you haven't," said Molly, sitting down in front of the fire again.

"Well, maybe not him but his footprints. Because they're so long, his toenails curl over, leaving a distinctive human print. And we can still hear his anguished howl."

"Nuh-uh. That's a fox or maybe a wolf."

"Think what you like, Sister Molly, but Sister Peg believes she saw him when she took leftovers out to feed the chickens and cats after dinner one evening. She said he was along the tree line, skulking like a raccoon, only this one was a man bent over like a hunchback."

Molly and Charity hugged each other. "Who was he?" they asked.

"Some say he was once Mariah's lover before she married John Fielding. She'd sneak out at night to meet her beau in the thick wood. They wanted to marry, but her father wouldn't allow it. She'd go against him and God's laws, however, and continue to meet him in the forest. Evidently, her father suspected or somehow found out because he hung around, hoping to see Edgar—that was her lover's name, Edgar—in the forest one night. When Edgar waited for his lover to come to him, Mariah's father sneaked up from behind and poured boiling oil over him. It melted his head, chunks of hair and skin dripping down his neck and arms. He was so deformed, he ran into the forest to hide himself and learned how to survive like an animal. When Mariah found out, she was irate with her father. But of course, he was her father so she had to marry the man he chose, even though the idea of sleeping with her new husband was repulsive to her. She still took walks in the forest but always hoped she wouldn't see Edgar because she knew he'd be deformed and felt so guilty."

"Did she love him?" asked Charity.

"Probably not. Would you love a man who looked that bad? I'm positive I would've thrown up. Anyway, after they recovered Mary's body from the pond, they buried her there in the forest so her gravesite would haunt him."

"Will you take us there tonight?" Molly asked.

"Good Lord, no. Eldress Evelyn wouldn't let us out at night."

"She lets us go out to the shed."

"That's only if you're sick. Otherwise you use the pots and certainly don't go to the forest. All sorts of men wander through these woods. Edgar isn't the only one yearning to sink his blade into a pretty young virgin!"

"Is that the story?" Charity asked. "I can't wait to see the headstones."

"Yes," said Elizabeth. "Did you like it?"

"Yes," the other girls agreed.

"Are you all right, Sister Lucy?" Elizabeth asked.

I pulled myself up. "Yes," I said, still feeling a bit shaky.

"Off to bed now. I'll have to come up with another story for next week."

"So you made it all up?" I asked her.

"Not at all. This one's true. Ask Brother Seth to show you the tracks he found out near Otter Creek."

My father, Marcus Hammond, had a commanding voice. My brothers and sisters and I could not help but listen. Even if we covered our ears, we could still hear him. One early spring evening after dinner in 1838, he gathered all five of us around the table, thrust his hands into his pockets, and announced, "We aren't makin' it here, kids. I talked to Mr. Broderick at the bank, and he said he has no more money to lend us. They're takin' the farm away. I guess you can't fight nature when she's turned her back." I watched Papa's eyes focus on me. "Your mother and I have a plan, though. We've heard there's more land openin' up out west. We have enough cash and supplies for some of us to make it there but not for everyone."

He stopped to listen to our gasps. My little brother Paul started to cry, and I put my arms around him.

"That doesn't mean we're leavin' any of you here permanent. We just have to get to western Ohio. Then we'll start sendin' for you again."

"Where do we have to go?" Willie asked. William was the eldest, nearly sixteen and big, with unruly hair, red as a cock's comb.

"There's a community near here that takes in children and educates them. All you have to do is learn their religion, and they'll take you in. You all need religion. We talked to them already, and they want to meet you, Lucy. The other girls are too old, and we need the boys to help set up the farm on the other end."

The air rushed out of my lungs. "Who are they?"

"They're called some long name I can't remember, but they have a beautiful clean place. Broderick calls them Shakin' Quakers, because they're peaceful like Quakers."

"Why are they shaking?" I asked.

"It has somethin' to do with the way they pray. They sort of dance when they worship. That sounds like fun, doesn't it, Punkin? It'll be like goin' to a ball every Sunday."

I gazed at the others and saw surprise unfurling across their faces.

"What about the rest of us?" Constance, my eldest sister, asked.

"We've got to check out some more places for you and Martha," he said. "And there's still the possibility little Paul will have to be left somewhere, requirin' us to collect him later."

Lydia, our mother, had not said a word. In fact, she was not even in the room. But, of course, Mama had little say once my father got it in his mind to abandon the farm and move west.

I recall my first day at Hancock because I could not believe no one had mentioned it was only a few weeks before my eighth birthday. I also remember hugging my brothers and sisters in the wagon because my parents would not let them go in.

"Are you scared?" Martha asked.

I squeezed past her knees to climb down. "No," I said, not sure how to answer. "You and Mama and Papa are coming back for me as soon as you're all settled. Mama said so."

Tears rolled down Constance's cheeks, but she turned away before I could hug her. I patted her shoulder.

"Let's move," said Papa. "The sooner we go, the sooner all will be settled."

Mama shot Papa an angry look. I took her hand, and she slowly led me up the walk. Leaving me at the door, she kissed my cheek, and burying my head in her collar, I threw my arms around her neck.

She knelt down and pulled me away. "The time will go fast, Lucy. I promise."

Removing the scarf that hung from her neck, Mama wrapped it around mine. Then she left. I hardly remember her face—mostly her back as she walked away without glancing around, and her smell, of course, though I suspect the scent of the scarf has changed over the years of her absence.

"Hancock Village is like a small town," Eldress Evelyn said, leading me into the members' dwelling to meet another eldress, Abigail. "This building's one house. There are two more like it near here. But the town has more than just dwellings. It also has businesses. Most of the buildings around here are businesses—places where we work."

I stood beside her, afraid to let go of her hand.

"You'll go to school in another month or so," she said. "Girls attend school during the summer months and work after classes. Because most of the heavy work is done in the summer, boys go to school in the winter."

I resisted the urge to insert my thumb into my mouth. My mother had warned me on numerous occasions I was too old to do it, but it made me feel so much better. "I go to school in New Lebanon next year. There'll be mostly boys in our class."

The eldress turned to face me. "Boys and girls don't socialize here. We're all equal in the eyes of our Lord, but we're separate. Sins of the flesh interfere with our work and make women inferior to men."

Having no idea what she was talking about, I stared at her.

"We're here on earth to await the second appearing of the Savior. He's coming soon and will be pleased by what we've accomplished," Evelyn continued. "It doesn't look like Eldress Abigail's here. I'll take you next door to the retired senior members' dwelling and show you the school, which is nearby. I'll get Sister Elizabeth to help you unpack your things. If you have more questions and can't get any answers, you may come to my office. You're to address me as Sister, not Eldress Evelyn. We're all working for God, and I'm no different from anyone else here."

I remember glancing over my shoulder several times to make note of our path. I needed to know how to get back to the wagon when my parents returned to retrieve me.

My first impressions of my new home were benign—at least they seemed that way. As I said, I have few memories of anything that first day. The buildings were painted and lined up in somewhat of a geometric pattern. The place was clean. We walked through the five-story brick dwelling to another a few yards away. This one was an imposing structure similar to the brick dwelling but with wood siding and only three floors. The eldress led me through a door at one end from which a long, wide passage traveled the length of the building.

"That across the street is the schoolhouse. Can you read? Most of the girls your age are still struggling with that, so if not, you'll be able to catch up quickly," she said, still holding my hand. "Always enter through the left-hand door and walk on this side, Sister Lucy. You'll have no need to cross over to the right side of this passage until you're older and have reason to be over there."

About halfway, we turned left into another passage that crossed in front of us.

"My office is this one near the girls' entrance. Next to my office is my sleeping quarters and across the hall is a small meeting room. If you have to wait for me, you sit in there. You rarely need to cross over to the other end of this hallway where Brother Thomas lives. Just as the boys must not come over here, you must never ever use the door at that end. Follow me," she said, slipping past.

I ran to catch up and grab her hand.

"Sisters your age live on the second floor," she continued. "At the end of this hall is the dining room, and on the right is the stairway the women use. When we came in through the meeting room door, there was also a staircase for the men. Did you see it?"

My head whirled. I was not used to so many rules and certainly did not understand why the girls had to use different doors and stairs than the boys. At the top of the stairway, we stopped at the first room that held five or six beds, a few sets of drawers, and along each wall, a string of pegs about chest high.

"Sister Elizabeth here will take over. She's your elder sister and holds the key to your contentment in the Community."

I must have stared blankly at the eldress, but the woman quickly turned away and left. I did not know if I was supposed to follow her.

"Your name?" Elizabeth asked curtly.

"Lucy Hammond." My knees shook.

"How old are you, Sister Lucy?"

"I turn eight next week." I could not wait and hoped Elizabeth would suggest we have a party.

"Your bed's over here by the window between Sister Molly and Sister Charity. They're a bit older but will be moved to the next room if more girls your age arrive. Leave your things on the bed and follow me," she said, twisting her hair between her fingers.

Her hands were too high for me to grasp. Trying to keep up with her fast gait, I followed. We traipsed down the stairs and stopped in front of the door at the end of the hall.

"This is the dining room. The girls eat at these tables on the right, and though there are no men eating with us, the men eat on the left. We're the first sitting. The senior members dine at the second," she said before quickly taking off down the next flight. "In here is the kitchen. We're lucky to have our own kitchen and dining room. Members of all the other families eat in the brick dwelling. Sister Peg, this is Sister Lucy. Sister Peg is in charge of our kitchen. You must listen to Sister Peg carefully because you'll spend a lot of time here."

"What's this?" I asked, noting more doors.

"This is the pantry. There's an entrance to another room from here inside the kitchen. That room's off limits to you."

"What is it?"

"Don't be nosy, Sister Lucy. That can get you into trouble. The space in that room is for goods going out to people all over the area. In the brick dwelling there's an assembly room. Businessmen sometimes gather there to do business with the elders. Most of the time, though, the world's people go directly to the trustees' house. The door to the outside from that room is over there up some steps next to the men's entrance, something you wouldn't notice because you aren't allowed over there. We receive goods from the world's people and sell them what we produce. Some of the boxes are stored in that room. I'm not allowed in there either, nor is our eldress. Outside business is done by the deacons and trustees and sometimes by office sisters."

I nodded, still unsatisfied.

"We usually start new children in the kitchen, so you'll stash your things and report down here to Sister Peg in about an hour. I'll introduce you at a meeting after dinner," Elizabeth said, starting up the stairs again. "Hurry up. Don't just stand there. You aren't my only charge."

I would learn that Elizabeth, though tall, was only twelve. She was the daughter of one of the senior elders, her whole family requesting to join the commune too. Having never committed to the Believers by signing the covenant to become members, her mother and two older brothers returned to the outside world months later. This was common. Many seemed to be dissatisfied with the so-called power-sharing by the sexes. Elizabeth had been here since she was three and was well versed in the rules set down by the elder ministers. While she was often dismissive, she was also fair, especially when one of us tattled about those who did not keep to the cherished rules.

The first few months were excruciating, because I craved the caress of my mother or one of my older sisters and wanted so badly for Elizabeth to offer me a sign of affection. I was not one of Elizabeth's favorites, however. I was impulsive and on occasion bent the rules when I could not help myself. Though her tongue was as sharp as a snake's tooth, to her credit, Elizabeth never swatted or punished me unduly.

Like her, I was plain. My brown hair was thin and stringy and my features unremarkable. Unlike her, no one had ever called me homely so I never suspected my appearance might get in my way. For years, Elizabeth did not see me as a competitor to her rise in the ranks and treated me with little deference. That said, I was fiercely independent and curious to a fault, both traits eventually destroying any hope of a relationship with her before it ever got off the ground.

It was Evelyn, the eldress of our dwelling, who taught me about my new family soon after I arrived. She sat me down in her small office and explained that our Community had been founded by a woman, Mother Ann Lee.

"Mother Ann arrived on our shores from England in 1774, and because it was so close to our war against British control, many people persecuted her," she said. "Mother Ann had begun winning over Americans in New York and then courageously traveled from town to town, converting others to her new religion. Many didn't like her. They threw stones and jailed her because they thought she was a heretic."

"What's a heretic?" I asked.

"They said she was sinning because she wasn't following their church laws. Nonetheless, she converted enough people to start a new church. We became the United Society of Believers. Early worshippers formed families, carving out the forests and transforming the land into big farms. It was difficult at first, but because they worked hard, look what we have today."

"Where's she now?"

"She's in heaven with the Heavenly Father and Holy Mother Wisdom."

"I thought this was heaven."

"No, Sister, this is Zion, heaven on earth. We're preparing the world for the second coming of the Savior."

"Is he coming here? When?"

"Yes. Because we've created a beautiful place for him, I'm sure he'll come here," Evelyn said dreamily. "But we must be ready—work hard to make our garden worthy."

"Where are the others?"

"The early followers are in heaven too."

"No, the ones who threw stones at her."

"I don't know," she said. "But that's not the point."

"Are they still around?"

"No. While some people object to our success, most of the world's people like us," she said, dismissively. "What's more important is that you keep your mind on heaven. You should do the jobs assigned to you and follow the rules."

That sounded ominous—the word echoed in my head. If I had a weakness, it was having to keep track of rules.

"And the Heavenly Father calls for us to work as one, that we are one owner of our farm, yet no one owns the property for it belongs to the Heavenly Father," Robert, our ministry elder, said, his voice echoing through the rafters of the meetinghouse that Sunday. "Our hard work and tenacity will be rewarded both here on earth and in heaven. We won't listen to those outside our Community who call us to follow their laws, their government. For the Heavenly Father's power supersedes all other governments, especially those of the lower forms, destitute without the blessing of the Heavenly Father—those who espouse marriage and individual possession of property, who fall into wars and debauchery because they lack conviction. The act of procreation makes us unequal. The rights of one spouse replace those of the other. When our minds and hearts wander from the Heavenly Father's purpose for us, we all become slaves to the act instead of proponents of his goals for us here on earth."

Hoping he was finished, I squirmed on the hard, backless bench. After his sermon, we all got up and danced. I liked that part. The others acted silly then. They stomped and pranced and shouted out their praises to the Heavenly Father. They did not act like adults at all. Even Evelyn became agitated, shaking and twitching. And I twirled until I was dizzy, bumping into the others.

Feeling invigorated by the dancing, we made our way back to the dwelling. A late breakfast of fresh eggs, bread, and preserves was to be served in the dining room an hour after the service.

"What's debauchery?" I asked Molly as we walked along the path.

"It's when people are wicked, Sister Lucy."

"What do people do to be wicked?"

"Things like flirting with boys," said Charity. "But you can forgive the world's people because they don't know it's a sin to do that."

"Do what?"

"Did you like dancing at meeting, Sister Lucy?" Charity asked, walking on ahead.

I ran to catch up. "I'm getting better."

"You shouldn't take Elder Robert seriously, Sister," Molly said. "He always talks that way about the outsiders. I guess he wants to warn us we're lucky to live here where it's safe."

Charity giggled. "Do you think about Brother Seth when you're dancing, Sister Lucy? I watched him on the other side of the room and he acted funny, like he thought you were watching him."

"Seth doesn't act funny," I said.

"You'd better not go anywhere alone with Brother Seth, Sister Lucy," Charity continued. "Sister Molly and I can stay with you so you two can keep your thoughts pure."

"Gee, Sister Charity, she's only nine," Molly whispered. "I don't think she knows what an impure thought is. Do you, Sister Lucy?"

"Well, Brother Seth does. He's going on thirteen," Charity said.

Molly smiled. "I know. What a waste for you to pair him up with little Lucy. He's quite handsome."

I did not understand. "What are you two going on about? I hate him because he always gets spots on his clothes and loses buttons. Then I end up having to restore them. I hate to sew on buttons. I hate to sew. I don't know why I always have to do his mending."

"They fall off because you can't sew," Molly said, laughing. "They always give new indentures young people's clothes to sew. When you get really good, they'll give you those belonging to senior members."

"How old do you have to be for that?"

"I'm already sewing the good stuff, and I'm only twelve," Charity said.

When we returned to our room to wash up, I sat down on my bed and reached under my pillow. Grabbing my mother's wool scarf and kneading the material between my fingers, I put my face down close and inhaled what I remembered of my mother's scent.

Those first few years were quiet. I watched my peers and followed what they did. I attended school and was good at my lessons. And needless to say, I did not flirt with boys. In spite of the dependable and therefore comforting cycle of seasons, my life would change forever one November when a young orphan came to stay at our dwelling. She would bring the best and worst of the world among us, and I would slowly begin to realize just how stifling the rules set down by my new family had become.

2. SARAH

With the rhythm of the changing seasons, my first years at Hancock passed fairly smoothly. I had friends who were older than I was and some who were younger, but I had no friends my own age. There were rules, and they were made quite clear to me. I was to do what I was told, and more importantly, I was supposed to stay away from the boys. The last part was easy. I was not interested in boys, and they were not interested in me. I spent my days in the women's shop when I was not in school. Switching jobs monthly, I mended clothes, did laundry, ironed, churned butter, milked the cows, and worked around the kitchen. But I also learned to weave cloth, harvest the hay, and pack seeds. These were all things women were encouraged to do.

But times were difficult for the Shaker Community. In the last century, what the elders first mandated as unalterable Church laws had to be modified to meet with an anemic national economy, ebbing religious zeal, and resistance by church members. Of course, as more industry moved into the area, the economy would rebound. But new wealth and materialism in the outside world would create even more problems within.

When I entered the Community in the late 1830s, young boys were not housed in the same dwelling as the girls but rather with another family a few miles north of Hancock. Unfortunately, in the early 1840s, that dwelling burned in a fire that would leave the third floor where the boys lived unusable. The elders moved them into our dwelling, planning to create space for the boys by shifting some of the retired members down from the third floor.

The remaining older members complained vehemently.

"Boys, no matter how well behaved, are boys, and the noise will make our quiet lives miserable," grumbled Zachary, a former ministry elder who was afraid the young boys would knock him off his feet when he staggered too slowly through the hallway.

Percival Walter said, "I've earned the quiet. I go to bed right after dinner. Don't tell me those youngsters won't make any noise."

Evelyn decided she had to bend one of the rules, so the boys moved into the rooms directly across from ours. Things were not supposed to be different for us. I mean, the rules for us to stay apart were the same. Now, however, they allowed us to attend organized and supervised weekly meetings with the boys, and Anson, the equivalent of Elizabeth, created children's stories and games we could play during our Friday night meetings.

There were other changes. Because our goods were noted for their quality, more businessmen came to buy them from the Community. But our customers' demands for extravagance also increased. Soon they wanted hats and gowns made with silk and furs and the latest species of plants in order to procure the finest seeds. Molly once told me she loved trying on the gowns. I saw her doing it once when no one else was in the shop.

"Don't you love this one on me, Sister Lucy? The material we wear is rough. This is soft, see? I'd let you touch it, but you might snag it and get us into trouble." She twirled. "Maybe a man will come here some day and take me away. He'll be able to afford the dresses and hats, lots of hats, because he lives in the world."

When our brethren saw what those in the outside world possessed, they apostatized, moving back into the secular society so they could experience the wealth like everyone else. Of course, the Community would have to have a revival so people would again think about God instead of material goods. A spiritual renewal happened just as I arrived in the late '30s. The result, however, would be temporary. Somehow, we always seemed to be short of young men.

When the crops grown in the outside world went bad or farms failed, more children arrived to fill the ranks. People like my parents could not afford to keep their young. The more children we squeezed into the rooms, the fewer members we had to train them, watch over them, or stimulate them about our religion. Business, however, was the ministry's means of survival. No matter how difficult it became to keep our minds on heaven, it was business that kept us from giving up.

Needless to say, my life was hectic, and keeping busy dulled the pain of loneliness. Even though I shared my room with five other children aged six through thirteen, I always felt isolated. But as my thirteenth birthday approached, my being alone would change too.

The night was cold. It had been frosty and damp for nearly a month. Stripping the remaining leaves from the branches, sharp winds blew in from the east. Aqueducts and fences were built or repaired in November, and the men and boys complained bitterly about their hands and feet. In the kitchen, Peg asked the girls to add more butter and cream to the potatoes and sauces to "get the fat on 'em." In her meeting room, Evelyn warmed her hands on the dying embers of the fireplace as wind and sand drummed against the windowpane. It was just after six, but it had already been dark for over an hour.

"So she brings property with her?" Evelyn asked the man

standing on the other side of a long table.

"Yes, ma'am. There's a list of goods here that would go with her in five years when she turned eighteen. Bishop's will states she's to live with the Shakers if she's underage and has no one else to take her. If necessary, her inheritance is to be given to you as payment for raising her."

He handed the list to our family elder, Thomas, who stood in the shadows in the far corner. The uncertain fire and two chamber candles on the table affording the only light, the room was dim.

I stood hesitantly in the doorway. Should I leave and come back or just wait for the eldress to be free? When I saw the room was busy, I did not back away but stared at the beautiful girl sitting at the table. The flickering flames streaked her face, and the brim of her velvet bonnet hid her eyes. But I still stood there, mesmerized.

"Sister Lucy, this is Sarah Bishop," Evelyn said. "Please stay close by. I'll need you to help her get settled."

Sarah removed her cap, letting her golden curls fall over her shoulders. Her eyes were a bright blue, like a robin's eggs, and the only flaws were shadows cast by the deep dimples impressed on either side of her wide smile.

Carrying in a bundle of logs for the fire, Seth cleared his throat. "Please move to one side, Sister. I need to tend to the fire."

He saw the vision sitting there and watched her as he dropped the logs on the hearth, one of them landing on his foot. He did not cry out, though I could see tears fill his eyes. He slowly piled logs onto the grate and poked at the fire until the flames roared. When he left, he did not look back. Had he done so, he would have seen her wink at him, her golden lashes waving as if in slow motion.

"And the items on this list are in your possession?"

"Yes, ma'am," said the lawyer, tightening his fingers around the brim of his top hat. "The items are all out in the cart, except for the farm itself and the equipment Miss Bishop sold. There's cash here to represent those items."

"Brother Thomas, please find Brother Jeremiah and tell him to pull the cart out of the storm for Mr. uh—"

"Mr. Richmond."

"Would you like some hot tea or coffee before you go, Mr. Richmond? This isn't a good night to be out."

"Thank you, ma'am."

"Sister Lucy, please ask Sister Peg to brew some tea and bring it up here."

"I'm supposed to work in the kitchen tonight," I said.

"Tell her I said you could take the evening off. After you talk to Sister Peg, you may take Sarah up to your room and get Sister Elizabeth to assign her a bed."

Sarah stood up, rustling the numerous petticoats supporting a green velvet dress. The gown was beautiful. I could not help but stare at it.

"And maybe Sister Elizabeth can find her a dress to wear. She won't be able to work in that."

I took Sarah's warm hand and led her down the stairs to the kitchen. "Peg, this is Sarah Bishop," I said, unable to take my eyes off my new friend. "We work down here much of the time, Sarah. Don't worry, I'll show you how."

"I can show you better teachers," Peg said.

"Evelyn also asked if you could serve the man in the waiting room some tea and biscuits," I said to Peg. "She says I'll have to work upstairs this evening. I hope that isn't too much of an inconvenience."

"Hmmph," the cook said, quickly returning to her work.

I took Sarah back up the stairs. "Don't worry. She's really very nice." I would not let go of my new friend's hand. "How old are you?"

"Thirteen," she said. "I just turned thirteen last month."

"Oh. I don't know if Elizabeth will let you stay in our room. I'll be thirteen in a couple of months, but I'm still in the baby room. I like your dress."

"It's rather old, I'm afraid—nothing special."

"It's beautiful. Do all your friends dress that way?"

"Yes. Velvet's fashionable, but this one's rather high cut. The new gowns out of Paris plunge right here."

"Oh, my," I said. "I'm afraid that would bother Edith. She's in charge of sewing and has lived here forever. Her taste in gowns is somewhat conservative."

Sarah slid over to the door across the hall. "What's this?"

"Oh, Sarah!" I said. "You can't go over there. That's the boys' room, and we aren't allowed to walk on the boys' side of the hallway."

"That's silly."

"No. It's the rule. The Community promotes equality between the sexes. But that equality requires that women not become subservient to men by letting men use them."

"Use them? What do you mean?"

"Sins of the flesh," I whispered, scanning the hallway to make sure no one was listening.

"That's even sillier. Men do use women when two people fall in love. But both sexes enjoy acts of intimacy."

"Well, I hear such acts as holding hands and kissing sets them off. The boys just can't stop."

"They can stop just as easily as you can."

"And it's a sin."

"Really? They think it's a sin?"

"Yes. You'd be in big trouble if you flirted with the boys here. And you'd get them into even bigger trouble."

"Is there someone out here in the hall?" Elizabeth asked,

coming to the doorway.

"Yes," I said, spinning around so fast my shoe scraped the floor. "Elizabeth, this is Sarah Bishop. She's thirteen and needs a room assignment and a dress."

Elizabeth bit her lip. There was one bed free in each room. She would have to determine which one the new child should occupy. "Do you mind, Sister Lucy, if we move Sister Louise in with the older girls? She's fourteen. Then Sister Sarah can have the bed next to yours Sister Louise has occupied for six months."

"That's great, Sarah. You'll be by the window right next to me. Isn't that wonderful?"

Sarah smiled. Elizabeth left a simple frock on the bed, and Sarah began to undress. I helped her take down all her petticoats.

"This is too big," Sarah whispered after she had slipped the new one over her head. "Not to mention it's downright ugly."

"Mine is too. They're supposed to be loose so we can be comfortable working in them."

"And take them off real fast?" Sarah asked.

I smiled, not really understanding what she meant. "Our Sunday dresses are prettier. You have to wear this kerchief around your neck so you don't spill on your dress."

"And where does that boy who delivered the wood live?"

"Seth? He's sixteen, so he lives in the room down the hall with the older boys. The ones across the hall are our age or younger. Are you hungry? Maybe we should get down to dinner before it's too late. I can show you where to sit, and after dinner, I can introduce you to our roommates."

"What? Not at dinner?"

"Another rule. We don't talk during the meal. Someone will be appointed to read prayers to us while we eat."

"So many rules. Don't they trust us?"

★ ★ ★ ★ ★

The next day, Evelyn assigned Sarah to the sewing room in the morning and then the women's shop, where Sarah would help set up a new fan loom Brother Richard had designed to make hats. Disappointed Sarah's work times did not correspond with mine, I went about my own duties, looking forward to sharing moments with my new friend at meals. I could not wait until school started in the spring, when we would finally be together all day.

"Lucy, this doesn't look right. Will you please check it?" Georgia asked. "I wish you'd keep your mind on the mending. What are you dreaming about when you get that lost look of yours?"

"I think of home—of our garden. The season's only a few months away. I wonder what I want to plant."

"You know we have a small vegetable garden beside the kitchen. I think Brother Jeremiah furrowed it after the growing season, but maybe you'd rather be doing that job."

"I asked last year, and they told me it was men's work."

"Try again. Brother Jeremiah wants to spend more time in the carriage house to be with the horses. I don't know anyone else who has the time or the inclination. It'd be a shame if we let that go to seed just because there are no men to do it. Ask Sister Peg this time. I know she has an interest in it and might approach the elders herself if you have a plan."

"I watched how Brother Jeremiah built up the soil last year and disagree with what he uses. Did you notice how puny the carrots were?"

"So you've worked with vegetable gardens before."

"Yes. My mother kept a vegetable garden. We planted flowers in between the rows, and the bugs seemed to like the flowers better."

"Brother Allen started a compost pile about ten or fifteen

years ago," the older woman continued, tying a knot and chomping down on the excess thread. "When he took ill, no one kept it up, but I know where it is. I can show you after we finish here. He believed compost would really help our crops."

"What about my sewing? I thought you'd want to make sure I could sew as well as you and Elizabeth."

"We can't all sew. If everyone sewed perfectly, there'd be no one to sew for anymore. We'd have all these gowns with no one to wear them or sell them to. Anyway, I don't think you really want to sew, do you?"

"I'd like to get this hole mended so I can move on to the buttons that have fallen off."

"What jobs do you have in December?"

"I have kitchen and laundry, and Brother Deke said he'd assign me to churn butter because I scare the hens when I collect eggs. But not all of us can collect eggs, can we, Sister? If we did, there'd be nobody left to do the other jobs."

"That's correct, Sister Lucy. Now you have it," Georgia said, continuing to examine my work.

Cups and dishes rattled loudly as one of the girls set the dinner plates on the counter. Lydia pushed a stack alongside a pile of flatware on the dumbwaiter shelf and closed the door. Then she ran upstairs and, tugging on a rope in the dining room cupboard, pulled them up. When she had removed the dishes and flatware from the lift, Lydia sent the shelf back down to the kitchen where I pushed more stacks onto it and signaled it was full.

While Sarah dumped a load of chopped onions into a large stockpot, I returned to the table, selected another loaf of bread, and began slicing.

Peg walked by the table and winced. "I can't stand to watch you do that, Sister Lucy. I'm afraid you'll cut your finger. You look so awkward."

"I already asked Sarah to dice the onions and carrots because those are slippery. I can't think of anything else you'd consider safe."

"Let me see. Last month you dropped the shelf and broke the dishes when I had you set the tables. Before that, you left the lid off the flour pot, and we found a dead mouse in it."

"Would you like me to fill the pitchers with juice?"

"Heavens no. Remember the time you served the men wine instead of juice? The brethren still ask for you to fill the pitchers when they're empty."

"There has to be something I can do."

"You're as flighty as down in a pillow fight, Sister Lucy."

"Why not stir the beans, Lucy?" Sarah offered. "I can cut that bread."

"I'm fine, Sarah. I can do this as long as I concentrate."

"We have fresh apple pie for dessert, girls," Peg said. "If you could watch the oven, I'll go upstairs and help Sister Lydia set the tables."

Seth pushed the outer door open and dropped a pile of wood into the box. Then he hoisted a few of the smaller logs onto his shoulder and carried them in. Sarah moved to one side so he could open the stove door just beside her knees.

"Do you have it?" she whispered to him as he forced logs through the grated doors.

He reached into a pocket and pulled out a little book. "Check it before I leave," Seth whispered.

"This is the right one," Sarah said after opening it up. "Thanks. I owe you."

I watched Sarah stuff it into her apron pocket. "What's that?" I asked her.

Seth closed the door to the fire and stood up. He glanced at me as he brushed himself off and, without a word, walked back out of the door.

"Well?" I asked again.

Sarah motioned for me stand beside her and stir the bean pot. "It's a diary. It was among the items in the wagon the lawyers brought when I came. Brother Seth was kind enough to find it among my family's possessions before everything was sold."

"I didn't know they stored your things somewhere," I said. "Why wouldn't they sell them?"

"Because when I came to the Community, my inheritance was turned over to them," Sarah said. "But there were a few things I wanted to keep."

"Is that permitted?"

"I'm sure they don't need everything. Who'd want to buy a used diary?"

"What else did you have Seth get for you?"

"A cloth doll and a few things that belonged to my mother," she said. "They would've been mine, after all."

"Don't get Seth involved, Sarah. He's very well-respected in the Community, and stealing is a serious offense."

"The way you sound, you must like him. Is that what this is about?"

My face felt hot. "No. This is about what we believe here."

"Don't worry," Sarah said, smiling. "I won't tell him. But one of these nights, I'm going to sneak out of here and bury the rest of my inheritance. I'm going to need it when I become an adult."

"The ground's frozen, so that won't be easy."

"I'm sure the wagon will still be there in the spring. It's crammed into a space in the carriage house, making it pretty difficult to get out."

That was the first time I heard Sarah say it—that she did not plan to stay at Hancock after she turned eighteen. I had not thought about it before that. I always figured we would both stay and continue to work in the Community. From that minute on, I began to listen to what the others said about the world and its people and wondered if what they said was true. Were the outsiders unhappy? Is that why they had persecuted Mother Ann? Sarah certainly did not seem unhappy. Were outsiders completely ignorant about the Savior's plan to come again? If Mother Ann indeed had a vision and knew exactly what made heaven on earth, why had so few people listened?

I did not sense my beliefs were changing quickly. Defending my family was still much easier than understanding how things worked on the outside. While I probably should have been more critical of Sarah's actions, I could not see her as anything other than someone who was misguided. And as her acts became increasingly defiant and unbeliever-like, I could see our elders draw the string tighter, almost creating more rules in order to hold us under their thumbs. But, of course, there was a good reason for the elders to bar the doors, as more and more followers left. At the same time, I believed Sarah's penchant for bending and even breaking rules seemed destined to get her in a whole world of trouble. As much as I feared her future at Hancock, my efforts to protect her from her own actions would probably fail to stave off the trouble everyone around us predicted.

3. The Garden

Like my brothers and sisters, I was impatient for the arrival of spring. At least once a week, I would take some time to sit on the window seat by Sarah's bed and watch the changing scene outside. I was not supposed to pause to contemplate such things. Brother Robert, our ministry elder, gave a sermon one Sunday, telling us one was not to sit and ponder one's feet when there was work to be done. Thus, realizing it was a grievous sin to gaze at what was going on behind the dwelling, I shortened the time spent watching such things. Instead, I reflected on what I had to do the rest of the week.

Not ten feet from the door at the back of the dwelling stood the boys' privy. Beyond the little outhouse, a small tract of land had been cultivated into a hay-growing area. A path led from the boys' door near Thomas's office to the road, which led to Pittsfield in one direction and New Lebanon in the other. This was a public road, and if I pondered long enough, I would see a carriage or wagon pass by. These were usually outsiders doing the world's business. The schoolhouse stood across the road. Waiting to see the boys get out of their class with Jerome, Sarah had spent some time at this very window on winter afternoons.

One evening during meeting at the end of our hall, Sarah imitated the boys' teacher. "Guess who I am," she announced, throwing her shoulders forward and walking like a duck.

"He's not that bad," I said, giggling.

Jerome was in his thirties and tall, taller than most of the

37

other brothers. He was so lean, Peg swore she would thicken him up by sneaking lard into his potatoes. His nose was long and sharp.

Sarah felt her nose. "I think he got his caught in one of those books he always carries around with him."

Sister Eliza Ann had been our teacher until she ran away with Brother Caleb in the fall. No one wanted or was trained well enough to take her place. The first month after the defection, we girls were told we would not go to school in the spring.

"You sisters might do well to take a year off from school and concentrate on the skills you'll need after you graduate," Lavonia, the ministry eldress, said one day as the Sunday meeting ended. "It isn't imperative that girls have a lot of book learning when there are so many chores in the Community that need to be done."

"But then who'll interpret Mother Ann's writings?" I asked.

The others looked at me as if I had spoken out of turn.

"I'm very good with learning and not so good at others things," I continued, hearing the buzz of voices behind me. I could not tell whether they agreed or not.

Before Christmas, however, Lavonia relented and asked Jerome to teach the girls after the boys were finished with their term in the spring. This, of course, was an immense relief to him. Being skinny and bookish and all, if he did not rise in the ranks to a leadership role, there was not much else he could do to contribute.

Beside the school, the ground rose gradually. This was the beginning of the forest where the brothers had cleared the underbrush away, leaving the maples and most of the birch. The trees were sparse, however, and if I looked hard enough, I could see the pond halfway up the hill. Beyond that was the real forest, where it was always dark with plenty of places to hide.

There were times when I yearned to walk to the pond and

kick my feet in the water. But that was in the summer when the days were long and hot. In the winter, the whole area looked eerie. On most days, a murky pall shrouded the tree trunks, a mantle hovering over the surface of the pond. Before the freeze, the wavelets' continuous movement cast the sun's rays in all directions like candles floating on a stormy sea. But today, this second week in February, all was quiet and hidden—and eerie.

It must have been one day this same week that I imagined I saw Edgar. It was misty outside and tracks of droplets made the windowpane blotchy. The miasma hung in between the trees like a shroud, but it was only two-thirty or three, too early for the darkness to overtake us completely. Someone approached the pond from out of nowhere. Emerging from the clouds, a dark figure slogged in front of the water, stopping and bending over as if to take a drink. Then he stood again and lumbered around the other end, piercing the cloud cover and vanishing into the forest. Unable to take my eyes off the scene across the road, I felt a chill and found it difficult to stand up.

Elizabeth came upon me before I had regained my wits. "Sister Lucy, I'm surprised to see you up here. Don't you have something to do before homework time?"

"Yes, Sister, I was just resting a second."

"You weren't resting," Elizabeth said. "You came up here to daydream. You must do it all the time. Is that what always interferes with your work?"

"I came up for my apron. Peg wanted to know where I'd left it."

"Please get downstairs this minute, or I'll have to tell Eldress Evelyn."

"Yes. I'm going right now."

I had to admit she was right. Sometimes I did like to reflect on faraway worlds when I should have been working. I promised myself I would not do it again—which would be easy because I could turn my thoughts to the union meeting in the large room at the end of the second floor hallway the following night. Anson had invited a group of us to come in and talk to some of the boys.

They sat in a line of chairs in the middle of the meeting room, and we in a similar line facing them about fifteen feet away. Seth was there, as was Ezekiel, a boy about the same age as Seth. I had known Ezekiel since his arrival, but he had come and gone from the Community more than once. His parents had indentured him but reclaimed him a few years later. Aware Ezekiel would soon be old enough to become a good resource for the Community, the elders objected to his removal. Their investment would be for naught if all the parents took their children back when they were old enough to prove useful in the fields. A few weeks after their first claim, the parents, demanding Ezekiel be released, brought a lawyer. Evelyn instructed me to wait in her office while she and Thomas spoke with them just outside the open door.

"We didn't place our son here so he could be stolen and forced to do manual labor," his mother said.

"But when you signed the papers, Mr. and Mrs. Parker, you told us you couldn't afford to give us property to pay for his care," Thomas said. "Most children come with effects that are given to us to repay the cost of raising and educating them."

Ezekiel stood beside his parents but did not say a word.

"You can certainly see our side," Evelyn said. "We haven't been paid for our investment."

"We can take you to court," the lawyer said. "I'm certain a judge would find it difficult to see your side in this matter. As far as I know, it's illegal to buy and sell children. If you offer to take them and then refuse to release them until you're paid, it's selling, as far as I'm concerned. As for the Parkers signing any papers, I'm sure that can be construed as duress. Do we need to bring in an official at this point? I don't think that would shine a good light on this so-called church, which is unorthodox and questionably lawful at best."

Ezekiel left with his parents but was gone for only a few years before returning on his own when he was thirteen or fourteen, insisting the elders let him be a courier for them. When he was not helping with the harvest or doing winter chores, he skipped school and traveled to other Communities with mail and goods to trade.

Usually, the union meetings were only with the younger children. This was the first time I had a chance to talk to many of the older boys, something that only happened because of the influx of younger children to the Community. At fourteen, I was one among a smaller group of older children. Molly and Charity sat next to each other, and I sat beside them along with Sarah and Elizabeth. At this point we all occupied the second room.

Anson stood up and recited a prayer. Then he began the conversation. "Who here wants to discuss their jobs with someone from the other room?"

Sarah was the first to speak. "I'm interested in what the boys are doing. Brother Mark, I understand you've recently harvested the ice. What did that take?"

Mark, a thirteen-year-old, cleared his throat. "I'm not sure I can explain it. I've only done it once. Maybe Brother Seth or Brother Ezekiel can tell you more."

"First we must clear the snow off the pond," Ezekiel said, holding a pointer in his hand and slashing it in the air as if it had a blade on the end. "Some of us dig up the snow with shovels like the ones we use to clear the paths. Then we slit marks in the ice so we can cut it along straight lines with long saws. Some fellows hold pikes like this, but with sharp ends that pull the ice blocks toward shore so we can extricate them with tongs. That's what I usually do because I'm bigger and can lift the heavy ice."

"But how do you keep the ice from melting?" I asked.

"We store it in the barn," Seth said. "You know the one, Sister Lucy. The floor is built into the ground. We fill up the whole floor with blocks side by side before we start on the next layer, sprinkling sawdust on top and in between the blocks to fill in the cracks. Even if the summers are hot, we rarely run out of ice."

"When you were working, did you ever see anything up there by the pond?" I asked, not even thinking to give the other girls a chance to talk.

"What do you mean?" Seth asked. "There are animals that drink out of the pond. Of course when we work up there, they don't come near. The horses are brought so they'll be ready to deliver the cart full of ice to the barn. We're all too noisy, scaring any deer and raccoons away."

"No. I mean people," I said, suddenly fearing I probably had not seen anything at all.

"Are you talking about Edgar, Sister Lucy?" Ezekiel asked, a smirk on his face. "I mean, you sometimes seem timid when you're outside."

"I thought I saw him," I said, dead serious. "Maybe I was too far away."

The gasps were evident among the girls, but I ignored them.

"It could have been anyone, Sister Lucy," Seth said. "It might have been someone from the world, collecting snow to melt for water."

"Why would someone camp in the forest when there's snow on the ground?"

"He came from the forest?" Molly asked, her voice unusually high.

"Yes. There was no wagon parked at the edge of the road.

Are you sure it wasn't someone planning to persecute us?"

"He could have been passing through on foot, Sister Lucy," Anson said. "Maybe he was destitute and couldn't afford a wagon. It does happen. Anyway, unless you're sure, I prefer you don't scare the sisters. Are there any more questions?" he asked, trying to get the others to join in.

It should not have surprised me, but during the Friday meeting that took place in the large meeting room in the dwelling, the spirit visited Sarah for the first time. Sarah was not herself. Usually so graceful and elegant, she screamed and kicked and writhed on the floor in front of elders, sisters, and brothers. Others stamped and danced in their designated areas, but the fervor slowed soon after Sarah began her performance. There was a point before her collapse where she chattered in tongues none of us could figure out.

Evelyn turned to Elizabeth. "I don't understand her," she whispered. "You don't suppose she could be speaking in an ancient language, do you, Sister?"

"Shhhhhh," Elizabeth said, her eyes narrowing as if she were concentrating hard. "I'm interpreting it. It's something in Arabic. Isn't that what the Savior spoke?"

Later in front of Robert and Lavonia, both ministry leaders appointed by the leadership in New York, Elizabeth, now assigned as an instrument designated to reading gifts, translated the whole episode for all the elders.

She rose in the middle of one Sunday meeting and announced, "Sister Sarah's heard from the Savior himself that he's coming to inspect our Eden. He instructs us to build an outdoor shrine, a sacred ground, by next summer so we can worship him and he can visit us." As Elizabeth's voice droned on about the details of such an undertaking, Evelyn took down her every word.

I was aghast at Elizabeth's knowledge of Arab languages. She had been able to interpret everything down to the minutest detail. What knowledge she possessed. How I wanted to be like her, so smart I could translate faraway languages and decipher a graceless ballet. Of course, Sarah remembered nothing of her contribution and was back to herself straightaway—after the elders finished cooing over her.

The mornings were still cold but calm. A few weeks after Elizabeth delivered her pronouncement, everyone trekked to the Sunday service in the meetinghouse. Sarah and I lumbered down the stairs and out the door. The frost on the walk crunched under our shoes. I liked that sound and continued to walk over the ice beside the stone path.

"If we turn this way, we can make it to the top of the hill before anyone sees us," said Sarah.

"Unfortunately, they'd miss you in the service. They'd get bored without you there to do that little dance of yours."

"What are you saying, Lucy? Are you telling me you think I'm a liar?"

"Well, not a liar. I just think maybe you dress it up a bit."

"Perhaps a little."

"You say you forget what you said, but I don't believe that either."

Sarah smiled. "It comes back to me on occasion."

"So what language are you really speaking when you say those things?" I asked, stopping in the middle of a puddle.

"They think it's Arabic, but they've never heard Arabic, so I doubt they really know. I don't even know what it is. It just comes out. Lucy, the water's staining your shoes. We'd better keep walking."

"Are you going to speak like that again today?"

"Possibly. I've been practicing something."

"Practicing?"

"Yes. I wrote, *You are my sweetheart and my love, Seth Deming* on a piece of paper. Then I put it up to the mirror in the washroom. I plan to say the words like they're read in the mirror, *gnimed thes evol ym dna treahteews ym era uoy.*"

I was thrilled my friend had taken me into her confidence. "Sounds like Arabic to me," I said, grabbing hold of Sarah's hand. "Perhaps you should teach Arabic to Jerome."

Sarah hunched forward and pointed her toes out, waddling down the path. "That's a good idea, Lucy. Then he can declare his passion for Seth Deming too."

Within a few weeks, the ground was soft enough to till. Since I was not allowed to use the horses, Jeremiah did that for me. Then I knelt down in the mud to sow the seeds in the little rows I had already planned out. The compost pile Brother Allen started years earlier was beyond the horse barn. Carrying a shovel and bucket, I headed to the end of the field. The compost pile was still there. After Brother Allen left, the others used it as a dumping ground for fruit and vegetable skins, tea leaves, and manure of all types.

I could smell it long before I got near it. That was why the pile was so far away from the dwellings. I never dreamed it could be so foul. Holding my breath, I walked up to the nearest corner of the heap and scooped a shovelful into my bucket.

Jeremiah was saddling a horse and came around the corner of the barn. "That's not the place, Sister Lucy," he said, smiling when he noticed the look on my face. "The aged compost is better. It's on the other side of the pile. To get there, you can slog through beside the barn over here."

My eyes filling with water, I began to gag but forced it back. Jeremiah laughed.

"Where are you going?" I asked him.

"I have business in Enfield. I'll be back tomorrow. Be sure and get the good stuff, Lucy. It'll make the vegetables grow so much bigger."

After applying compost over the ridges, I headed for the kitchen entrance.

"You aren't coming in here, Lucy Hammond," Peg yelled, waving her arms. "Oh my Lord. You smell like you've been playing with the pigs. I'll get a bowl of water. You'll have to wash out there."

"It's cold and everyone will see me," I said, starting to cry.

"Why you wanted to do men's work, I'll never know," Peg said, handing a bowl of warm water out to me. "Surely the elders didn't think about the consequences of letting Lucy Hammond out to play in the mud. If it isn't bread dough all over you, it's something else. I'll have to get you removed from kitchen duty tonight. You won't come near us with that stench."

I rinsed myself off as best I could outside and then tiptoed barefoot up the dwelling steps. With hot water from the kitchen, one of the girls filled a tub upstairs. While I believe I looked much better when I showed up in the dining room for dinner, still no one would sit next to me. The reward would come weeks later when I handed Peg a bowl of the best-looking squash and beans she had ever seen.

Spring finally arrived but it was late. Rain still flooded the fields, and in May, we trudged through the mud to the schoolhouse. Jerome was beside himself. Before we stepped onto the classroom floor, he forced us to remove our shoes, and the sight of all those wiggly toes under the thin gauze of the girls' stockings seemed to disrupt his normally stern tone.

"Good morning, Sisters," he said, his voice cracking nervously and his eyes level. "We must get started because we have a lot to cover this year. Your brothers made it through the *Millennial Laws,* discussing and memorizing them pretty easily. They also proved to do well with the manipulation of numbers. I don't expect you to get that far, however—nor would you ever need to learn it all. Sister Evelyn thought we might study the spiritual *Testimonies* published in 1816, so you're more aware of those who knew Mother Ann personally. Remember what you have already learned about Mother Ann Lee. She lived and nearly starved in that small cabin in New York and had to convince her companions to keep going, because the converts would certainly show up eventually. And when the crowd heretofore attending different revivals in search of a religious leader finally arrived, she and Father James Whitaker preached that sins of the flesh are the principle causes of poverty and cruel treatment existing in the world. They couldn't discuss the blessings without first being certain their new followers realized they must give up their marriages, made only of the flesh, because such behavior is a 'covenant with death.' "

"But some people were angry with her," I said. "Didn't some of the world's people rise up against her?"

"That has nothing to do with the *Testimonies,*" Jerome said. "But yes, there are stories about the difficulties early followers experienced when they tried to practice their new religion. In Harvard, some bullies whipped them and drove them out of town."

"But that wasn't all," I said, shaking down to my feet because I was not sure I wanted to hear the story again. "The outsiders actually kidnapped her once, didn't they?"

"That's correct, Sister. In Petersham, there was a meeting in the home of David Harris. Father James was reading the Bible to a crowd of attentive listeners when a group of scoundrels managed to enter the building and put out the lanterns. They attempted to kidnap her. When they failed the first time, they came back later that night and dragged Mother Ann out of the house by her feet. Throwing her into a sleigh and tearing her clothing in a reprehensible manner, they committed acts of cruelty against her. They claimed they wanted to make sure she was a woman and not a British spy."

The other girls whispered among themselves.

"Does the world still dislike us?" I asked, hoping for reassurance.

"Who knows what they think of us? While we practice the tenets of Mother Ann and dwell in the Garden of Eden, they live the filthy sins they commit. You must avoid the world's people at all costs," he said, his eyes sparkling with conviction. "But now we must get back to work. We'll discuss more of the *Testimonies* later. In addition to the stories, we must also take some time to cover all of the skills sisters should know in order to choose the correct apprenticeships."

But I was too busy thinking about the look on Jerome's face when he talked about the world's people. Was he as scared as I was about meeting up with one of them in the forest?

Sarah raised her hand and waited to be called.

"Sarah?" he said, his face lighting up.

"What if the Spirit takes us during class? Will you paddle us if we're so disposed?"

"If the Spirit renders a gift for us in this classroom," he said, smiling for the first time, "I certainly won't tell it to go away. It's very unlikely, however, we'll be visited, as all such spirits know how important our work is here. They've been instructed to visit during meeting and rest hours only."

Sarah shined.

I should have seen it back when Sarah's vision became the center of our thoughts. I should have noticed Elizabeth did not seem to bask in the attention created by Sarah's spectacle. Being an instrument was Elizabeth's chance to catapult up the line and become the kind of eldress she desired. Perhaps because it was Sarah who had received the most attention during and after her performance, our elder sister stepped back after her pronouncement and let the elders meet on the subject by themselves.

It was Sarah who met with the elders and calmly described each step. It was my friend who was commended for her ability to receive gifts from the spirits of our Savior and the Holy Mother. And because of this, the elders began to turn to Sarah for advice about how one crosses over to speak to Holy Mother Wisdom. Peeking out from under her bonnet, Sarah's gold hair shone and her loose gown swished in such a way everyone stopped to watch her when she strolled by. My Sarah became a celebrity. I wanted her for myself but had to share her.

Elizabeth and I continued to do our work and to concentrate on our worship, but somehow we were always like stained linen that could be rubbed with lye and still not come clean. It did not bother me that much, but I am not sure how Elizabeth felt. She became irritable, her melancholy lasting longer than usual. While the others did not detect it because she plastered a smile on her face when she was among them, I did. I noticed because she did not take her disappointment out on those involved with Sarah's glorious gift, the elders, or on Sarah herself. Elizabeth took out her indignation at being overlooked on me. But that would not last long. Just as spring brings leaves to the bare branches, Elizabeth would find a way to squeeze back in and outshine Sarah.

4. THE SACRED SHRINE

Spring slithered into summer, and the days turned long and warm. I loved summer because I could do more jobs without feeling tired. We would all rise at four-thirty and make our way to our first assignments before breakfast. My task in July was to milk the cows, and I was getting quite good at it.

It is one thing to get up at four-thirty in the summer and hear the first peeps of hungry birds and feel the warmth of a new sun on your back. It proves to be another to trudge to the dairy shop in the dark of winter. My gloves were cut off at the fingers, and it was hard to bend them around the teats in the freezing temperatures. I had the urge to stick both hands in the warm milk. That was not allowed for obvious reasons. But this was summer, and I actually looked forward to sitting on a stool, easing the discomfort of an obviously tormented cow.

After breakfast, the elders permitted me to tend to my garden, which was looking very fruitful indeed. Then I went to school with the rest of the girls. Following class, I would hang laundry and then pack seeds until dinner. By dinnertime, I was usually starving. Shortly afterward, I would retire to the second floor to work on homework before it got dark. Some evenings we had a union meeting where we would continue to discuss work. Anson and Elizabeth encouraged us to talk about our spiritual passions.

"What do you think is an important lesson we could teach the world's people?" Anson asked one evening.

"I believe they should stop fighting so much," Sarah offered.

"But what should we do if another country attacks us?" Elizabeth asked.

"We don't need to fight, because the Heavenly Father will protect us," Molly said. "And that includes the surrounding hills where Brother Ezekiel says he goes fishing."

The elders banned gossip during the union meetings, but sometimes Sarah or Molly slipped some in before Anson could change the subject again.

"I don't think Ezekiel's the only one going to the hills," Sarah said. "I heard Sister Harmony was seen kissing Brother Alex on Blueberry Hill just last week."

"Really?" asked Molly. "How did they get out without being caught? Blueberry Hill's at least a mile north of here, isn't it?"

"I ask you all to keep your minds on the lesson today. I'm sure the Heavenly Father's angry when we talk about such lurid events—especially when they aren't true."

My favorite activity was tackling class assignments. I loved to read books. The elders discouraged reading when the school session ended. So not only did I look forward to the summer weather and the start of school, but also to each evening when I could let myself slip into pages describing bizarre characters in exotic locations. Only then did I feel truly alone—without the barrage of elders and sisters telling me what to do. Of course, I was not permitted to read just any book. Jerome was only able to get hold of ones examined by the ministry elders first. Even with the books the elders embraced, most of the pages carried me away from the often drab existence of our Community.

In addition to reading, I also enjoyed writing. For a while, I kept a journal of our daily experiences and hid the notepad under my pillow, afraid someone else might decipher my deepest secrets. When I read my words later, I realized nothing at all had really occurred during my stay and dropped the practice.

My thoughts were probably the same as all the girls there, though I did not dare write about boys in my journal.

I also loved doing sums. Solving problems was sometimes the only excitement I got all day. When I finished my lesson, I often helped Sarah with hers. But even though she spent long hours studying with me in the meeting room downstairs, she would get lost when confronted with the easiest of word problems.

One evening, I took my reckoning book and a sheet of paper to the room at the end of the hall. Usually the area was empty because few of the other girls studied. I was surprised to find Elizabeth and Seth sitting at the table side by side. I questioned, though only to myself, the wisdom of their sitting close together when the rest of us so diligently practiced separation to prevent the boys from needless torment.

"Sister Lucy," said Elizabeth. "Why are you in here?"

"I study in here."

"Can't you study in our room tonight?"

"Why?"

"You may study in here, Sister Lucy," Seth said. "Sister Elizabeth and I can do this with you present. Do you mind if we whisper?"

"What are you doing?"

"We're writing down my visions," Elizabeth said. "And if you don't keep your nose out of our business, you'll get a gift on Sunday."

I understood immediately. Ever since Elizabeth became an official instrument, she had been handing out gifts at meetings. Heavenly spirits gave out gifts to inspire us to work harder for the Savior. We were often rewarded directly during meetings by letting the spirits guide us in a special song or dance. That is what Sarah supposedly received when she was moved to wriggle on the floor and speak Arabic. In Mother Ann's time, gifts were numerous and quite stirring. But most of us today had trouble understanding Mother Ann's zeal and sometimes let our minds wander during meetings. We often thought about our secular work and achievements instead of worshiping the Heavenly Father.

The ministry hoped receiving gifts the spirits had delivered through special messengers or instruments might provoke passions in our religion similar to those felt by devotees of Mother Ann herself. Molly received a gift from a messenger during the meeting, telling her Mother Ann had noticed she chewed her food with her mouth open, and in Eden, our paradise here on earth, a lady always closed a mouth full of food.

Charity got a gift telling her the Savior wished she would stop primping her hair so much because it was a sign of vanity. Even Sarah received one. Hers mentioned Holy Mother Wisdom wanted her to quit putting on a show during the meetings because it drew too much attention to herself. Pride is sinful. Of course, each gift was read in front of the whole congregation and even to worldly visitors attending the meetings to observe our spiritual practices. Until then, I had no idea that, as a proclaimed instrument, Elizabeth was interpreting the spirits' messages and delivering them to unsuspecting children.

"How do they come to you?" I asked.

"How does what come to me, Sister Lucy?"

"The spirits. Do you actually see them? Is there anyone else around who can see them too? Have you seen them, Brother Seth?"

"Don't be stupid, Sister Lucy," Elizabeth said.

When Sarah received her gift, she ignored the messenger's warning, crumpling up the piece of paper and dropping it along the walk on the way back to the dwelling. I remembered our discussion.

"It doesn't matter what Elizabeth thinks," she told me. *"Her spirits*

can't speak Arabic, so I doubt they're real."

"But, Sarah, how do you know it was from Elizabeth? I know Elizabeth says she hears instructions from the spirits, but others have received instructions too."

"Have you actually seen her receive them?" Sarah asked.

"No. I don't know when she talks to them."

"That's because she's making it all up."

"I'm just glad I haven't received any warnings, Sarah. That would be devastating. I try to be good. I think I'm a good believer. No matter what Peg and the others say. At least I'm good at that."

"Are you talking to the spirits right now, Elizabeth?" I asked, coming to my senses.

"No, Sister Lucy," Seth said. "We're just writing them down now. Sister Elizabeth's already had the visions."

"Why are you helping her, Seth?"

"Because he's got better handwriting than I do," Elizabeth said, turning to face me. "But I'm getting a vision about you now. Oh yes, Holy Mother? Is that so? I didn't know that about Sister Lucy. I'm sure she'll be very pleased to receive a gift on Sunday, knowing you're trying to help her to mind her own business."

I left, holding back my tears.

Summer was also the time when the Community had to fulfill the wish Sarah had prophesied. My friend had not really envisioned a holy place for outdoor worship on high holidays, but Elizabeth supposedly translated her Arabic that way. While most of the men stayed, working the fields of summer crops and tending the animals, a few of them went along with most of the women and children to search for a suitable site on which to build a monument.

Carrying picnic lunches, our large group scoured the hills beyond the pond. The forest was as dark and thick as Peg's molasses beans, but a trail cut through all the way to the top of one of the hills. We came to a clearing where wildflowers peeked through long blades of grass and sat down in the meadow to eat our sandwiches. Sarah veered off to sit near Seth, but one of the sisters cut her off before she could secure a spot among the boys. Evelyn got up and said a prayer, and we dove into our picnic packages.

While we all ate, Elders Robert and Thomas and Eldress Lavonia walked to the edges of the clearing and talked among themselves. Finally they came back and announced this very spot was to be called Mount Sinai.

"Once in May and again in October, the Community will worship in a special meeting right here at the top of Mount Sinai," Robert said. "The men will spend the rest of the summer chopping down trees and building a spiritual pool. At one end, the men will erect an altar-like stone as a fountain. There's no water at the top of this hill, however. That's why the fountain and pool will be 'spiritual.' Many of our gifts won't be seen by the human eye, but our strong faith will make them real."

I was glad when, later that afternoon, the group emerged from the woods at the bottom of the hill. I was hungry and sleepy from exercising in the warm sun.

The men started work on the project the very next week, and the women and girls were given fabric of vivid reds, greens, oranges and yellows so we could make costumes for everyone. In meetings at the dwelling, all the children learned new dances that would be performed at the October celebration. I enjoyed this immensely. Any meeting without Elizabeth's gifts was fine with me.

Adding the new jobs to an already busy day was almost too much. I still arose at four-thirty to milk the cows and went to breakfast after that. I still tended the garden, but I somehow had to squeeze sewing costumes into my busy schedule.

Instead of studying one school night, I went to the women's shop to sew. When I heard the school bell the next morning while still in the garden, I realized I had not only left my lesson unfinished, but that I had no time to wash up before class. Rushing to the water bowl Peg had put out for me, I quickly rinsed my hands before heading across the street to the schoolhouse. Jerome insisted we girls be prompt. We had to be in the classroom and seated before the last ring of the bell. I stepped over the threshold just in time.

"Sister Lucy," he said. "Because I saw you, I continued ringing the bell so you wouldn't be late. Where's your work?"

I reached into my pocket and pulled out the half-finished assignment. "I'm afraid it isn't complete. I had to sew costumes last night."

"And it's dirty. Please unfold it for me. I'm surprised you think you can hand in such messy work. And look at you. Your face is red and sweaty, as if you had run all the way here. It isn't proper to come to me in such condition. I'll have to give you an extra assignment."

"Yes, Brother Jerome."

"I'd like to show everyone what kind of work I do accept. Sister Sarah has handed in a perfectly beautiful paper. Her lines are straight, and there are no smudges because she's proud of her work," he said, holding up the paper.

I leaned over to Sarah and asked, "When did you have time to do the work?"

"I didn't. I think it's Seth's. It's easier for me to be neat when I can copy it off another page. I hope the answers are correct. I wonder sometimes if Seth is as smart as he lets on."

"Seth's very intelligent, Sarah. You're lucky he's helping you."

"Do I sense a bit of jealousy here?"

"Jealousy?"

"I think you're the one who wants to attract Seth's attention. I'm sorry he doesn't help you, Lucy. Maybe you should ask him."

"I can do my own work, Sarah. We aren't supposed to be paired up with the boys."

"There's far too much chatter in the classroom," Jerome said. "Did you two get the assignment?"

"No, Brother Jerome. I'm afraid I was advising Sister Lucy on how she could better use her time. Would you please be so kind as to repeat your instructions?"

"Yes, Sister. I can see you're serious about your learning. I've assigned pages one through twenty in your lesson book."

Jerome crumpled up my homework paper and put it on the table in front of me. "This is to be redone and handed in tomorrow," he said, continuing on to Sarah's end of the table. "Your work's wonderful, Sister Sarah. Perhaps we should talk about letting you go ahead with your studies."

"Ahead?"

"I can tutor you."

"I'm not sure our elders would agree with that."

"If I can get permission, do you think you could work with me for an hour or so each evening? I tell you this because Brother Whitley's moving to Enfield, and they'll need a replacement in the office of the trustees."

"What's that?"

"You know. The trustees are the ones who take care of the business. Even as an office sister, it's a very important place to work. There are books to be balanced and legal papers to be kept. All the world's people from miles around come to the store. You'd know what's new in the outside world and get to experience seeing and touching material goods the elders prefer we don't see."

"What do I need to study to be in the trustees' office if all I need are skills to work with the world's people?"

"Your numbers," Jerome said. "There's calculating and balancing to do. I'm not sure an office sister would be allowed to work with the businessmen directly. Think about it. I'll get back to you."

It was odd Jerome had enticed Sarah this way. I could not fathom the passion he must have felt, talking about the outside world the way he did, as if he lusted for its material goods. But was he conveying his own sentiment, or did he talk in that manner because he thought Sarah's passions would be roused by attractions only available outside the Community? I guessed it was a little bit of both.

Weeks later, I received a message before dinner, asking me to go to Evelyn's office. I tried to hide my feelings from the messenger, but she must have sensed I was nervous about going.

"I don't think they're mad at you, Sister Lucy," Charity said, putting her arm around my shoulders. "They didn't look angry when I saw them."

"I know they're upset with me, Charity. There's always some reason, though I try so hard to please them." Tears filled my eyes, and I could not speak.

"You can't be that bad, because you never do anything that would make Holy Mother or even the Heavenly Father angry."

I'm forever grateful to her for showing so much compassion when I was about to fall apart. I knocked on Evelyn's door with a trembling hand and then walked over to sit in the waiting room.

The eldress emerged from her office all too soon. "Sister Lucy, please come with me to Brother Thomas's office. How's the garden? Sister Peg says it's giving plenty to the kitchen."

"Yes. We've been lucky this year. We have so much squash Peg has to come up with more ways to cook it."

Thomas's office was not far. It was across the dwelling in front of the boys' entrance. His office was the exact reverse of Evelyn's. When she opened the door for me, I was even more terrified. Jerome sat across the table from our elder. I quickly checked my smock for spots and looked at my hands. He did not stand up when we entered. He did not even look in my direction.

But Thomas did. "Please sit down, Sister Evelyn."

I stood in front of the table, imagining I posed completely naked in front of my judges. Jerome passed a sheet of paper to Thomas.

"Sister Lucy, we have a serious problem in the Community," Thomas began. "I believe you're aware of the recent apostasies. There have been more brothers and sisters coming in to replace them, but we don't feel they've been prepared well enough to sign the covenant. They'll need time to make their decisions and are thus classified as novices. Each new member has been examined by the ministry elders, and he or she seems to lack the basics. The reasons for joining appear to have little to do with spirituality because no one can give us evidence he knows anything about our doctrine." Thomas sighed and looked up at me. "I'm not sure you understand the tribulations we've been experiencing, and I don't want you to think these problems are a threat to our peaceful Community. It's simply that we must adjust. We must adjust," he said under his breath.

"Yes, sir," I said, wishing he would get to the point.

"I have here a sheet of paper Brother Jerome says you handed in a few weeks ago."

My knees began to shake, and I leaned against the table to steady myself.

"Are you aware no one else was given this assignment?"

"That's not true. The others had an assignment too. One of the sisters . . ." It was as if my mouth had taken off, and I could no longer control it.

"Yes?"

"I forgot what I was going to say."

"Is this your work?" he asked, handing me the sheet.

"Yes, sir," I said automatically. But to my surprise, it was not the same homework Jerome had so ceremoniously rejected. "I had a lot of cross-outs because it took a while to figure them out. I tried to be neat, but for some reason my head just wasn't working right that night." I noticed Jerome give me a side-glance but pretended I did not see it. "I would've copied it over onto a clean one, but I thought using another precious sheet would be wasteful. I apologize if I didn't make the right decision."

"But you verify you had no one help you find these answers."

"Yes—I mean no. No one helped me."

"Brother Jerome here says he doubts you're getting help because he's aware of no one else in the Community aside from himself, Brother Eli, and Brother Leonard who know their numbers this well. He tells me he tried to tutor other students on the same concepts, but they couldn't figure the problems out. You know we don't have a single woman as trustee here at Hancock. Mother Ann said we must have an equal number of women to match the number of men in managerial positions. I'm sure she meant these women should also be members and not novices or minors. You haven't committed to the Community because you must be eighteen to be spiritually mature enough to make that commitment. It's with great difficulty, therefore, that I ask you to work in the office of trustees as an apprentice to Brother Eli. You won't be an official trustee until we come to terms with our doubts about the meaning of Mother Ann's instructions or until you pledge your desire to stay here when you turn eighteen. Your handwriting must improve because Brother Eli's a stickler for clean and legible books. This is a serious commitment."

"I'm very honored, but I have a question. Must I give up the garden?"

"Sister Lucy," Evelyn said, "You'll continue to go to school and have kitchen and laundry rotation, but I'm afraid you'll have to give up the other jobs. You won't have time."

"Perhaps she can get a helper for the garden," Jerome said. "She can teach one of the younger children what to do to finish the season. The job can be reevaluated before the spring, and based on Sister Lucy's progress and the success of the garden, we can decide its fate."

"Well?" Thomas asked. "What do you wish us to do, Sister?"

"I too would like to try working in the trustees' office. If I spend the day indoors it'll definitely be much warmer this winter."

"That's good. Brother Jerome will get you a garden helper immediately, and you can start at the office next week. Please give Sister Evelyn your current schedule."

"I already have it and am finding replacements for the other jobs," Jerome said. "Certainly the new members can be trusted with the milking."

I am not sure what I did right after talking to Thomas. I told no one of my luck, afraid I was somehow dreaming a meeting with Jerome and the elders would be positive. I could not tell by Jerome's expression if he were happy about the decision or disappointed his protégée had failed to succeed. But whatever he thought about me, I would become a friend for life. I would be his guardian angel and protect him from any future questions about his zeal for the triumph of the Believers.

Yes, using our hands for God would produce the goods that keep the Community going. No one realizes this more than a trustee. But using our brains is just as important, and Jerome would have the intelligence and judgment to keep us on track too—that is, unless his devotion for Sarah somehow lured him away from his obligations.

5. THROUGH THE WINDOW

Each drawn out summer day moped along like a brooding slug. While the well-being of the Believer Community depended on the hard work of every one of its members, there were still days when a few of us were allowed some fun. I believe it was Sarah who first mentioned the need for a break, claiming to be going blind from the grueling amount of homework Jerome assigned and from the vibrant colors of the fabric we had to sew together to make costumes. Evelyn suggested she go to the infirmary for spectacles, but Sarah swore the disability was only temporary.

Elizabeth had a better idea. Sarah and I could go on a picnic in the woods. Evelyn gave her permission, as long as we did not go on a school day, and only after Elizabeth agreed to accompany us as a chaperone.

The day started off sultry. We were glad no brothers accompanied us so we could remove our neckerchiefs and unbutton our collars as soon as the buildings had disappeared from sight. We had hiked for a couple of miles around the hill before Sarah suddenly stopped.

"Holy Mother, it's hot!" she said, pulling down the top part of her dress and continuing along in her shift.

Elizabeth and I soon followed, trying to guide the breezes, if there were any, through our chemises. We stopped by a creek about half way up the hill, and off came the rest of our dresses. I removed my shoes and stockings so I could wade in the cold water, but that was a mistake.

"This feels so good," I said. "Come on in."

When Elizabeth and Sarah stepped onto the rocky bed, Sarah slipped, sitting down in the rushing stream.

"That must have been a trick," she said, giggling and splashing water in my direction.

A water fight ensued. I do not think Sarah wanted to be the only one wet. We hung our dresses over some branches and bathed in our shifts, rinsing our hair before grasping hands, dancing in a circle, and daring the moving current to knock us over.

For the first time, I noticed how Elizabeth had changed from the plain gawky teenager she'd been when I first arrived. The thin cotton chemise clung to her seventeen-year-old body, revealing a full but beautiful shape. Nipples erect from the cold water, she bounced around like a child, unfettered from the strict rules of chastity that controlled our daily lives. Untied and wet, her tresses curled into ringlets, and the sun highlighted gold strands in the otherwise mousy brown hue. Her gray eyes, wide with excitement like I had never seen them, looked longingly at Sarah, who teased us both mercilessly by trying to measure the size of our breasts with the cup of her hand and then reaching inside her shift to check her own. Then we lay down on some flat rocks, letting the sun dry our shifts, and raising our knees to let any light breezes run up and down our skin.

"I'm bored," Sarah said suddenly. "Let's get dressed and go up to see how our new shrine is coming. Maybe, if we're lucky, some of the boys will be working. If we're quiet, they might not see us and still have their shirts off."

"I think I heard Seth say he would be up there today," Elizabeth said, pulling her dress back over her chemise. "That should excite you, Sister Lucy. I wonder if he'll be embarrassed seeing you."

Walking was difficult because the damp cotton twisted and

clung to my skin. But soon, we arrived at the top of the hill. All was quiet. Nobody was working at our holy site on Saturday, and the others seemed disappointed. We pretended to be celebrating that holy day in October when we would all climb the hill and perform for the Savior. Sarah sang a hymn, and she and I danced down to the fountain or altar, a flat-topped stone, which had been placed at one end of the dry spiritual pool. We marveled at how the men had dragged it onto a wagon at the bottom of the hill, pulled it all the way up, and heaved it on top of some pillar stones.

"I wish we'd been here then," Sarah said. "I can just see them now, their tawny chests awash in sweat."

"The men have to come back to carve a prayer in the altar stone," Elizabeth said. "I'll find out when, and then we'll sneak up here again and hide so we can watch them work. I'm sure they'll remove their shirts for that too."

Sarah got up and walked directly to the stone. Along the way, she had collected a sharp rock. Stretching out on her back, she began to carve her initials on the underside of the altar. I was too shocked to object. I could not believe she could be so bold and was surprised Elizabeth said nothing to stop her. After all, Elizabeth would soon sign the covenant, committing her life to the Community. There was no doubt she would. When Sarah was finished, she handed the stone to me, but I threw it down.

"Elizabeth, do you want to do it?" she asked. "Evidently, office sisters are too righteous to play."

"No thanks," said Elizabeth. "I plan to be a ministry eldress, and if those initials were ever discovered, it wouldn't look good for me to have mine under there either."

It was then Sarah did something that took my breath away. She suddenly turned around and slid up onto the altar, pulling up her dress so that she sat on the stone directly. She looked at me. "What? The stone's warm against my wet drawers."

"Sarah," I said when Elizabeth ignored her actions. "In the meeting, Robert told us the stone was sacred. No one is to touch it with impure hands after it's set in place and blessed." I tried to hide the smile that twitched at my lips when I looked up at her. "There'll be a bowl here where those who are allowed to stand near the stone can wash their hands before handling it. It's a grave sin to touch the altar let alone desecrate it with our . . ."

"With our what, Lucy? Bottoms?" she asked, beginning to giggle. "When the elders insisted this part of our bodies remain untouched by our brothers, I thought it was the most holy. I concluded, therefore, it's also the cleanest part of me."

"I saw a paper about the altar in the trustees' office. It said anyone who defiled the altar stone with dirty hands would be cursed and live only a short time after that," I said, beginning to snort in an attempt to hold back my laughter too.

Elizabeth also began to snicker, "I think, dear Sarah, the concept of a clean bottom refers to virgins only. And technically, Lucy, Sarah didn't defile the altar with dirty hands."

"What are you saying, Sister?" I asked Elizabeth. "Sarah's a virgin as am I."

"At the risk of upsetting you, dear Lucy," Sarah said. "We should all refrain from talking about virginity. What'll we do next, Lizzy?"

"I thought this was supposed to be a picnic," I said. "Where's the food?"

We both looked at Elizabeth, who had described our outing as a picnic to Evelyn.

"I had to say that or she wouldn't have let us go out," Elizabeth said.

We proceeded down the trail that wound through the thick forest past the pond to the dwelling. The afternoon sun was starting to fall behind the hill, and the shadows beneath the trees stretched out across the path. I had never seen the woods so dark. I tried hard to keep up with the others who raced each other down the trail, turning the corner ahead of me. Each time I lost sight of them, my heart raced. I thought about Edgar. I would stare ahead, humming so I would not hear the rustle in the bushes flourishing under the forest canopy. Just before we reached the pond, the two disappeared once again, and Elizabeth slipped into the overgrowth, waiting for me to pass. When I turned the corner, she jumped out at me, making me scream at the top of my lungs. I was still jittery and holding in tears when we arrived at the dwelling, hoping Peg had some scraps left over from lunch.

August brought about the official change of jobs. In July, both Sarah and I did the mending, laundry, and sewed costumes for the October meeting. And now we both had kitchen duty. But our other jobs had also changed. Sarah switched to needlework as an apprentice under stone-faced Edith. Sarah was very good at that. Delighted with each item she finished, I loved to watch her.

"Oh, I love it, Sarah," I said, one day when she brought me a pincushion she had created. "Look at the embroidery work on it. It's perfect."

"Actually it isn't. Normally my cushions go to the trustees' house to be sold, but this one has a tiny error on it, and Edith told me I could keep it. Put it under your pillow, though, because Evelyn frowns on our keeping worldly gifts out in the open."

Because my mother's scarf was already under my pillow, I hid the little pincushion under my mattress and would take it out every night and stroke the soft material.

I once worked with Edith too, but after a month, the woman asked that I no longer be included in the rotation.

"Your work, Sister Lucy, isn't up to par. With all these holes, it looks like you filled this fine silk with buckshot. Ladies have the privilege of doing this kind of work because they're blessed with patience and elegant fingers. Your nails are never washed. You bring the garden in with you and smudge the creations."

I do not think she liked me too much either. I tended to ask too many questions, and Edith was not fond of chitchat. She only wanted to sew. I really wished to produce beautifully hand-crafted pieces like the other girls, but mine just did not turn out that way. It might have been because I could not keep my mind on sewing. I could neither sit still nor stay quiet for long, and unfortunately needlework, knitting and weaving all required what Edith called the "patience of a saint." Obviously, my being what Peg described as "flighty" made it difficult for me to qualify as one. She reported me to Evelyn.

Thus banned from the sewing room at the girls' shop, I had to find something else I could do for the rest of my life. Of course, I thought I had found it. The garden did indeed thrive under my careful watch, and I was loath to leave it to Benjamin, a ten-year-old. To my surprise, he was enthusiastic and learned quickly. I kept an eye on the garden for the whole season after I started to work as an office sister, but it was determined at the end of summer Benjamin was knowledgeable and talented enough to continue the custom when the growing season started again. While the garden was taken care of, the sisters who faithfully packaged the seeds missed me. Packing seeds was a woman's job so Benjamin did not fill in for me there.

My first afternoon at the trustee's house whizzed by. Jerome was correct when he told us an office sister would not deal with the businessmen who visited to pick up goods each day or the world's vendors who delivered the few goods we at the Community could not grow or make ourselves. But that was all I learned of those who waited in the lobby each day the first summer I worked there. Eli hurried me to a room on the second floor of the house where other women worked. I would take care of the business from this room. He would come up for the last hour of each day and show me how to fill in the books and calculate the results.

I soon learned the other women did not do the same kind of work that I did. Some of them were messengers. Each day they collected goods from storage and from the various girls' shops, labeled them, and put them into another storage area on the first floor. Orders would come in throughout the day. They conveyed the instructions to the appropriate workers and returned with the goods if the items were ready. Others filed papers and contracts. Usually those papers went through me at one time or another as I recorded orders, drew up invoices, and collected the money or recorded the items businessmen brought in for trade. The balance of each patron's account was at my fingertips, and even though I did not tie the account names to faces, I soon learned the state of most of the world's businesses. To me, the names were figures as I rated the clients' abilities to pay their debts, and even what we might provide to improve their status.

At first, I thought I would never understand it. Each afternoon, Eli brought me a pile of papers and cash, and I had to figure it all out. If I got lost, he usually tried to help me.

"What seems to be the problem, Sister Lucy?" he asked me one day.

"Must you bring me so many sheets at once? I'm afraid I'm getting confused."

"I've checked all your work, and it's fine. You seem to finish it on time. What's confusing you?"

"I guess it's just that my chest seizes up whenever something new comes."

"Mmm. This last pile seemed to be cleaner than the others. I could almost read the numbers without figuring the arithmetic out first."

With his help, I managed to learn and even gain some confidence. Eli rarely complained after the first few weeks. He did not talk much, and when he did, it was usually about my smudges or handwriting. But he did not comment often, as I tried hard not to make mistakes in the first place. I am not sure if my handwriting miraculously became legible or if Eli just gave up a few months after I arrived. But somehow Eli learned to read what I wrote, and my handwriting was never mentioned again.

While I spent most of my extra hours at the trustees' house, I also still had duties as a sister. It was summer, and I had to devote time to school and schoolwork. Jerome showed more respect for my abilities and was careful not to give me long assignments or berate me in front of the others, but I could not miss school or kitchen duty in the evenings or on all-day Wednesdays. Nor did I wish to miss them. Being with Sarah brought me so much happiness, I could not bear the hours I was without her. On Wednesdays, Sarah and I would laugh and tease Peg, allowing the older sister to let off steam by making jokes at our expense.

"Sister Lucy, will you please help Sister Lydia by filling the shelf with flatware and dishes so she can pull them up? And be careful. Don't overfill it like you did before."

And later.

"Sister Lucy, will you collect some more flour to thicken the gravy? Please put back the lid. Sister Sarah, will you follow Sister Lucy and make sure she's sealed the flour canister while she heats the butter and mixes in the flour? Then you, Sister Sarah, can make sure Sister Lucy doesn't burn the gravy."

It was a game and we would all play along. We dutifully saw that dinner was served but also spent a lot of time mimicking Peg behind her back. Peg gave an order, and I repeated the order in a poor rendition of her voice as I did the job. Then I would heave my body around the kitchen scolding the others, my finger wagging like the tail of an excited puppy. I believe Peg enjoyed hearing our imitation of her and would give us more orders just to listen to each of us mimic her.

Wednesday was the day bread was baked all day long. On kitchen duty, Sarah and I would spend the whole day together, forming dough, kneading it, letting it rise, and then punching it down for baking. Class was always short of students on Wednesdays during the summer. The month before, Molly and eight-year-old Betsy were always gone. In August, it was Sarah and I who did not show up for school. Bread-baking always took precedence.

I enjoyed the day off because I would spend it with Sarah, and likewise, Sarah would not have to put on airs for Jerome, who seemed to have fallen hopelessly in love with her.

"Did Jerome ask you if he could study with you tonight?"

Sarah smiled. "Today I dropped my assignment on the floor just to watch him rush to pick it up for me. I believe one of these days he's going to fall to his knees and beg me to marry him."

She knew she had him hooked and played with his affections mercilessly, and I, having sworn to protect him, barely understood about such things as love and attraction. I just watched, hoping he would see the absurdity of his infatuation with a capricious fourteen-year-old before the elders did.

While Sarah performed for Jerome, her affection for me was unquestionably real. We seemed to be linked, and no one was going to interfere with our fondness of each other. In the kitchen, every time Peg passed our bread-making line, she would have to move closer to my station.

"I swear you two were born attached," she once said. "You don't look alike or talk alike or act alike, but you are still fastened like a button and hole."

We both laughed uncertainly. I do not think either of us understood what she meant. Who was the button and who was the hole and which was it better to be?

While we had fun at dinner one August Wednesday, my efforts to sleep that night were not successful. Something ate at me as I continued to toss and turn almost an hour after we retired. Had I forgotten to do something? It could not have happened at work, because I had not been to the trustees' house all day. I created a list and went over it in my mind. Sister Peg would be furious if I did not finish a chore in the kitchen. Hopefully it was not something that would burn down the place.

After hours of trying to reconcile my actions with the list, I finally had to get up to check. First I rose onto my elbows to make sure Elizabeth was asleep. She seemed to be. I slithered out from under the covers and tiptoed into the dark hallway. Touching the wall with my fingertips, I blindly made my way down the hall and carefully descended the two flights to the kitchen.

Moonlight swooped in through the windows, illuminating a small patch not two feet in front of me. Broken dishes, sugar, flour, and torn pieces of bread littered the floor. I stepped forward to have a closer peek. The whole kitchen looked like it had been in a storm. I could not believe my eyes.

Suddenly, a breeze blew past my face, a cold draft that made the fine hairs on my cheeks stand on end. Frozen and barefoot in the middle of the kitchen, I was unable to flee or make a sound. I stared forward at the bank of windows along the wall.

For the protracted minutes I stood there, I could still hear—

and hear things I did. There was a rustle from somewhere. Was it in the pantry? I could not tell. The next noise was a crackle. Was someone taking a step? Did I hear the *crunch* of glass underfoot? Suddenly a shadow crossed the floor, shutting out the light from the first window on my right. While my eyes refused to follow, I could still hear its careful footfall, make out its slow but steady movement, and see a large slab of darkness begin to overtake the next window.

I could hear myself breathe, short crusty breaths that sounded like a band playing in my ears. I refused to exhale, but the thump of my heart kept the beat of the drum, and the resulting pants started the next verse. The shadow even stopped once, as if to listen and ascertain where the music originated. But the shape did not stop for long. As soon as the second window was blocked out, the first one cleared, releasing the moonbeams to spotlight the garbage-strewn floor. Was the figure in front of the window or on the outside? I could not tell, but as it approached the third pane, I could see the fracture, the hole from which the outside breezes were sucked in. And as the shadow passed beside it, a piece of glass that had previously dangled, refracting the stream of moonlight, suddenly dropped onto the counter and splintered into a thousand tiny crystals, dancing in front of my eyes. It was not the spectacle that caught me by surprise, but the sudden loud chink I heard as a crash! The sound woke me up. But stemming from my throat, an involuntary sigh was all that was needed to catch the shadow's ear. It stopped right there in front of window three. I let my eyes continue on. The door to the mudroom was just after window five.

I spun in the direction of the unlit corridor, and somehow missing the mess around my bare feet, dashed up the stairs with such speed, my toes barely touched the treads.

I did not awaken Anson, who would know how to use one of the rifles stored somewhere in the dwelling. I did not rouse

Elizabeth, who still snored away in her bed. But I hurried back to my room and buried myself under the covers, wanting so badly to see the faces of my sisters and the sunlight streaming in through the windows when I awoke from my ghastly nightmare.

6. THE OUTSIDE

I awoke to a stream of light across my face and sat up with a start. Rolling over, I felt for my bonnet. Instead of sitting on my head, it was neatly folded on the pillow beside me. Perhaps that ghastly experience the night before had all been a nightmare. Glancing around the room, I noticed everyone else was gone. They must have been out working, leaving me the only one still in bed. Something had happened, but I was not sure I wanted to know what it was.

I descended the stairs ten minutes later. The hallways were quiet. Only the clang of dishes and utensils hit my ears, and I walked into the dining room to see if breakfast was over. Actually, it had not yet begun. Sister Lydia stopped distributing plates and stared in my direction. It was the first sign of what was to come, but I thought only of my stomach and the need to fill it.

Burying any thoughts about the events of the night before, I slinked down the next flight, still hoping to somehow sneak into the kitchen so no one would notice I was late. To my surprise, the place was clean and bustling like it was every morning.

My misstep, being late, was a serious one but forgivable because it did not happen all the time. I was not usually tardy and it was not that late. Actually, it was almost impossible to be tardy. Not only would one find it difficult to sleep through the other girls' struggles to wash and dress for work, but not one of my roommates would allow it. The sleepy girl would be taunted

75

and prodded onto her feet. We just did not give one another the luxury of time in the morning when we could actually remember our dreams. Somehow I had managed to sleep through all of that this morning. I was, therefore, surprised when Peg came around the corner. Stirring some sort of batter, she suddenly let the spoon fly out of her hand. One of the other girls rushed to clean up the spill but said nothing.

"I believe Sister Evelyn's waiting for you in her office," Peg said when she came to her senses. Her voice was not implacable or vindictive, but strong and steady.

The other girls stared in my direction, and as if their eyes conveyed the truth I had succeeded in expunging from my memory, it hit me. I gazed at the bank of windows, noticing a sheet of wood now replaced one of the panes, and experienced the sheer terror of my nightmare once again. But this time, I felt I was somehow responsible for the damage that had occurred. If I could not convince myself Edgar had actually been here in the kitchen, how would anyone else believe me?

They must have seen the look on my face because Peg, dear Peg, just as suddenly softened the blow. "We had an accident here last night, Sister. Evidently someone from the world, too embarrassed to ask for a handout, forced the lock instead. Needless to say, we had a mess. I don't know why he didn't just take what he wanted instead of damaging the whole place. But messes can be cleaned up. If you could please talk to Sister Evelyn and then hurry back here and help us, we'd all be grateful. Girls, please get back to work. I'm sure our brothers will soon be hungry and would appreciate it if we were prepared."

The walk to Evelyn's office was a long one. I desperately tried to remember the details of my nightmare so I would be ready with an answer, but the boundaries of the dream began to shift, making what I saw as facts transitory and erratic. That, and I worried about its plausibility.

None of the others had ever admitted seeing Edgar. They assured me I was too gullible, that his story was lore. Charity had reminded me on numerous occasions that I should look at the numbers I was so good at. He would be too old to be alive. It had been over sixty years since Mother Ann first sought converts in this area. If Edgar were twenty when he fell in love with Mary, he would be in his eighties now. How many eighty-year-olds have secreted themselves in the forest and terrorized people who had nothing to do with the original crime? It just did not add up.

I knocked softly on the door and then walked meekly toward the waiting room. Before I had taken two or three steps, the door opened, and I turned back to see Thomas standing in the entry.

"Sister Lucy, please come in. We were hoping you'd be up soon."

I entered reluctantly and stood in front of the table facing Evelyn. Thomas circled and sat down beside her.

"As you may have heard, Sister Lucy, the dwelling experienced something last night that is both appalling and disturbing," Evelyn said.

I could not get my lips to move. They were trembling, and I bit down hard on the bottom one.

"Sister Evelyn and I have two reasons to think you might have some idea about what happened and would very much appreciate your assistance here," Thomas said. "The first was speculation on Sister Peg's part. She claimed you were in charge of closing up last night. Is that correct?"

"Yes. I remember locking the doors."

"She also told us you sometimes have trouble with small details concerning your responsibilities in the kitchen."

"I must confess I do forget things on occasion," I said. "I've tried to think of something I overlooked last night. I mean, I had the feeling I might have forgotten to do something, but I couldn't think of what it was." My voice trailed off. I was unable to remember the question.

"But because your indiscretions are usually so minor, she didn't think of suspecting you might actually have had something to do with the incident until she found a bonnet on the floor with the rest of the garbage. When Sister Elizabeth checked and found you asleep without one, Sister Peg guessed you might somehow have been involved."

"I confess I do make mistakes in the kitchen, and Peg's warnings about my possible missteps make me try harder to prove myself. But the more effort I put into it, the worse I seem to get."

"Sister Lucy," Evelyn said. "It surprises me you should be so exact with your calculations in the trustees' house that you keep intricate figures so accurately, while you seem to fumble over the uncomplicated tasks in the kitchen. That said, I'm going to ask you a straightforward question here. Were you in the kitchen last night?"

"Yes."

"Why?"

"I don't remember why I got up. I couldn't sleep because something troubled me. I feared I'd forgotten to finish all the jobs in the kitchen."

"Do you remember the events clearly?" Thomas asked.

"Yes," I said. "At least I think so. Part of what happened seems like a dream."

Thomas and Evelyn sat silently. "Well?" they finally asked.

"I went down the stairs to the kitchen in my bare feet," I said, trying hard to think of every detail. "I stopped near the entrance because it was a mess."

"You could see that in the dark from the doorway?"

"No. My feet were bare. I could feel crumbs or something on

78

the floor, but it was what I thought I saw that troubled me. The place was a mess."

"But you didn't hear anything?"

"Not at first. I just saw broken dishes and flour and bread crumbs on the patch of floor the moon lit."

"Why didn't you come and get us?" Thomas asked. "We were only one flight away. Even if you continued up to your room, Elizabeth was only a few yards from your bed. Why didn't you get someone to search the area?"

I shuffled my feet, unable to come up with a response.

"Are you covering for one of the others?" Thomas asked.

"I think I saw someone."

"Who?"

"The one who made the mess. But he was outside the windows."

"What do you mean, Lucy?" Evelyn asked.

"He walked along the windows on the outside. When he saw me, he stopped. I worried he'd come in the door so I ran back upstairs."

"What did he look like?"

"He was hairy and had long teeth."

The elders looked at each other.

"But you didn't get help," Thomas said, frustration growing in his voice.

"I thought I was dreaming," I said, my voice little more than a squeak.

"Do you normally dream about men breaking into the dwelling?"

"Yes. I mean no."

Thomas pushed his chair back with a loud screech that made my teeth ache.

"Lucy, you know there are people in the world who have no source of income," he said. "Sometimes the world's people ignore them and encourage them to move on. Sister Peg often saves scraps and puts them out for beggars who are in need of food."

"I know, but he was all hairy. He was a man, but I don't think he's one anymore," I said, the tears starting to fill my eyes.

My interrogators looked at each other. "Edgar," they said in unison.

"My God, Lucy, you can't possibly believe you saw Edgar," Thomas said. "Edgar's a myth. He doesn't exist. You're acting like a seven-year-old."

"I'm going to have to stop this once and for all," said Evelyn. "Because we have no witnesses, and other than the bonnet and this ridiculous story, there's little evidence that you, Sister Lucy, were even down there. I hereby officially conclude you had some kind of dream last night and walked downstairs in your sleep. Ungrateful for the food Sister Peg offered, someone broke into the kitchen. Sister Peg's doing an inventory to make sure nothing was stolen. I expect Brother Eli's anxious for you to return and will thus excuse you to go to your duties. You'll speak with no one about what happened, and none of us will talk about it further unless more evidence turns up."

"I worry Edgar might seek revenge."

"Nonsense, Sister Lucy," Evelyn said. "The world's people around here know we're pious and industrious people. No one wants to hurt the Community in any way."

I backed out of the room, still unsure why a poor traveler would bother to destroy the kitchen when all he wanted was food. I waited hours for them to announce I would be tied to a tree for a night in the forest to prove Edgar did not exist. In the days that followed, however, nothing more was said about that night by anyone.

But the silence did have its downside. It left a vacuum in

which every rattle or creak in the house was Edgar, trying to find the person who had witnessed the fit of madness that made him wreak havoc on the kitchen that night.

As October began, the woods outside the dwelling window displayed a rainbow of colors. The heavy boughs that veiled the pond became bare within a week. Edgar, or any strangers at all sloshing through these woods, would now pass neither quietly nor invisibly. I doubted anyone would trouble us further and looked forward to hiking with my sisters and splashing my feet in the pond before school started.

But while the woods next to the schoolhouse seemed inviting, wandering beyond, into the jungle, would take more daring than I was able to muster. Fortunately, we were too busy for such frolics. Fall was the busiest time of year. The harvest was upon us, and gathering the vegetables was a job for both brothers and sisters. I did not mind. Getting up at four in the morning to work for a few hours among the rows of herbs and vegetables was a chore I relished. I still spent the rest of my days in the small office in the trustees' house and often looked dreamily out the window at the others bustling in the fields.

Through my office window one day, I watched Sarah help the others load squash and other vegetables into a wagon. She was beautiful, her bonnet having slipped off the top of her head to reveal strands of gold. I must confess I was not sure Sarah enjoyed gathering the acorn squash as much as frolicking with the brothers.

She looked almost helpless, collecting the items in her skirt and hurling them onto the cart, only to have some of them hit the ground instead. The brothers greedily took turns assisting her. I longed to be with her—watch her expressions of surprise as she tried to pick up a large pumpkin only to drop it on her foot before getting it to the wagon. I saw Seth talk to her once.

He pointed to the wagon. Sarah nodded and attempted to clamber up the spokes of the large wheel. Seth finally gave in and, clasping her small waist with his strong hands, hoisted her up into place before climbing in himself. The wagon took off to transport the load to the barn for sorting.

But as the harvest slowed and the men looked forward to preparing the grounds for the winter snows, October's final Sunday brought a cool but perfect sun. Of course, Mother Ann would have to make it perfect because it was a holy day for us. The following Sunday, we would don colorful costumes that would have rivaled nature's show just weeks earlier, and hike up to Mount Sinai, offering our homemade gifts of music and prayer to the Savior. We would prove Hancock, which had now officially been named "City of Peace," was indeed heaven on earth.

My costume was a little big. We had to pin it up in places so it would not drag on the ground. But Sarah looked magnificent in hers. The colors shimmered like her hair.

It was still dark when we lined up in the field. We brought our candles with us so we could light the path through the forest, an idea I supported wholeheartedly. Edgar would undoubtedly hesitate to attack a procession of flames, already having experienced burns to his skin and all. I held my candle up and dared him to harass us, not thinking he might be so tired from another night of incursions into neighboring farms that he would be asleep in the deep bowels of his shelter.

In the clearing, the sky sprawled over our heads. A pink cast on a perfect slate blue was gift enough for me, but I was ready to return before we blew out our candles.

Lining up around the fountain, we watched Robert scrape the last crumbs out of the grooves forming the newly-carved letters. He then turned and read the words. I wondered who had actually etched the saying into the stone and if the bare-chested artisan had discovered Sarah's initials on the underside. As the sun's first rays slid over the top of the smooth surface, I imagined I saw the faint mark of Sarah's damp bottom on the edge of it and smiled to myself. Then we all began to sing our new songs to the glory of the Lord.

By the time the meeting was over, it was late morning and I was starved. The sun was cool, thank goodness, because our costumes, fitting over our usual Sunday dresses, were not. I needed both water and food.

After standing in one place for what seemed like a whole day, Lavonia said a short final prayer, "May we all thank the Lord for this beautiful day so we can pay tribute to his great work here on Mount Sinai."

We lined up to start down the hill once more and were only about half way down when the procession stopped. I could not see the front or the cause of the sudden delay because the line was long, and we were quite a ways back. When it did not move again after several seconds, I crouched in place, exhausted. We sat in the middle of the forest for nearly forty-five long minutes. Word of a problem spread.

Charity, several rows toward the front, yelled back, "A traveler's been sighted with one of Sister Peg's bowls, and Elder Thomas has taken off after him."

Lydia soon gave another reason. "Eldress Abigail's fainted, and the brothers are having trouble lifting her."

Abigail, though very nice, was quite plump. Peg had teased that the eldress liked to help Harriet, the cook in the brick dwelling, by tasting each dish with her finger before it was served to the others.

Finally the line began to move once more. I am not sure which story was real. I tend to believe it was the one I heard just before breakfast, that Jerome had taken ill. He was forced to go quite deep into the autumn-stripped forest to find cover so he could relieve the cramps that had overtaken him. When he tried to return, he became lost, and two brothers had to go out looking for him. By the time the procession reached the field, Jerome had already been taken to the infirmary, unable to partake of the spread Peg and Harriet had prepared for us. And I, of course, was relieved they had found him unharmed.

The next year passed in a swirl of activity. Sarah and I busily worked through a winter with little snow and another summer with picnics and hikes before and after the school term with Jerome.

Autumn was short. Too short. Soon the winds howled, initiating the new season with two inches of snow. The brothers had not finished cutting all the wood. They had hoped the pile would not be depleted too soon, but the family needed it right away. The window above Sarah's bed whistled. We could feel the draft blow across our faces and had to snuggle even farther down under our quilts.

"I'm cold," Sarah whispered.

It was late. The others seemed to be asleep.

"It can be cold like this in the winter, Sarah. We're lucky last winter was an unusually warm one. I used to sleep in a bed with my two sisters, Constance and Martha. They made the bed feel so warm. I pretend they're with me now."

"We had a fire burning in our room, but if it got too cold, I'd climb in with my father," Sarah said dreamily. "I think my toes have fallen off. I can't feel them. Why don't you move over here with me? We can keep each other warm."

"We can't."

"Why not? It's an emergency. My toes are about to fall off."

"Maybe for just a few minutes. But we can't get caught

together. What if someone gets up to use the pot? They'll see us and tell Elizabeth."

"Do you look closely at all the other beds when you get up? Scrunch up your quilt, and they'll think you're still in it."

I got up and slipped in beside Sarah. "Your feet are cold. Here, put them under my nightgown."

That was the first night I fell asleep next to Sarah's warm skin. And once I felt how warm and wonderful it was, I continued to sleep with her throughout the cold winter. Somehow I always roused in time to crawl back under my own covers before Elizabeth woke us up.

At first, we would whisper to each other about our families and pets. But soon our conversation began to move in another direction. I had never spoken to anyone before about secret feelings for our Shaker brothers. But Sarah was open about her own feelings, and I discovered a whole new world. After a few weeks, the subject of boys dominated all the others.

Sarah liked boys and had not lived with the Shakers long enough to make any effort to put her lurid thoughts away for the benefit of the other girls. Do not get me wrong. She was careful about what she said, even creating a secret code to be used in front of the elders. But I knew what the code meant, and it was hard to hide my chuckles in school or during the day when she would say something shocking about one of the boys or men.

"Look at what I have," Sarah said one night, pulling a pile of papers out from under the blanket.

"What are they?"

"They're pictures Sister Camilla drew. The sewing ladies used to make underwear to sell. Look at this one."

"Ouch! That looks like it hurts," I told her. "I don't think my waist could get that small. I didn't know they'd let any of us draw these, especially when we never wear them."

"They don't anymore. When the ministry elders found out about these, they shipped Camilla off. They must have been shocked."

"Where did you find them?"

"The men had them. Seth told me the brothers look at stuff like this. They keep it in the barn, buried in the hay."

"I don't believe you. Seth would never have this."

"I thought you knew him better than that. You've known him for so long and still don't talk about it."

"About what?"

"About what men need from women. It's nature."

"I don't want to talk about it now," I said, pulling the quilt up under my chin.

I did not listen to it then, but the subject would come up again. Eventually I would learn so much about the people on the outside, the world's people would soon become the objects of my fantasies too.

Sarah was only a few months older than I, but she seemed years ahead. I watched her stretch in the moonlight, dark spots pushing at her nightgown. I wanted to touch her, caress her soft creamy skin. It seemed perfectly natural to me that my admiration of Sarah's splendor would end in this unusual fascination. Forced to feel no physical attraction to the young men around me, who else would satisfy the physical longings of puberty? Would Sarah reciprocate with equal interest in me? Over the next few years, our friendship would indeed grow, but her real interests, while a surprise to me, were evidently obvious to the other brothers and sisters. Sarah's determination to achieve her aspirations could not help but affect not only my life, but also the security of the whole family.

7. A REAL TRUSTEE

Not even thinking to get a good look at his face, I failed to recognize him. I would never be able to identify the intruder, which made it difficult for me to put the dread of another break-in to rest. After darkness fell, Edgar-like destitutes often danced in my head. But I should have put the fear aside because something else needed my attention.

I ought to have been more frightened by the consequences of sleeping with Sarah. I tried so hard to obey the rules governing my relationships with my brothers. But perhaps because our daily lives forced us to hide our attraction to members of the opposite sex, I did not even think those rules might also pertain to a fascination with another sister. Was I drawn to Sarah the same way a woman is drawn to a man? That is difficult to answer. I had never felt an interest in any of the boys or men at Hancock and worried I had not. If I were to continue to live in the Community, the fact that I was not attracted to my brothers would only serve to make it easier to give my passions to my work and the Heavenly Father. At the time, I guess I did not realize feeling Sarah's allure might cause the same pangs many of the others felt for men. But it is my belief I needed some kind of affection, a bond with another, and if I could not look for it among the brothers, I would seek it out among those who were closest and most convenient.

While I tell you boys did not excite me, that does not mean

we refrained from talking about them. Sarah and I whispered incessantly about boys those nights we were side by side. I am not sure if my daily spying on my brothers was the result of an arousal of interest on my part or the consequence of my trying to keep Sarah from finding me boring.

"I saw Seth today," I told her one night. "He was at the pond when Molly was there. He was checking the ice and didn't talk to her. I wonder if that upset her."

"Most likely. What was she doing at the pond? Did she walk out on the ice and try to get his attention?"

"No. I think she was collecting pinecones for the dinner table."

"She shouldn't have been there alone."

"I don't think she was alone," I confessed. "She was with Charity, I believe. It seems he doesn't like either one of them. It appears he's more interested in Elizabeth. Have you seen him with Elizabeth lately?"

"No. But I talk to him quite frequently."

"You do? Are you two alone when you talk?"

"Sometimes. I can't believe you didn't see us together yesterday. We were having a discussion over by the carriage house. I gave him back the underwear catalogue. Our hands touched."

"I don't think you'll be able to get him to leave the Community with you, Sarah."

"Why would I do that, Lucy? I wouldn't want to run off with him anyway. I need someone who's already established in the world, not some kid who has no skills to run his own farm."

"What about Ezekiel?" I asked. "I hear he's back from one of his trips."

"What about him? He's a pimply-faced, smelly kid who's reached his potential. I'm not interested in him. Good God,

Lucy, I'm not going to waste my time talking about boys if you don't take their futures seriously."

As spring approached, the sun streamed in earlier and earlier. I soon decided I could not rouse quickly enough to change back to my bed before we would be seen, so I moved back permanently. I missed Sarah. I missed the bond we had formed. I was her confidante, listening to her describe her escapades with certain brothers, exploits that to me were fantasies any young girl might have when her every move or reflection was controlled.

As if the spring sun was another beginning, I turned most of my thoughts to my work. I awoke each morning at four-thirty and headed to the laundry, where I spent the hours before breakfast washing and hanging sheets, towels, and clothing. After breakfast, I went to the trustees' house, where I would enter orders and invoice customers or balance their accounts. After dinner, I returned to the laundry to finish ironing or mending clothes. It was an easy schedule. I had enough hours to finish one job before moving to the next. And at bedtime, I was too tired to say more than a just a few words to Sarah before I was asleep.

Thankfully, Sarah and I were no longer sleeping together when the epidemic hit—when girls were up several times a night with endless fits of coughing or sniffing or to ease the cramping of their irritable stomachs. Not only would we be more likely to pass the ailment on to each other if we still slept together, but of course, our sleeping arrangement would almost certainly be discovered. But sleeping in the same room with afflicted girls made it more likely we would become sick ourselves, even if we did not feel inclined to help our ailing sisters personally.

It felt good to be able to rouse and go to work and not have to stay with them. And while I feared daily I would be the next to contract the transmittable illness, I realized I had no power over it when it went outside our room, to the other dwellings and beyond the Community itself.

One day, Eli came to my office, a handkerchief over his mouth. "You must come downstairs. I have to show you what we do up front."

"Are you sick?" I asked.

"No, Sister. I'm trying to stay well!"

That was the first time I had ever seen the front room where the world's people came in and did business with the trustees. Its simple beauty surprised me: sanded wooden benches facing a long counter. I wiped my hand on the smooth countertop. It was beautiful.

"Where's Leonard?" I asked.

"In bed. I summoned you here so you could help out. You're the only one besides me who knows what to do."

"It doesn't look too busy. Can't you do this yourself?"

"I've been working closely with Brother Leonard and am not sure how long my health will remain like this. I need to teach you how we do it because we can't afford to shut everything down. You're lucky most of the world is in bed. Otherwise it would be very busy here."

Sure enough, early the next day, Eli went to his room sick and left me in charge of the store. It was not busy. I thought I could handle it.

"Can I help you, sir?" I asked a gentleman sitting on one of the benches.

"Yes, miss," he said. "I'm here to pick up a couple of hats I ordered for my store in Lee."

"What's your name?"

He handed me the receipt, and I found his order in the large

90

storeroom at the back. It was not that difficult. I brought out the items, and we both examined them. Satisfied, he paid what he owed on his account and left. But he was not the only customer, and things would soon begin to get complicated.

Ezekiel entered and handed me a pouch of money. I told him I would balance his account later when I got a chance, but he insisted I do it then, leaning over the counter and smiling at me.

"I can't believe you're here by yourself," he said, his grin revealing yellowing teeth.

"If you go round back, the brothers can help you refill your cart. I'm really busy right now."

"Sister Lucy, I hear you saw old Edgar a few months ago when I was assigned a district in New York."

"This isn't the time to talk about your business, Brother. We can work on the account later."

"It's just if anyone wanted a witness to the happenings of that night, I might feel obligated to volunteer."

I looked him directly in the eye. My bravado belied the fact that under my skirt my knees shook. "If you have something to report about the night the kitchen window was broken, maybe you should report it. The elders are anxious to hear from any eye witnesses."

Suddenly the door opened, and another man walked in. Ezekiel stepped back but still did not leave. The first business-man was soon followed by two more. I was definitely busy now. Running to fill orders and taking items in to settle accounts, I did not notice when Ezekiel slipped out, but by the time I could close up and go to dinner, he was nowhere to be found. I did not tell anyone he had confronted me in the shop, afraid the elders might find reason to return me, a young woman, to the back room. When I heard nothing from the elders in the days that followed the incident, I suspected Ezekiel was lying about being a witness. I wondered what he was up to.

We were losing money. Business was down because so many people were too sick to come in or feared they would become sick if they were exposed to us. Jeremiah suggested we take a cart out and deliver the goods directly to the farms and stores. The elders were concerned neither Eli nor Leonard was strong enough to make the trip, and a trustee would have to be present and responsible for the goods.

"I think Sister Lucy here is capable enough to fulfill that job," Jeremiah said. "She knows what needs to be delivered and recognizes what on the accounts requires immediate settlement."

My ears perked up. He never even mentioned to me the possibility I go with him when he asked me to attend this meeting. I do not think the elders would have listened to such a preposterous idea had any of the other brothers proposed it. But Jeremiah was highly respected. He had once been a deacon, a supervisor in the furniture-making shop, and never made any trouble. The thirty-five-year-old loved his new work, caring for the horses in the carriage house full time, and was enthusiastic about his worship. He had been asked to take preparation to be a ministry elder but graciously refused the invitation, explaining he would miss his horses, Dakota and Mamie. He told me on more than one occasion he felt it was his calling to care for them.

"I'm concerned about the safety of an unsupervised young woman out in the world," Thomas said. "Sister Lucy's too young to commit to this Community and therefore very open to influence from the outside."

"I find Sister Lucy has a good head on her shoulders," Jeremiah said. "She's very responsible and doesn't talk about boys or giggle when she's around boys. I can't say that about the other young sisters."

I cleared my throat, more to remind them I was present and that they did not need to talk as if I were not.

"I can send a chaperone with her," Evelyn said. "Sister Georgia has an affection for Sister Lucy. While she's too old to help unload the cart, her presence might convince me Sister Lucy would be safe."

"And I can bring Brother Seth with me so the two of us can unload the cart," Jeremiah said. "Brother Seth's very sensible too, and last fall, he made a strong commitment to our cause."

"Is that all right with you, Brother Thomas?" Evelyn asked. "Do you have any other questions?"

"No. I'll want a list of farms and stores you plan to visit, however, and a report from you when you return. I'll need something to present to Elder Robert and Eldress Lavonia, who are currently visiting the Harvard Community. On the next trip, we'll have to have their blessing, because I'm afraid we're bending more than one rule here."

"Which is your prerogative, Brother," Jeremiah said, standing. "Sister Lucy, will you please inform Sister Georgia we'll all meet at the carriage house at nine, right after breakfast?"

Georgia and I ate quickly. It seemed she was as excited as I was, even though she had been out in the world several times already.

"It's always fun to go to places you don't see often," Georgia said. "I grew up around here. I went to school with Beth Barnard, Amos's wife. I'd love to hear news of their family. Over the years, different elders have either discouraged correspondence with the outside or ignored the fact we were writing letters to friends and relatives. It depended on how pressured the leadership was—if the apostasy rate was high or if they heard we were writing letters complaining about our mission. We've never been officially allowed to visit with the outsiders directly."

Seth approached us from the carriage house. "We need your help, Sister Lucy. The cart sits by the trustees' house. Brother Leonard has let us in, but we must have the account papers to know what needs to be delivered today."

I read the names from my sheets while the men, trying to keep orders together, loaded the items onto the wagon. Then Seth helped Georgia up front with Jeremiah, and Seth and I climbed into the filled wagon, sitting on some bales of hay that were to be delivered to Mr. Osborne, owner of the farm just over the hill from us.

The scenes around the borders of our Community were gorgeous but not as stunning as the gardens I saw beyond. The yard in front of Mr. Osborne's farmhouse had a host of blooming yellow iris and garlic mustard.

I climbed down from the wagon to examine the flowers. "Mr. Osborne, these are beautiful. Are they from our seeds?"

"The garlic mustard is, I believe, Miss Hammond. What did you bring me today?"

"I understand, Mr. Osborne, that besides the hay, you ordered some seed. The carrots and onions should probably be planted soon. You also asked for a new leather yoke. I think that's here in the wagon."

"I like these chairs. Who are these for?"

I glanced at my list. "Miss Wright on the other side of town ordered one, and so did Mr. Marshall."

"How do I order a chair like this?"

"Right here, Mr. Osborne," I said, taking out another sheet of paper. "You can probably pick it up in August, there being several orders in front of yours. Anything else?"

"My hat," said Mrs. Osborne running toward the wagon. "I ordered a hat and some material."

"Yes. It's right here. Seth, will you hand Mrs. Osborne her order?"

I slipped Mr. Osborne the bill, and he paid me right there with some cash and a crate of chickens. Then I climbed back into the wagon and repeated the actions with three more farms as we drove into town.

I had never seen West Stockbridge. It was a lot like Hancock, with a line of houses along the main road. When I was a child, my father would take us to Great Barrington, but that did not have the mining trains carrying loads of iron to big buildings on the edge of town that West Stockbridge did. Some people, planting seeds in their yards waved, and I waved back. A little farther into town, a man in a straw hat and gray suit with a walking stick strolled along the road. I have to admit I gawked as we passed him. I had met many of the local businessmen over the last few days, but this man had not come into the trustees' office. I would have remembered him. After we past, he waved his staff, but I was too nervous to wave back.

Jeremiah pulled the wagon up in front of Barnard's General Store and jumped down. Something flew by. I caught the object out of the corner of my eye. It landed on the front of Jeremiah's shirt. Soon there was another. Two young boys approached us.

"You dance with no tune. You hop like a loon. You say you're so good but dance naked in the wood," the first one recited.

Grabbing a cloth from the floor of the wagon, I threw it to Jeremiah so he could wipe off the front of his shirt. The rancid odor of the rotten egg began to waft in my direction. I stood up to climb down, but Seth leaned over and grabbed my wrist.

The second boy was older, and though nearly as tall as Jeremiah, much more gangly. He stood behind his friend. "Why don't you share your women if you're too busy to use them yourselves?"

I'd had enough. I wiggled my wrist away from Seth's grip

and turned to climb over the side. I did not see him approach. I only heard the splatter as another egg hit its target. By the time I turned around to confront the boys, the man with the walking stick had swatted at them, causing them to retreat across the street.

He offered Jeremiah his handkerchief. "I apologize for the children," he said. "I'm sure their parents would be quite shocked by their behavior."

"It's not the first time. There are a few people in these parts who choose to remain ignorant," Jeremiah said, continuing to wipe his shirt with the rag. "We haven't seen you before. Are you from around here?"

"No. My name is Daniel Aldridge. I'm from Springfield and am staying at the hotel in town. Please let me help you unpack your goods."

"No need. As you can see, I've brought plenty of hands with me."

I believe Mr. Aldridge expected an introduction, but Jeremiah offered none. Seth came around to help Georgia down from the wagon, but as Evelyn had cautioned us, she did not offer to help us unpack. Instead, she walked up the street to a fabric and dressmaker's shop. Mr. Aldridge held the door open, and I grabbed my notebook as well as a box and followed Seth into the store. I looked at Mr. Aldridge more closely as I passed. He smiled and nodded. I could not touch my face because my hands were full but knew it felt hot. I had just turned fifteen and, for the first time, was uncomfortable around a man, worrying that maybe my bonnet was crooked or there was a spot of breakfast on my neckerchief. I put the box down near the counter.

"Mr. Barnard, good morning," Jeremiah said. "I'm not sure you've met Sister Lucy. She's the trustee and will work out the accounts with you while we unpack some of the goods."

"Ah yes, Mr. Johnson. I haven't seen you around town lately."

"I've been busy in the Community."

"I hope you brought more peppermints. We've been out of them for almost a week."

"Yes, Mr. Barnard, how do you do?" I said nervously, aware Mr. Aldridge was examining some shelves along the back wall. My ears burned. "How's your wife? I hope she's improving."

"Yes, yes. I don't think I caught your name, Miss—"

"Hammond, Lucy Hammond," I said, realizing he probably felt uncomfortable addressing me as Sister Lucy.

"Mrs. Barnard's doing better. Thank you, Miss Hammond."

"I have here a list of the goods you ordered. I believe you'll especially like the seed selection we have this season. They're the very finest, especially the garlic mustard."

Mr. Barnard watched Jeremiah unpack the boxes. "Yes, yes," he said somewhat absent-mindedly.

"I have an invoice," I explained, placing the piece of paper directly in front of him. "And this gives me the perfect opportunity to take your next order so you don't have to make the trip to our place right away."

Mr. Barnard continued to look toward Jeremiah as he listed his needs. "I liked the fabric you brought last time. It went real fast. Do you have more of that, Mr. Johnson? Do I need to show you some of it?"

"No, Mr. Barnard," I continued. "I have it listed in my books. Was it the blue with flowers?"

"Are there other colors or prints of that same fabric? My wife doesn't want the same look with every dress," he said, finally gazing down at me.

"I'll see what I can find," I said. "Maybe your wife would like a hat. We have fan hats that look pretty with that print."

Mr. Barnard cleared his throat, seemingly uncomfortable with the subject. "I should ask my wife," he said, looking back up at Jeremiah.

"We also have canned fruits and vegetables," I said, trying to get his attention again. "I noticed your stock's kind of low. I can pick out a selection for you if you'd like. And the brooms— those aren't ours, are they? It looks like you're out of our new flat brooms. If you move the ice tongs and shovels out of here because they're no longer in season, you'll have some room for barrels of potatoes. We have a new variety this year."

Mr. Barnard smiled. "Maybe you should be behind the counter instead of in front of it."

"I usually stand behind a counter, Mr. Barnard. Rarely do I get to stand on this side. So you agree you need some more canned fruits and vegetables?"

Jeremiah indicated it was time to go. When we got outside, he looked at my new list and smiled. It was then I remembered we forgot to deliver a crate of leather straps. I grabbed the sides of the box and returned, immediately walking to the rear of the store where I had seen an empty box. Mr. Barnard was still standing at the counter, talking to someone through a doorway behind him. Mr. Aldridge listened to the conversation with his back to the door. Neither seemed to hear or see me reenter the shop. I went directly to the shelf and knelt down to refill the box.

"I'll take one of those if you can order it for me," Mr. Aldridge said. "Maybe you should have ordered it from that young lady when she was here. Will she be back?"

"No, no. I don't think so. They don't come into town too often, especially the women."

"I don't understand."

"Oh yeah, you aren't from around here, are you? She's with the Shakers. Some call them the Shakin' Quakers, but that isn't what they call themselves. Ever heard of 'em?"

"Yes. In fact, I was trying to find out more about their farm.

People seem to come and go there quite frequently, don't they?"

"Oh, you mean for your investigation into that bank robbery in Springfield? Not too often. I think more come out lately than stay in. But I guess if one were hiding from something, he might . . ." Mr. Barnard said. "Don't think of getting too close to any of those sisters though, Mr. Aldridge."

"Oh?"

"They have a vow of chastity there. They live together but supposedly don't do anything. Sounds fishy to me. Mrs. Barnard's on a committee at church here in town. They're trying to get Pastor Davis to preach to some of those ladies, it being sinful to live with a man, or maybe even more than one of 'em, without the benefit of marriage. I doubt their leaders would ever let one of those sisters like that Miss Hammond go out alone."

Not wanting to hear another word, I stood up and smoothed my dress. My face must have been flushed if not completely red, but I threw my shoulders back and picked up the crate. "There, Mr. Barnard," I said. "I noticed you were short of leather straps and pouches. If you need anything else that isn't on the list, I'm sure Brother Leonard will be well enough to take your order at the trustees' shop." I walked directly to the door. "Mr. Aldridge," I said, nodding my head.

When I got outside, I did not wait for Jeremiah to come around and help me up but climbed up the wheel and sat down on an empty crate. There were still items to deliver, but I said nothing the rest of the trip. I only longed to go home.

8. Caught

Late spring brought a lull in my work in the trustees' office. Both Leonard and Eli were healthy and did not need me full time in the store. Neither wanted to keep the books, so I spent a few hours each evening reckoning the accounts. But during the day, I was free to do what I chose, and there was always a dearth of hands to help with the planting. I spent much of the time in the mud of the vegetable fields collecting seeds. And after cleaning up each day, I spent a few hours with my old friends packing what I had collected. To tell you the truth, I could have done this every day for the rest of my life, but the trustees' office had given me opportunities I could never have dreamed of: a glimpse of the world just down the road.

My days delivering our goods were relatively few. The epidemic lasted only a week or two, and not being a regular salesman for the Community like Ezekiel was, opportunity to travel outside did not materialize for a long while after that. Mr. Barnard came to the shop fairly regularly, and I ran into him on occasion when I settled his account. Our meetings were always awkward, however. Though I never let on I had overheard him that day in his store, he was never quite sure I had not and stumbled over his words when he spoke to me. I appeared quite comfortable, I think, but the pretense was just as thorny for me.

Mr. Osborne entered the store frequently and was very nice. "I'd like to see some of the gowns made from silk that might go with the hat you delivered last week, Miss Hammond," he said in an unusually loud voice. "Mrs. Osborne really loves that hat and needs a gown to go with it."

"Edith has created several gowns in that color, Mr. Osborne. Perhaps Mrs. Osborne should come in to give us specifications on her size."

"You've sold me, Miss Hammond. It's so wonderful to work with a businesswoman who's so convincing."

I, of course, would not order what he requested in his paced voice, fearing Mrs. Osborne would appear at the door to reproach us all for selling her husband unnecessary trinkets.

"By the way, Miss Hammond, how are Mindy and Mandy, the hens I gave you?" he asked one day.

"Oh, Mr. Osborne, Peg served them for dinner last week, and we enjoyed them immensely," I mistakenly said, not realizing he had brought in a pouch of special grain for them. Fortunately, he did not hold the comment against me.

Mr. Aldridge never came into the shop, which was odd because he was supposedly looking for a criminal in our midst. I wanted to tell him about Edgar breaking into the kitchen, because I thought Edgar was probably his bank robber, but he never gave me the opportunity. After several weeks, I did not think about the detective anymore, figuring he had returned to Springfield. There was little time for him anyway. Men just did not fit into my environment. He would be happier on the outside, I thought, where he could actually meet and eventually marry a beautiful heroine. My future lay in the Community, worshipping the Heavenly Father so he and the Savior would see we had actually created heaven on earth.

I have to admit, being outside with my hands in the dirt was my favorite chore, my calling.

"Sister Lucy, get your knees up off that dirt," Peg called to me from the door of the dwelling one day. "You're the only one who has work dresses worn at the knees."

"I'm sorry, Peg. My legs got tired." I got up and looked at the mud stains on my dress. It was a good thing there were still a few months before school started.

Brother Seth came up beside me to help.

"How are you doing, Brother? At the meeting on Sunday, I heard you might make an announcement concerning your plans for the future."

"There are more important events than that, Sister Lucy. We have visitors. Justin from the Millerite group is here. You remember Mr. William Miller. He spoke the summer before last on the urgency of readying the area for the second coming."

"Yes. Has he pushed out his carefully planned prediction of the Savior's second coming again? We've gone through the same activity twice already. We even dedicated Mt. Sinai as a holy area in preparation for his last prediction, but it never happened."

"There are others who are disillusioned. He claims his calculations contained errors."

"He could have asked me to look at his books. I would've pointed out the errors before we did all the work."

Seth smiled. "You probably would have, but then we wouldn't have had the bonus."

"What bonus?"

"Miller attracted many new believers to his church because people were hoping for the Savior's second coming, right? When he erred the first time, we got his apostates. The people were so stirred with love for the Savior they wanted to continue their worship with us. Then, he went out and drew in a new flock. Now his followers are turning to us again. This man, Justin, is going to talk about bringing Miller's people in. That's great. We'll need them for harvest in the fall."

"Why, Seth, I had no idea the ministry was so sneaky."

"What harm did it do to back him as long as we didn't instruct our own members about an imminent second coming? We know we already have heaven on earth, even if the Savior doesn't visit for generations to come."

"You should be in the ministry, Seth. You think like a minister."

"Between you and me, I've already been asked. They need leadership in Ohio and Kentucky. I'm not sure I want to go that far. I'm hoping they'll find a need closer to home before Mother Hanna makes up her mind."

"I hear Elder Ramsey in Tyringham is ill. He may want to retire."

"Until then, we've got a busy summer. I don't need to think about it until it happens."

"Tyringham would be nice. Then you wouldn't really be leaving. I could still see you from time to time. I'm proud of you, Seth, but I'll miss you if you go far away."

"You're too busy. You have one of the best jobs in the Community, and I hear you're very good at it. You'll probably be a full trustee the minute you commit," Seth said, getting up and looking across to the barn. "Anyway, I should go help out with the cows. I'll talk to you later."

I was in the laundry when the message came. Wearing a grave face, Molly approached. I would not have been alarmed had her expression been different.

"Eldress Evelyn would like to speak with you in her office," she said.

"Why?"

"I don't know, but Sarah's already there."

"What did she do?" I asked, assuming they caught Sarah doing something bad. I broke the rules so little, it would be difficult to pin anything on me this time.

I returned the iron to the stand and removed my apron before walking down the lane to the dwelling. Just inside the girls' entrance, I realized something was wrong. Evelyn's office door was ajar. I could make out Thomas standing behind her desk. I pushed the door open and peered in.

"Sister Lucy," Evelyn said, her voice a piercing staccato. "There's been a report of something that concerns the elders here deeply."

I stared at the back of Sarah's head. It was bowed, and she did not turn to look at me.

"Please sit down," Thomas said.

I watched the side of Sarah's face as I pulled out the chair and sat down. Tears made tracks down her cheeks.

Evelyn cleared her throat. "I'll get right to the point since you girls are old enough to know the gravity of the situation. It was reported to me you two have been sharing a bed for quite some time. Sister Sarah here has confirmed it. What do you say in your defense, Sister Lucy?"

"I don't deny it. It was a cold winter, and I couldn't bear the icy sheets. The beds don't seem to warm up at all which makes me have to—" I stopped, realizing Thomas was standing over me, and I did not want to detail how many times I had to get up to use the pot.

"And why didn't you tell Sister Elizabeth so she could provide you with another blanket?"

I did not dare tell her Elizabeth would not have given me one, that the elder sister thought we would all be better off if we learned to put up with what she called "inconveniences." I did not need Elizabeth's wrath on top of everything else. "We haven't slept together since March," I said to her.

Evelyn began to pace the small area behind her desk. Even Thomas moved farther into the corner to give her more room.

"You can't begin to comprehend how serious this is," she

said. "Perhaps we didn't make it clear. Just as we can't give all of our energy and love to the Holy Father if we are having marital relations, the same is true of other types of relations."

I stood up. "But, Eldress, we didn't have a relationship. We only kept ourselves warm."

"If that were true, Sister, it was only a matter of time. I think we'll have to address this problem in a union meeting. Heavens, if this is occurring in the girl's shop, just think what's happening on the other side."

I must have gone pale. My head whirled. "You mean we have to discuss it with our brothers?"

Thomas looked embarrassed. "Perhaps a union meeting with the adolescents is a good idea. I'm not sure we've addressed the subject of alternative . . . well uh, carnal expressions of love with them at all. I'm sorry our sisters here have even thought of such things. Perhaps the idea was brought in from outside the Community, but it might be best if we don't hide the possibility of an outbreak. We can reveal its sinfulness so other families can watch out for it too. I'll talk to Elder Robert. This should be addressed in a Sunday meeting so all the families are aware of its dangers."

"Yes, Sister Lucy, just the older brothers and sisters," Evelyn added. "The two of you could use some humility. You're lucky we haven't asked you to remove yourselves from the Community."

I must have wrinkled my brow here, not understanding how our removal was possible when we were just fifteen. Did the Believer Community make provisions for orphaned or abandoned outcasts? If not, where would we go?

"Brother Thomas recommends you both be discharged from your apprenticeships for six months, but we need you to continue to work somehow, because we're short of hands. Sister Sarah, you'll go to the vegetable garden outside the kitchen.

Sister Lucy, you'll sew with Sister Edith and learn how to embroider. I'll make sure the others are told."

Sarah began to weep.

"What about the trustees' house?" I asked. "It's beginning to get busy there. What will they do without me?"

"I'm afraid you should have thought about that before now, Sister Lucy," Thomas said. "Working there's a privilege. Brothers Eli and Leonard will have to make do and will probably be very upset with you. But your offense is so serious, I must ask for their tolerance while we address a crisis that concerns the entire membership."

We stood up and repeated, "Yes, Brother Thomas, Sister Evelyn." Our heads were bowed until Thomas left the room.

Evelyn waited for him to close the door. "Oh, yes. And Sister Lucy, you may switch beds with Sister Agnes. That way you'll be closer to Sister Elizabeth. She can help you get extra blankets when you're cold."

Sarah rose and opened the door but stopped to listen from the doorway.

"But Agnes sometimes wets the bed," I said. "I don't want to sleep in a bed with that kind of odor."

"You and Sister Sarah can scrub down the bed or get one of the brothers to replace the webbing. But I think if you just switch your mattresses, it'll be enough. Perhaps it was a mistake to put you two next to Sister Agnes in the first place. Her problem is exacerbated by her ability to sleep through a twister. Had she roused more easily, we could have stopped this nonsense early. I won't have either of you talking to anyone else about any affliction Sister Agnes might have. That applies to the meeting, too."

The union meeting was held in the large room at the far end of the second floor just a few evenings later. It was set up like a regular union meeting and besides me, included Sarah, Agnes, Louise and Phoebe, the last two under fourteen. Sister Molly had committed to the Community and now lived in the brick dwelling. Charity was busy preparing to sign the covenant and was therefore excused. I had not expected them to become members. Both girls, though fun to be with, were a bit scattered. But I guess I really had no reason to imagine them in the world with families either.

The boys were different, too. Calvin and Gilbert were both very new and about fifteen or sixteen. George had been here from the beginning but was very quiet. Then there were two biological brothers, Martin and Russell, one sixteen and the other seventeen. Sarah had evidently already met them.

"When they moved to the Community with their family last year, they already knew they wanted girlfriends," she whispered to me.

It was difficult to hide my shock, and I immediately tried to shush her up.

"He touched me right here," she continued, showing me where Russell had stroked her arm.

"Isn't he seventeen? I believe he'll be in the world more than a year before you get out, you know," I said. "You probably won't even recall his name when you turn eighteen."

"I'll always remember him in my heart as my first and most cherished love," Sarah vowed.

Elizabeth brought the meeting to order. Her face went blank when she introduced us, almost like we did not really exist under her supervision—like she did not know us. "I haven't had a chance to introduce you to my sisters, Brother Damien. I'd like you to tell them about yourself first."

Damien Rathburn was Anson's replacement. I had never witnessed such elation as on the day Anson found out he was assigned as second ministry elder. I heard he never wanted to be an elder brother, overseeing the welfare of the Community's young people. The position had been described as one of the worst. Most of the young men, and Anson was well into his twenties, did not want to look back on their own youths. The responsibilities of the elder brother were great. I remember Anson's reaction when eight-year-old Davis Blanchard fell off a horse and broke his neck. The boy should never have been on the horse. But no one was watching when he managed to climb onto a fence and then onto the horse's back. Anson took months to recover after the boy's death, swearing to this day it was his fault for walking away for a few minutes to get the horse some oats.

Damien was a novice, and because he was a new convert, they were able to get him to watch the boys as an elder brother. No one had a chance to tell him how difficult the job really was. I thought about it a minute. If naive novices were the only ones they could get to watch over the children, how were the young ones going to pick up Mother Ann's intentions? How was she a model for us to live our lives every day? There was another question here too. Why was Elizabeth still an elder sister? Why had she not left? When she committed, she should have been able to pursue another position. Did she love us that much? I did not think that was the case, especially when I saw her expression before the meeting started.

Damien stood up. He was good-looking—tall with dark curly hair and shrewd brown eyes. I looked at Sarah and saw her face light up. She smiled in his direction. Gone was the penitent expression she promised to keep through the whole meeting.

"I come from Hudson, Massachusetts. My father's a preacher in a church there. I wasn't interested in my parents' way of life and looked far and wide for a form of worship that appealed to my nature." He said nothing about liking children or looking forward to working with young people.

Elizabeth stood up. She stared across the fifteen-foot expanse at him and threw her shoulders back, making her bosom look much bigger than it actually was. "Thank you, Brother Damien. I believe we ought to start our meeting with a little prayer. Please, Brother, would you lead us?"

Damien removed a piece of paper from his pocket and opened it up. He looked at Sarah, who was beaming at him. "Lord, hear us today as we clear the way for prayer. In our joy to serve ye, we sometimes forget your laws are essential to keep our hearts free to acknowledge your gifts and our heads lucid so we can heed your words."

Elizabeth smiled and clapped her hands as if it were the best prayer she had ever heard. "We're here tonight, brothers and sisters, to discuss a problem that has occurred in these very quarters," she said. "Let there be no question about the rules of this house. Perhaps Sister Sarah and Sister Lucy would like to stand and explain what they did, so Brother Damien and I can go over the rules yet another time."

Sarah gazed at Damien. When he looked up, she finally lowered her lids, perhaps to contemplate her transgression. She turned as if she were introducing me and began, "Sister Lucy and I shared a bed."

The others gasped in unison, the rush of air rustling my hair.

"We didn't do it with the intent of having a relationship but to keep warm and to talk about our brothers," she continued.

Gilbert giggled right there, and Calvin elbowed him. I was reeling and did not know why I had not fainted right there in front of everyone. The whole scene was appalling. If it were like this now, what would it be like on Sunday?

"I certainly didn't sleep with Sarah out of any sort of attachment. Nor did I stay in her bed to talk about brothers," I said.

I did not think for a moment that perhaps Sarah was trying to send a message to Damien. Telling everyone we were talking about boys was evidently some kind of code to them, though when she told me later that it was, I still did not understand it. She evidently felt the need to let them all know she was interested in *them,* not another sister.

Elizabeth got up and turned, gesturing for us to sit down. "We aren't here to judge our sisters. The aching they feel in their hearts will last far longer than any punishment that has been exacted. The problem here is sharing a bed, whether with the opposite sex or with one's own, is strongly forbidden. The impure thoughts, and in this case, unnatural acts, set you against both the Heavenly Father and those outside our Community who already see us as insincere and malicious. Is there anything you want to add to that, Brother Damien?"

Damien stood up and smiled at Sarah. "No Sister. I think you've said it sufficiently. I don't believe the sisters intentionally sought to perform unnatural acts. What my boys should get from the situation is that sometimes one's intentions aren't very important. What might seem innocent in the beginning could lead to unnatural yearnings in the future. If anyone's so troubled by his vow of celibacy that he chooses an aberrant bond with a fellow brother, he should seek the advice of an elder immediately. We all have to fight the urges to fulfill our carnal fantasies. You, brothers, aren't alone."

I was no longer ashamed. I just sat there, my mouth open. I could not believe what he had just said. It was one thing to experience the feelings; it was another to talk about them in front of everyone. Perhaps he and Sarah belonged together after all.

"Now then," Damien continued. "I believe this meeting's over. I'll recite an ending prayer. Please help us, O Lord, to save the souls of Sisters Sarah and Lucy. Please guide them along the correct path so they, too, can join ye in the garden. We already forgive them for their deplorable sins, as you indicated forgiveness is necessary to healing. We also ask forgiveness from our dear Mother Ann Lee, who'd be horrified by the events that have occurred in this house."

We all got up and rushed for the exit. Sarah made sure she went out the women's door to the hallway at the same time Damien passed through the men's door right beside it, an endeavor aided by her pushing Elizabeth forward into the hallway. But Elizabeth won the scuffle in the end when she tripped and fell. Damien was at her side in an instant and helped her up. Sarah would have to settle for Gilbert once more.

While the others felt the union meeting resolved the issue once and for all, this assembly was actually only the beginning of a year of confusion for our family. The Community and our beliefs did not cause my disorientation. It was my affection for Sarah that would change. In the vacuum created by my departure from Sarah's bed would come an interest—indeed an obsession—with a man who lived among the world's people.

9. THE PENALTY

I made it over the first hurdle. While totally humbled at the union meeting, I survived the whole evening unscathed. Even the persistent chatter between Calvin and Gilbert about sex and unnatural liaisons eventually died down. None of our sisters took part in joking about us. Nor had the older boys. I thanked Holy Mother Wisdom over and over our brothers did not attend school with us, or the incessant titter about sex and body parts would have had the whole class yearning for cooler weather.

The next obstacle for the return to normality was the Sunday meeting. My stomach churned as Sarah and I, clad in our Sunday clothes, strolled over to the meetinghouse.

"I think we should run off to the forest and wait for it to be over," Sarah said.

I tugged at her hand. "Don't worry. It'll be over soon. We haven't done anything wrong, and there's nothing the elder minister could intimate that would change that."

As soon as we were all seated, Sarah and I in the back row, Robert stood up and began the prayer. I listened, looking down at my hands, unable to see the reaction of those around us.

"Brothers and Sisters, we're gathered here in prayer so our rejoicing hearts can sing," Robert said.

We all stood up with our hymnals and sang out.

When we were seated once more, Robert continued, "I believe we oft forget, when we receive such gifts from God, we have to show him how thankful we are. Today Sister Peg has prepared a nice breakfast for us. We must sing for the blessing of the early summer harvest and thank Brother Benjamin and, of course, Sister Lucy for bringing us such a great return on the hard toil they have put into the garden."

Of course I was grateful he associated my name with the garden at all, since most of the hard toil this year was certainly Benjamin's. But this was the moment of truth. This was the time he would have to talk about the sins committed over the last week. Although Robert did not usually list the transgressions of the Community, he was known on occasion to bring up a few instances where a brother or a sister had gone over the line. These set examples for us, reminding us of what we ought to avoid.

I held fast to Sarah's hand with the clamp of a tightened vice. In order to avoid the unwanted glances of the young brothers across from us, I watched the worlds' people sitting on some benches against the wall. At least those from the outside would not be able to recognize the names of the sinners about to be clearly enunciated to all the ears in the room. But I was wrong. In the middle of the assemblage was one face I recognized. My eyes passed him once but immediately darted back to rest upon him. He stared straight at me. My face must have taken on a bright red hue, because the clash of the hot and cold chills that ran through me brought a flurry of fireworks. I looked down once more, crouching to hide myself.

And then Robert cleared his throat. "Before we begin the dancing, I'd like to bring up something that occurred this week. It isn't often I must speak of such grave problems as I must do now."

My stomach churned again at such a speed I was not sure if I should run out of the room or vomit right there on the floor at my feet, something that would reveal itself when we moved the benches against the wall so we could dance. I tried to picture

Edith stepping in it and sliding out of control around the room, but even that failed to bring a smile to my lips.

"The Whitewater settlement in Ohio has had a fire with much damage," Robert said. "Those afflicted number about three hundred. The survivors of the incident, and all of the Church members did survive, have been moved to the North Union Community and promise to help the new group become stronger. At the same time, most are eager to rebuild, and we must pray they can become comfortable in their new home soon. In both prayer and celebration that they're safe, please move your benches to prepare for a dance. Think about the gifts our Holy Mother Wisdom has given us and see if you can transfer these gifts to our brothers and sisters in Ohio."

That was it. He did not even mention unnatural acts in the children's dwelling. Before getting up, I clasped my hands together and thanked Mother Ann for the fire in Ohio. I knew it was wrong to rejoice in such a catastrophe, but my joy and relief could not go unacknowledged.

And when we sisters formed a large circle on our side of the meetinghouse, Sarah and I led the group with the loudest foot tapping and swinging. When Sarah fell to her knees because the spirit took her, I fell too, doing my best to look as natural as possible.

And then Sarah started to sing out in Arabic, "*Neimad ot traeh ym evig I.*" She looked at me to do the same.

I stopped short, remembering that Mr. Aldridge was watching. I was not about to profess my love for anyone.

While the fear of our exposure to the entire Community was no longer a threat, Sarah and I both had to face our punishments. I am not sure who would suffer more: Sarah getting her nails dirty in the garden or me having to spend time with Edith.

The older sister looked as dismayed as I was when she learned she would have to work for a couple of hours each day with her least talented student. While this was meant to be my sentence for having what the elders thought to be an illicit affair with another young woman, I am sure Edith felt equally punished.

I was to meet her at Evelyn's office, and she would take me someplace to give me the lessons. I waited outside of the eldress' office for no more than thirty seconds when I heard a screeching and pounding inside. Someone was complaining bitterly, an event that rarely happened in the dwelling. Living in a place where teamwork was the goal, arguing was discouraged. We all had to make an extra effort to get along, and tattling about another who had hurt your feelings or rankled you personally was strictly forbidden. So when I heard the squabbling coming from Evelyn's office, curiosity got the better of me, and I decided to stay put until Edith arrived to drag me away. To my surprise, when the door finally opened, it was Edith herself who emerged, her face streaked and jaw set.

"I believe the waiting room's free, Sister," Evelyn called after her.

I followed the upset woman into the waiting room, and the two of us sat down on the bench while Edith, soothing her ruffled feathers with a series of deep sighs, removed two hoops and a swatch of cloth from her bag.

"Have you ever embroidered, Sister Lucy?" she asked. "I would think you would've done so in school before you came here. It's a must in the good schools in the area."

"No," I admitted. "I didn't go to school before I came here."

"No school? What were your parents thinking?"

"I believe they thought I was too young. My older sisters and brother went to school, but I was too young."

"Well, first I'll show you how to put the cloth in the hoops, and then you do it for me."

The first hour passed very slowly. Edith, dear soul, was a

perfectionist. I must have stretched the cloth in the hoops at least fifty times. She was patient at first, but her disappointment in me began to show after about half an hour of repetition. Finally, she accepted my offering, and choosing the colors for me, began to thread my needle so I would know how to do it in the future.

It was around this time that I heard footsteps. Edith had left the door open. The room had no windows, and the doorway offered the only conduit of fresh air. It was early summer and already hot outside. The hallway often became stuffy by mid-afternoon, and the smaller rooms even sooner. I sat on a bench that looked back at Evelyn's office, and Edith sat across from me, busily preparing her own hoops. I watched her close one eye as she put the needle beside her nose and brought up her thread. The moment she was ready to shove the thread through the eye, her tongue came out and curled like a reptile catching a meal.

I was stunned. I did not think I could do it her way. But just as she began to poke her needle through her own pattern, I heard them—more than one set of voices crossing the transept, probably from Thomas's office. Not caring where it was supposed to go, I quickly stuck my needle through the cloth. If I had done it her way, I would not have been able to watch the hallway just outside the door. If I raised the hoops to pull the thread through, I could look across the embroidery work without being noticed by Edith.

Thomas approached Evelyn's office and knocked on her door. I had expected him to appear. But I did not imagine the other set of footsteps would belong to Mr. Aldridge. Both had their backs to me, but I recognized the detective immediately, suddenly gasping when my heart began to pound too hard.

"What's the matter, Sister Lucy? Are you sick? Do you have gas? Maybe you should go to the infirmary."

"If I do that, Edith, Evelyn will see that we make up the lesson."

"I believe you're leaving off the titles, Sister. I'm Sister Edith to you," she said, her voice as squeaky as a parched hinge. "Oh my, what have you done? You've ruined your work already. You can't stick the needle just anywhere, Sister. I can't fix it now."

She whined so loudly, Mr. Aldridge turned around. Seeing only me facing the doorway, he smiled and nodded.

"I'm sorry, Sister Edith. It was my fault," I said softly, my cheeks still hot. "I can cut these threads and start over if you'd like, but I can't do it now. I'll redo it by tomorrow."

When I looked up again, Evelyn had evidently opened her office door and let the men in because they were no longer in sight.

"Are you sure you can do this on your own time? I mean, you have school just after lunch, don't you?"

"Yes. I can do it tonight. Just give me a few colors, and I'll work on it later. And if Evelyn looks for us today and asks where we were, I'll tell her we decided to work outside in the sunshine."

Edith's eyes gleamed at my willingness to deceive the elders in order for us both to gain a little freedom from an indisputably unwarranted sentence. "Maybe we should work outside tomorrow anyway. Perhaps you need more light."

I smiled back, hoping this meant she now viewed me as a partner. "I have to work in the laundry. I must go now."

I did the work Edith expected, and we started off on a better foot the next day. I helped her pull a bench out the door into the sunshine where we both labored over our projects with little interaction at all.

I never finished that assignment, however. The following day I was summoned to Evelyn's office once more. Unfortunately, I had not seen Mr. Aldridge again and dared not ask about his visit two days earlier.

"Good morning, Sister Lucy," she said. "I have a problem. Brothers Eli and Leonard talked to Elder Robert this morning, complaining they can't handle all the work in the trustees' house. I don't know what you've done to the books, Sister, but they claim they can't decipher the figures and therefore aren't able to do without you."

"Well, I . . ." I began, not knowing how to respond.

"I'm therefore reassigning you to the trustees' office. I assume you've learned your lesson and that there won't be further fraternization with Sister Sarah."

"No ma'am," I said, feeling the eldress needed more convincing. "I had no idea an indissoluble attraction would form between us if we continued to share the bed and that no one here would be capable of severing that bond."

The eldress glared at me.

"And I don't think it would be fair to make Sarah remain in the garden if I were released, Eldress," I said, venturing out farther along the ship's plank.

"Sister Sarah's my concern, not yours," she said. "I'll find when I talk with Sister Edith you two have learned to co-exist, won't I?"

"I believe we got along quite well," I said, thinking about our little enterprise. "She'll miss me, but I doubt she'd let on about that in front of you."

"I'm positive she won't," Evelyn said. "And I think if you hurry over to the shop now, you can get in an hour's worth of work before lunch."

I nodded and backed out of the office. I was well away from the dwelling on my way to the trustees' office when I let out a whoop! I had not seen a brighter day all summer.

Eli and Leonard seemed very pleased to see me. I explained what had happened.

"I heard already, Sister," Eli said. "I guess Brother Leonard and I are supposed to say 'shame on you,' but your sin is actually minor compared to what's gone on in the boys' dwelling over the years."

"I believe it's called experimentation and is almost endorsed by the elders because it happens so often," Leonard said. "They sometimes call the younger brothers creative."

"I'm sure the elders are relieved you two couldn't elope like Brother Alex and Sister Harmony," Eli said.

"I didn't know that happened," I said. "Aren't they too old?"

"It's not as if temptation disappears when you become a member, Sister Lucy." Eli said. "It's a curse that exists for a long, long time."

"Did you hear Mr. Aldridge was here in the Community?" I asked.

"You mean the detective? Was that his name?" Eli asked. "Yes. There was a bank robbery a few years ago, and this detective thinks the culprit's hiding out here."

"How did you know who he was?"

"We have valuables here, Sister Lucy," Leonard said. "If there's a thief among us, we should know."

"He's asked us for a favor," Eli continued. "He'd like one of us to write down the dates our brethren in sales were away from Hancock and where they went. The years are scribbled in this column here, so it won't be difficult to figure it out even though you weren't in the Community at the time."

"Crimes?"

"Yes. There have been more than one over the last few years. I thought you could take the time to write down the information for the detective. You're very good at figures, and your handwriting has become more legible."

I worked very hard on the request, wishing my work would help Mr. Aldridge solve the crimes. Of course, I did not know the details so I could not solve them myself.

Days later, Eli came to my office and asked for the sheets. He scanned them and smiled. "You did a good job," he said. "Elder Thomas and Elder Zachary from the brick dwelling are both in the shop. Come with me so you can explain the details of your work."

When I entered the shop, I was surprised to see Mr. Aldridge with the two elders. Thomas looked over the sheets and asked me a few questions, but I do not remember exactly how I responded. Hopefully my answers were adequate.

"This doesn't prove all the brothers went directly to their destinations," I believe I said. "That information, though, could be looked at if you went to the destinations yourself, Mr. Aldridge."

"Yes. That's a good idea. At least I know who wasn't here on what days."

"Mr. Aldridge, this is Sister Lucy, one of our trustees," said Thomas.

"I know," he said, removing his hat. "We met at Mr. Barnard's store."

"During the epidemic," I said.

"And these papers are just what I need, Miss Hammond. Thank you very much for your efforts."

I nodded and backed away. No one noticed my exit, except Mr. Aldridge, of course, who also watched as I backed into the wall, missing the door by several feet.

Dinner was the first time I could talk to Sarah all day. I was anxious to hear if Evelyn had removed her from the garden work. Of course, we were not allowed to talk during the meal. Using sign language or disjointed whispers, we usually tried to communicate anyway. During dinner, however, Sarah made no attempt to talk to me. I tried to grab her hand under the table, but she pulled away. When the meal was finished and we had carried our plates to the counter near the dumbwaiter, I asked her how her day went.

"If you're asking if I no longer work in the garden, I was moved back to the sewing shop," she said, not even looking at me. "But don't expect me to thank you. If it hadn't been for you, I never would've had to work in the garden in the first place."

"What do you mean? We were both punished for sharing the bed."

"You came into *my* bed, Lucy, and you insisted on repeating the crime night after night."

"But you asked me to. You said you were cold."

"You knew the rules and came anyway. I'll never trust you again."

"I don't understand. What did I do? I didn't tell them, Sarah. Someone saw us. Why would I confess to it? It got me into trouble too."

"I'm just afraid to tell you anything," she said. "You let them know about the diary. You informed them about the boys. You told them I'd kissed some of them."

"I did no such thing, Sarah," I said, my head spinning. "I never mentioned the diary because that would get Seth in trouble. I didn't say anything about boys. You did. And if you kissed any of them, I didn't even know about it."

"So I was right. You *do* like Seth. You always liked him."

It was then I noticed the silence that surrounded us. There were several sets of eyes on us. I wanted to die right there. Word would inevitably get back to the members' dwelling where Seth now resided. But Sarah did not seem to care she had embarrassed herself. She passed me and started for the stairs. I began to move too as soon as I realized the Heavenly Father was not going to take me. I turned and ran out to the shed before the tears that stung my eyes fell down my cheeks.

That night I planned to make sure Sarah knew how much I wanted to be her friend. I would wait until the others were asleep and then crawl over to her bed and apologize. I must have drifted off for a while because when I awoke, the moonlight shone right through the window and lighted the beds beside me. I rose onto my elbow and looked across the room at Sarah's bed. She was not there. I stayed awake for nearly an hour, thinking she had gone down to the shed instead of using the pot in the corner and would return in a short time. But as the long minutes past, I began to drift off again.

In the morning, Sarah lay scrunched up under her quilt and seemed to be in a much better mood. Not wanting to ruin it, I said nothing about her disappearance in the middle of the night.

On the way to breakfast, she took my hand and whispered, "I shouldn't have shown my temper at dinnertime."

I smiled at her, relieved but also a bit uncomfortable. From that day on, Sarah's behavior got more and more bizarre. I still loved her, loved her golden curls and her energy and confidence. But her forays in the dead of night made me uneasy. What if the destitutes were still about? Would one of them catch her when she went out by herself? Maybe she was not even by herself.

I swore right then I would try my hardest to protect her. One time soon, I would stay up all night, follow her when she went downstairs, and see for myself how she did it and where she went. Of course, I feared Edgar more than anyone, having already witnessed the destruction he caused. But my relationship with Sarah was too important. I swore I would follow her out in the next week or so and learn for myself what she was doing.

10. Command Performance

It must have been no more than a week or two later I found Sarah in the dressing room one Sunday morning before meeting. Her face was red and covered with white welts.

"What happened? Are you all right?" I asked, pulling a piece of straw out of her hair.

"The milk I drank last night must not have agreed with me. It's given me a reaction of some sort."

"But milk has always agreed with you before, Sarah, hasn't it? Could it be the hay?"

She shot me an angry look. "I don't know what you're talking about, Lucy. A little hay in my hair doesn't mean I had it near my face."

"It looks like the rash has traveled down your back too."

"What am I going to do? We have meeting in less than an hour. Maybe I shouldn't go to meeting."

"That's fine with me, but Evelyn will send you to the infirmary if you don't go. They'll have to investigate what caused this. Do you want to know what your skin reacted to?"

"If *you* think ill of me, you can be sure the sisters at the infirmary will think worse. But I can't possibly go to meeting like this."

"I suppose some soda and milk might help the welts. It'll take only a minute or two for me to go down and get a bowl."

"And what will you tell Peg?"

"She should be getting ready for meeting. I don't believe

she'll even be in the kitchen. But I'll warn you now. You ought to stay away from haystacks, Sarah Bishop, especially if you have the inclination to roll around in them."

I got Sarah's skin to an acceptable color and assumed if we kept our heads down and sat in the back, we would make it through meeting with little notice. I had not figured correctly, however. To our surprise, Jerome had planned a special gift-imparting session from the school children.

Our worship started out normally. Sarah and I did succeed in entering through the women's door and finding seats in the back. Neither of us giggled nor did anything that might attract our elders' averted eyes. That achievement alone should have drawn their attention because Sarah and I were rarely angels during meeting.

Robert rose and said a prayer of thanksgiving, whether we should have been thankful or not. "This morning we sing a hymn to show our appreciation for the fine-looking harvest that's only weeks away and for the return of Brother Caleb and Sister Eliza Ann, who tried to build a life on the outside a few years ago. They've now returned, asking to be taken back, and brought with them a small child, ensuring extra hands to allow Zion to continue into the coming decades. The decision was made to house Eliza Ann in a cottage with the East Family so she could care for the youngster while her husband lived in a dwelling with the North Family."

"They must no longer have the urge to have relations to make them want to live apart from each other," Sarah whispered in my ear.

I remembered what Eli told me about feeling the urge for a long time and thought maybe Sarah was mistaken. Either way, it was difficult for me to understand why their faith might supersede their union. I glanced at the outsiders along the wall.

Mr. Aldridge sat there seemingly lost in thought. I wondered how any woman could tire of him so much she might want to live apart from him.

The next voice shook me out of my reverie. It was Jerome's, excited and breathy. "Today Elder Robert, I'm pleased to show everyone the gifts the students have brought to this service. I have here some poems the children have written about our Zion and the Heavenly Father. As I call each name, I hope he or she will come up beside me and recite a poem to everyone here. The first poet is Brother Andrew, who created his piece last winter when he was seven."

That announcement was the beginning of the end of our plan to behave. Sarah and I tried hard not to giggle as he read.

"I wonder if Brother Jerome has any beard. I believe he's a woman in brother's clothing," Sarah whispered.

Jerome missed the bench when he sat down, and I clapped my hand over my mouth. Tears began to roll down my cheeks. Finally Elizabeth stood up from the bench near the front and came back to ours.

"Move over, Sister Lucy," she whispered, plopping down between us.

That promptly quieted us, though I must admit it remained a struggle to keep from bursting into laughter.

As if Holy Mother Wisdom were watching, a bolt of lightning suddenly sobered me up when I heard my name called next. Elizabeth grabbed my arm and pulled me out of the row, knowing full well I was not going to leave the cozy seat on my own.

In the middle of both sets of benches, Jerome turned me to face the outsiders and handed me a sheet of paper. To my horror and consternation, I recognized the poem as something I had written when I was ten or eleven. I shot Jerome a glare before straightening out my piece of paper. He stepped behind me, nervously making noises in his throat.

My voice came out all squiggly—the kind of whine a three-year-old might offer. "I saw a bird up in a tree. He saw me too and flew to me. And when he soared, his wings so free. I knew right then that it was He."

Jerome did not have to push me to my seat. I was already to the end of the benches by the time I finished the last line.

Some satisfaction came just three students later when Jerome called Sarah to the front. Standing tall, she read out, "The Lord has given me a gift today. The blood runs high into my cheeks. I shall die if we do not commune again. Though my rapture will last for weeks."

I knew she had written hers more recently because she told me it was about Damien. Lost in love for his student, Jerome must have wanted to flaunt her skills as a talented poet. Normally I would have been upset by his desire to show her off at my expense, but something happened that diminished whatever anger swelled within me.

While Sarah did not appear embarrassed reading her poem with a loud clear voice, her face had turned a deep red. Not only that, but huge white spots grew out of the red, making her look like she had a pox or the measles. I put my hand to my face just as a loud snort emanated from my mouth and nose at the same time.

I need not have worried, however, as the whole congregation let out a collective *"Oooooh."*

Evelyn rushed forward to drag Sarah out of the meetinghouse before she had contaminated us all. Thus content, I did not even notice Mr. Aldridge had left the room before the end of the meeting.

I would see Mr. Aldridge a few days later when he appeared at the shop. Leonard came to my office and told me to follow him. He said I could talk to the detective on the benches. That way, I suppose, there would be a full audience while we discussed the paperwork. Mr. Aldridge removed his hat and smiled when I came through the door. I glanced over at Leonard, who looked nervous about leaving me with the visitor. He remained in front of the counter at the end of our bench for some minutes before finally deciding there were others in the room to keep an eye on us.

"I enjoyed your poem on Sunday," Aldridge said.

"I believe we have business to talk about, Mr. Aldridge. I'm not sure we should discuss what we worship here." I do not know why I said it. It was not like it was a rule or anything, but I could not afford to reveal the embarrassment I felt in front of my friends and strangers when I was supposed to act like a businessman.

Mr. Aldridge smiled and continued, "I wanted your opinion about the people you gave me statistics on."

"You want me to tell you who I think robbed your banks? I don't believe I'm qualified to tell you that. I'm not sure what a bank robber looks like."

"No," he said patiently. "I guess you've probably never seen one. It's just there are several people on this list who do business with the outside fairly regularly."

"And were on the road when the crimes were committed?"

"Yes. Have you ever seen anything in your dealings with these brothers that might give you a clue they did more than conduct their business?"

"When did these robberies take place? In the winter, summer, when?"

"One occurred last summer. Were you here then?"

"I'd just started as a trustee and am unsure I would've been aware of a brother's return. Let me see," I said, trying hard not to think about the man sitting beside me. "I remember Allen bringing back a deer he'd killed. We had lots of venison that year, but I don't think that makes him a bank robber."

"Did anyone else return with gifts?"

"Max turned up with a wife. That was just before he left us, of course. I don't remember if she wore anything that made her look like she'd come into money. In fact, she looked rather poor."

Mr. Aldridge laughed at that, though I did not mean it to be funny.

"Richard came back with a book on American history for Jerome. It was beautiful. It had a leather cover with gold lettering. That looked expensive."

"But bank robbers usually don't have that kind of taste, do they?"

This time I smiled. "I promise to think about it when I go back to the dwelling. If I come up with something, how do I get a message to you?"

I watched his hands as he fingered the notes I had prepared for him earlier. They were strong hands, as if he used them to hew trees or clear land. I guess his being an investigator gave me the idea he rarely worked with his hands. I was concerned if he were to marry and settle down, he would not have the skills to keep a wife and family.

It is not like I thought about him all the time. It would not do for me to dream about an outsider when I did not remember what it was like to live on the outside. I would be reading a book about the world when my thoughts would slowly turn to Mr. Aldridge or a man like him. He would become the character in my book. Or I would think about him as I brushed my hair, wondering how he would like me to wear mine if he were courting me. Of course, I would always end up pulling my hair back into a bun, but I dreamt of piling it high, with ringlets bouncing every time I turned my head. I put him out of my mind when I went to bed at night, fearing I would not get the sleep I needed to rise at four and help out in the kitchen.

"You can send it with someone going into town. I'll be back some time next week if you can't find such a messenger earlier than that. I have another idea. If you could slip into some of the rooms of these brothers and see if there's evidence . . ."

"Oh, no, Mr. Aldridge. I don't think I could do that. We aren't allowed in the men's rooms," I said, only then realizing he might not know that. I bit my lip until my mind caught up with my mouth. "Maybe I could somehow help out with the cleaning. There are sisters who clean up the members' rooms, but not often. The brothers usually keep up their own. I'll have to look into it and see what I can do."

"Thank you, Miss Hammond. I'd appreciate any help you're allowed to provide. Here's a list of the brothers who were on the road on the key dates. I trust you'll discuss this with no one. It's imperative that it be done in secret. Not even Mr. Robert Tyler, your Sunday minister, knows the details of this investigation."

I pocketed the slip of paper, proud as well as overwhelmed he had trusted me with details about which the ministry elder remained ignorant. I sat there until he walked out of the shop and then strolled back to my office, thankful neither Eli nor Leonard approached me with any questions.

While Mr. Aldridge's investigation was important, it reminded me I had my own to conduct. I would have to stay awake soon in order to follow Sarah on one of her nightly jaunts. Less than a week later I did just that. While I dressed in my nightgown with the others, I had placed my dress under the covers of my bed. When I heard the snores and sighs of my roommates, I quickly changed out of my gown and pulled the dress over my head. I would carry my shoes down with me. It felt odd wearing the dress without any underclothes, but of course, no one would see me, and if they did, no one would be able to tell what I wore under my dress.

I managed to stay awake until what must have been close to midnight when I heard a slight rustle sweep past the end of my bed. She was so quick and quiet, I barely realized it was Sarah. I rose and looked at her bed but could not tell it was empty because she had stuffed her pillow and maybe an extra blanket under the quilt. Having little time to do the same, I slipped my pillow under my bedding and tried to ruffle the comforter. It did not look real, but it would have to do.

Then, in my bare feet, I ran down the stairs, trying to catch a glimpse of her. I did not see her turn at the bottom step and stood there puzzled for a moment. Surely she would not be brave enough to exit either door directly in front of the elders' rooms. The only other possibilities were the accesses to the dwelling meeting room at the end of the hall and the exit from the kitchen another floor down. I did not hear the door close at the end of the hallway, so I sneaked down to the kitchen, stopping only long enough to make sure there were no shadows in front of the windows. Then I headed for the exit. It was unlocked, something Peg would not have let happen since that terrible night when Edgar turned the whole place upside down. I knew Sarah had used this door to exit.

As I sat on the step, the warm summer night hit me. I leaned forward to lace up my shoes, my feet feeling odd without stockings. Standing, I ran my fingers along the wall of the dwelling until I got to the corner. A full moon offered ample light to the back part of the house. The only shadow was the tall oak tree, and a big shadow it was, making me wonder how many destitutes could hide there and watch me move in the light along the side of the building. I stuck close to the dwelling, passing directly under our window, wishing I were back up in bed.

It was then I heard what sounded like a chuckle. It was in the distance across the road, and I strained my eyes to see beyond the tree. Was she in the schoolhouse? Because only Jerome would have a key, had she agreed to meet *him* there? I stopped and waited for another clue. Suddenly I heard the crackle of footsteps. I drew a breath and disappeared into the shadow of the oak, making it to the road and across until I was behind the schoolhouse. But the noises that followed were still far ahead of me.

The forest commenced about twenty feet from the back of the classroom, and I was not about to go there. Farther up the road, the ground rose to the pond. There, the forest floor had been cleared. I tiptoed from tree to tree, trying to make my way up the hill without fracturing any debris littering the ground. I did not succeed, but the giggling was louder the higher I got so I could tell that no one had noticed my approach. I stopped to catch my breath and leaned against a tree trunk when I heard a splash in the water. Was she swimming? I moved to another tree to get a better look.

Suddenly something clung to my skin, tangling me up when I tried to brush it away. The webs surrounded me, not letting me go. I fell to the ground and rolled, trying to extricate myself. I must not have let out a sound, because the swimmers continued to splash around, seemingly undisturbed. But I certainly felt the need to scream. I tugged hard at my assailant's sticky arms only to discover it was a nightgown—probably Sarah's. Afraid the moonlight would reflect off the white of the cotton if I picked it up and hung it on the branch again, I threw it down, involuntarily wandering farther toward the path that led up the hill to our shrine.

It was obvious one of the swimmers was Sarah. Her wet hair glowed in the moonlight. But I could not see who was with her. If it were a boy, I never managed to discover where he had stowed his clothes, nor did I desire to chance another attack.

Instead, I crouched low to the ground below a tree and watched and listened, trying to make out what was being said.

I sat there at least ten minutes or so when I heard a snap of twigs about thirty feet away. Was someone coming down the path? Would he find us out here on this summer night and report us all? Or was it something worse? Edgar's deformed face flashed through my mind. Would he be friendly or see that I was a Believer and persecute me?

I did not wait around to find out. I was up and running before he could take another step. I did not care if the swimmers heard me and were disturbed by the idea a marauder lingered close by. In fact, I hoped they were alerted to some danger lurking in the forest around them. I raced across the road and slipped into the shadows of the oak. By now I could see in the darkness without strain and was at the door and inside in an instant.

But then I hesitated. If I locked the door, Sarah would not be able to come back in. If I left it unlocked, a possible intruder could enter and do more damage or worse. I stood there, shivering. Finally glancing down, I noticed I still wore shoes. Bending over, I pulled them off. Alerting anyone else of our sinful adventures at this point would only add more pressure to an already awkward situation. Finally deciding to leave the door unlocked, I tiptoed back upstairs and into bed, clothes and all. I did not hear Sarah return. The exertion left me exhausted. If a destitute or Edgar did follow me into the kitchen, I would find out in the morning and probably be in big trouble once more.

11. Undercover

The chill and damp evenings of fall were upon us before we knew it, but that did not stop Sarah, who seemed to take off several evenings a week. I, however, could not muster the energy or the courage to follow her every night. It would take me weeks to recover from the first trip, waking up every hour to listen for Edgar and keep an eye out for Sarah's return. I usually dozed before managing to witness either.

But fall brought two main events that would affect me and the others in the Community. The first was the harvest. When I was not in the trustees' house, I joined in the festivities. Gathering squash as well as pumpkins, Benjamin and I busied ourselves by tending our little garden, which was no longer so little. These perishables were to go to one of the barns to be crated and sent to the other Communities and local markets. I enjoyed being outside in the dry warmth of the sun.

The other event was Sarah's birthday. Of course it was more subdued. We observed such anniversaries in our dwelling by serving cake and applauding the celebrants. Her eighteenth birthday would be more momentous than this because she would have an important choice to make that year, but Sarah's celebration was special too because no one expected Sarah to be here when she turned eighteen.

"What do you mean, Molly? Of course Sarah's still here. Why would she leave? She's legally indentured until she turns eighteen and knows she risks jail if she leaves before then."

"Dear Sister Lucy, I'm afraid you aren't seeing her with open eyes. She isn't happy here and could run quite far before the eldress considered doing anything to get her back."

"I believe she's happy. The dresses she makes are exquisite. I hear so many compliments about her talent because I talk to those who are ordering them and watch many of the gowns packed into carts to be delivered to faraway places. I tell her about the comments, and she's very pleased."

"But your telling her how good she is might make her realize she could live in the world and do well, don't you think?"

I should have seen it but did not. She had just turned seventeen, and it was obvious by now she was not going to commit on her next birthday. Legally, however, she was obligated to stay for another year. I was there to make sure she at least made it, if not to try to convince her to stay on after. I therefore did go downstairs in the middle of the night one more time with different results. This time, Sarah and I planned the night out together.

"I think I'm ready to have you come with me now," Sarah said one day. "You wouldn't tell anyone, Lucy, would you?"

"Of course not. I figured you went out all the time anyway, and I haven't discussed that with anyone."

"Very well. Tomorrow night."

"Who are we meeting?"

"What do you mean?"

"Which boy are you going out to meet?"

"I'm shocked you think I go out at night to see the boys, Lucy Hammond."

"Then why do you go out?"

"It's so wonderful with the trees and night animals. I can't explain it. I go out there for the thrill of being free. God knows, I feel imprisoned here. There's a rule for everything."

"So we aren't going out to meet anyone?"

"I'm not sure. Sometimes there are others out there. Maybe we'll meet someone. You never know."

That night came so quickly, it was a miracle I was ready. I made the same provisions I had the first time I went out and grabbed the garden boots by my bed as soon as Sarah jiggled my bedpost. To my surprise, Sarah, still wearing her gown and carrying no boots or shoes with her at all, turned left at the bottom of the stairs. I caught up with her before she turned left again at the transept and grabbed her arm.

"Where are we going?" I whispered.

"Out the closest door. Anyway, this one remains unlocked so the boys can use the privy. Our door is unlocked, too, but is on the wrong side, and Evelyn doesn't sleep soundly."

"I still think it's wrong to use the boys' door, Sarah."

"So what? The rule's ridiculous, Lucy. I can't believe you haven't reached that conclusion before now. How old are you? Oh, yeah, only sixteen."

"Shhhhh! Someone's coming," I said, my stomach churning.

"It's probably Elizabeth."

"Who?"

"She said she was coming too. I wiggled her bed post, but she's a bit slow, if you know what I mean."

I was confused. "Why are we going out?"

"For the adventure. We're going out to commune with nature," Sarah repeated, speeding up to get out the door.

Once outside, I sat down to slip into my shoes.

"Not here. This window is Thomas's room. He might hear you," she said.

I got up, my heart beating wildly. I followed her along the side of the house to the oak tree. In the shadows, we stopped and waited for Elizabeth, who showed up in her gown too.

Elizabeth was not angry but excited. "Who else said they'd

be out here?" she asked.

"Damien sometimes comes out," Sarah said. "But I don't know if he'll appear."

"Didn't you ask him?"

"No. I just tell others I'm coming out. It's always interesting to see who else comes. Please don't ask about Damien again, Elizabeth. Next time you can ask him yourself," Sarah said, putting out her arms and floating across the road like an angel.

Elizabeth and I followed her as she climbed the hill to the pond. "Do you want to go to the shrine?" Sarah asked.

My heart in my throat, I could not protest.

"Sure," Elizabeth said. "There's a good moon out tonight, but what about shoes?"

"I know where we can get some," Sarah said, her eyes lighting up.

I could not believe what they were about to do.

"Come help me, Elizabeth," Sarah said. "I'm certain Lucy will refuse to assist us. She'll just lecture us on our failure to bring shoes in the first place."

The doors to the shop were always open. We rarely needed to lock them. Theft did not happen often because we were a family that depended on each other for everything. I wondered why the destitutes never bothered to break into this shop. Surely they would find shoes a valuable commodity.

The two young women returned in a few minutes with new shoes and sat down to slip them on. Neither pair fit perfectly, but they were at least practical and not ones that Ambrose had created for worldly consumption. Most of those were satin with higher heels, which could be ruined by the hike. I did not know if Sarah and Elizabeth planned to return them when we were finished.

"Very well, follow me," said Sarah.

"Where are we going?" I asked.

"To the shrine. I have to check my stuff."

"What stuff?"

"Elizabeth knows. We'll show you when we get there."

"Have you gone out with Sarah before, Elizabeth?"

"Yes, once. At the time it scared me, but I couldn't wait to get out here again. I hope you aren't afraid, Lucy. There's nothing to be afraid of. It's exhilarating. Feel the freedom? I could be a member of the Community forever—as long as I'm able to escape once in a while."

"I didn't know you questioned your commitment."

"I don't believe any of the younger members feel totally committed, do you, Lucy?" Elizabeth asked.

Actually, I never thought about it that way. I always felt if you were going to sign up to become a member, you would harbor no doubts. If I had doubts about my desire when the time came, I would not choose to stay, and I thought everyone would do the same. On the other hand, it's probably easier to remain inside, especially if you have grown up among the members and are comfortable with the Believer ways. Perhaps both Sarah and Elizabeth were sticking their toes into the water to see if they might feel comfortable on the outside.

I followed the two girls up the hill, trying not to look around me at the darkness that hung under the tree branches. Their pace was quick. We did not have time to dawdle, and though out of breath, I did not dare stop to rest for fear they would leave me there.

At the top of the hill, Sarah ran across the field to a tree beyond the fountain, pulled away some dead branches, and retrieved a crowbar and a shovel hidden underneath. Elizabeth stopped at the edge of the spiritual pool, and when Sarah returned, they both climbed in. The pool was always dry, the water being imagined—a spiritual gift rather than a physical one. Our religion was based on faith, and we had to have a lot of it at the shrine.

I climbed in too and sat on my heels as Sarah lifted four tiles and began to dig. Not ten minutes later, she pulled out a large bag like the ones we used in the laundry.

"What are those?" I asked.

"They're my things."

"What things?"

"The items I came with. Seth showed me the wagon soon after I first arrived, and I retrieved what I wanted to take with me. You aren't going to tattle, are you, Lucy? I thought I could trust you because it would mean getting Seth into trouble, too."

"But I remember you telling me the elders sold that stuff."

"They did soon after I got what I wanted. It's lucky I took these items before it was too late."

"What do you have?" I asked.

"Some clothes."

"Aren't they too small now?"

"No. These are my mother's dresses and some jewelry. And there are toys in here and some books."

I could not believe she had taken so much of value. "I won't tattle, Sarah. It would be hard for me to part with my family's things too. Did Seth know you were going to take them?"

Sarah smiled. "I'm sure Seth understood the reason I wanted them. Why? Did you think he was honest? He's just like us, Lucy. Are you still in love with him?"

Elizabeth giggled. "He doesn't even notice you, Lucy. You're just a baby to him."

"Now that I know it's all here, shouldn't we go down and see who else is roaming about?" Sarah asked.

"Do you think Damien is out here somewhere?" Elizabeth asked.

"I told you not to speak about him."

I was stunned. It was one thing for Sarah to check her

treasure, but with all her talk, I had believed her when she told me she was not going out to meet boys. The two girls skipped down the hill, and I ran to keep up. About halfway down, Sarah stopped short, letting Elizabeth and me run into her. I looked over to my left and saw a flicker of light through the trees.

"Come on," said Sarah, veering off the path. "Let's go see who's camping nearby."

I could not move. The two girls walked boldly through the trees, pushing aside branches and climbing over rocks. My heart raced. I was unable to decide which way to run if one of the girls began to scream or I heard Edgar roar. But that is not what I heard. Instead, their voices echoed back to me in normal tones.

I finally moved forward and wriggled my way through the numerous obstacles. Stopping behind the last branch, I waited and watched. Sarah and Elizabeth both sat next to the campfire chattering away.

"Sister Elizabeth, I haven't seen you out at night before," Ezekiel said, turning a stick over the fire, roasting what looked like a rabbit.

"Good evening, Ezekiel. I thought you lived in the brick dwelling."

"No. Too stifling. I'm still unsure I want to commit. Elder Zachary wants me to take the time I need, so I have little supervision."

"And you eat here, too?" Elizabeth asked.

"I eat what I catch."

"Year-round?"

"Yup. When I can. There are plenty of sheds on the property to give me shelter when I need it, and Sister Peg puts scraps out. I eat those when I can't catch anything."

"But what about your room at the dwelling?" Elizabeth asked.

"I use it once in a while . . . when I have to."

"So the elders know you're out here?"

"I suppose so. Elder Zachary's never said a word about my absence at meals or meetings. I just camp out on the property here, living my own life."

"Have you seen Damien?" Sarah asked.

"He visited earlier this evening. He didn't ask about you, though."

"What did he talk about?"

"Just questions about what he wants to do."

"Is he thinking about leaving?" Sarah asked.

"Not really. Like me, he has doubts about what's best for him. Unlike me, he wants to sign the papers."

"You shouldn't try to talk him into leaving, Ezekiel," Elizabeth suddenly said.

"Oh? Do you have a problem with that, Sister Elizabeth?" He glared at Sarah.

"She had no problem with it, Zeke. She's been out with me before. I know she won't tell anyone, because then I'll inform everybody she wants Damien for a sweetheart."

"Are you going out to look for Brother Damien?"

"Maybe. Maybe not. Where's Lucy?" asked Sarah, suddenly looking around for me.

I stepped back farther into the shadows.

"Sister Lucy's here?" Ezekiel asked, standing.

"She probably ran back to the dwelling," Elizabeth said.

"I'd really like to talk to Sister Lucy," Ezekiel said, his teeth gleaming in the firelight when he smiled.

"I guess she got scared," Sarah said. "She doesn't really like being out."

"That one's a saint," Ezekiel said. "Eldress Lavonia better keep an eye on her back. Lucy Hammond's gunning for her job." He began to snort. "She's like a scared rabbit about that Edgar. All I have to do is mention I've seen him, and her hazel eyes get big. She's real pretty with that tiny waist of hers."

"Why don't we go and find Damien?" Elizabeth asked. "Maybe we should let Ezekiel and Lucy dream about each other on their own."

Sarah laughed at that, knowing full well I could not stand Ezekiel. "No. It's getting late," Sarah said. "Perhaps it'd be better if we return the shoes and head back."

"But you promised, Sarah."

"I promised nothing, Elizabeth. This was just supposed to be a night out. If you complain too much, I won't take you again."

"Didn't Sister Sarah tell you she and Brother Damien sometimes meet in the barn?" Ezekiel asked, snickering. "I can still hear them panting over each other."

"Zeke," Sarah said, before turning back to Elizabeth.

But Elizabeth had already walked away in a huff. Both Sarah and I listened to her footsteps as she made her way down the hill without returning to the path.

"Well, I've got to go too, Zeke. I'll talk to you some other night if Elizabeth doesn't prevent my going out again."

"Wait," he said, grabbing her arm.

"Let go."

"I need to tell you something," he said, pulling her back toward him.

I wanted to help her but could not move.

"Let go of me, Ezekiel. You can talk to me without touching me."

But his arm had already encircled her waist. I glanced around for something to throw at him. When I looked up, the two had disappeared from the light of the campfire. Mustering all my strength, I cupped my hands and bellowed Sarah's name before ducking and retreating to the path. When I got to the trail, I did not stop but ran all the way to the dwelling, not heeding anything along the way that might call attention to the offense—

that I was out of the dwelling at night. But I had little need to worry. There was no one there when I got near the dwelling. Elizabeth was nowhere in sight. I thought about going back to the shoemaking shop to look for her, but fear discouraged me from doing that.

I made my way to the kitchen door to let myself in, but it was locked. Remembering we had exited through the boys' door in the first place, I quickly scampered around the corner and up the hill to the entrance only to find it locked too. Ready to cry, I sat down on the step.

About ten minutes later, I heard someone rouse and a door shut somewhere inside. I scurried over to the stairs leading to the basement storage room and crouched in the shadows. Thomas soon came out onto the doorstep and made his way toward the shed, leaving the door ajar. As soon as he shut the one to the privy, I darted to the top and slipped inside.

As I climbed the stairs to the bedrooms, I worried for Sarah's safety, but not enough to awaken anyone. Who would I wake up other than Evelyn? When I crept past Elizabeth's bed, I heard her snore. At least Elizabeth had returned, though I had no idea which door she had used. Perhaps she had locked the boys' door on the way in.

The next morning, I found Sarah in the dressing room, nursing her bruises.

"Are you all right?" I asked, not wanting to reveal I had witnessed Ezekiel's attack. "What happened?"

"Nothing. I just fell down. What about you?"

"I was afraid when you and Elizabeth went toward the campfire," I said. "What if it was Edgar? I ran home. Those are nasty-looking bruises."

"I'm fine. The campfire belonged to Ezekiel."

"Doesn't he live in the dwelling?"

"His room's next to Seth's, but he's rarely there."

"I'm surprised you weren't hurt."

"I could've been, actually. Something scared Ezekiel. I'm lucky, because he can be a bit rough when he plays around. Watch out for him, Lucy."

"What do you mean?"

"There was someone else out there. We both heard him yell, and the noise distracted Ezekiel enough so I could escape into the trees. I circled back to the shoe shop before returning here."

"Where's Seth's room?" I suddenly asked, curious about where certain brothers were located in the members' dwelling.

"On the third floor in the men's wing. Why? Are you planning to meet him there? Remember to watch out for his roommate."

"That's funny, Sarah. Actually, I'm simply nosy. Glad you weren't seriously hurt last night."

It was easy to get permission to clean the men's rooms in the members' dwelling. When I asked for permission to talk with her, Abigail was making a list of women to do the semi-annual job. Benjamin was too efficient clearing the garden for next year's planting so I told her I needed some extra work. She was delighted and asked me if I could handle the men's rooms on the third floor. I suggested the east side of the building, but Abigail assigned me to do the whole wing because it was not very big. I agreed.

"I'll tell the brothers to be out on Thursday so they don't interfere," Abigail said. "Can you do it during the day?"

"How about morning? Before breakfast," I said. "That way it won't interfere with my other work."

Just as Abigail described, the men's area on the third floor of the dwelling was not that large. I only had four rooms to clean.

Armed with a broom and mop, I began with the chamber closest to the entrance. I did not know which was Ezekiel's. Ezekiel
was one of the brothers on Mr. Aldridge's list of those with opportunity.

The first room was relatively neat already. I had brought a
bucket of water up the stairs and decided to sweep the rooms
and then follow that with the mop. But first I had to find out
who lived in the abode. I headed for one of the cabinets. I did
not need to open it, however. There were objects on top of a
chest next to the closet. I recognized Seth's prayer book right
away. Beside that sat a book on machines. Inside was the
signature of Richard Stevens, a brother who worked in the
mechanical shop. Already I had identified the occupants and
quickly moved on to sweeping and mopping. I followed the
same procedure for the second and third rooms, cleaning them
as soon as I recognized who lived in them.

Tired but determined to check out the contents of Ezekiel's
room, I left the mop and broom outside the fourth and slipped
through the door. Inside, I quickly inspected the contents of
each bureau, unable to identify the owner of the clothes in any
of them. I then did the same for the cabinet near the closet. I
did not discover anything in my search but inadvertently
knocked over a boot at the bottom of one of the cabinets. I
reached in and pulled out the pair, dropping them with a thud
on the floor. That noise sounded wrong for a leather boot, and
when I looked down, a piece of cloth peeked out of the top. I
started to bend over to examine my find when the door suddenly burst open.

"Well, well, Sister," Ezekiel said. "Are you planning to shine
my boots too?" He crossed the room in two steps and swept up
the pair, returning them to the cabinet. "I'm sure Eldress Abigail will be very interested in what I found in my quarters.
Maybe I should search you to make sure you haven't robbed all

the others," he said, stepping forward.

I retreated farther into the closet.

He stood in the doorway and leaned against the sill. "Well? Am I allowed an explanation?"

"Yes. By the looks of this room, you need a good pick-up before I attempt to clean it," I said, mustering some confidence before pushing past him.

He grabbed my arm and pulled me closer.

"You're hurting me!" I said. "I think I know some of your secrets, Ezekiel. Perhaps we should talk about this in front of one of the elders."

He released me, but then pushed me down onto one of the beds. "Tell me what you're going to tell them, and maybe I'll let you go unscathed," he said, his knee on my arm.

I could smell the foul odor of his breath and feel the heat brush my cheek. It was then I heard it. Someone was ascending the stairs. Ezekiel looked back at the door, and I fought to sit up. To my relief, it opened. Zachary stood in the doorway. To say he was shocked was to put it mildly.

"I heard that you, Brother Ezekiel, had been seen coming up the stairs. Because you weren't at the meeting last night, I wanted to warn you the sisters were cleaning the chambers today," he said, pausing to look at me, my hair disheveled and sleeve torn. "I'm glad I came up. Sister Lucy, please take the cleaning items back downstairs and wait in the room across from Eldress Abigail's office. Meeting in the men's private rooms is a very serious offense, and I'm surprised you'd do so, considering your position in the Community. Brother Ezekiel, come to my office in half an hour. We can deal with this and with your absence from the meetings then."

I wanted to cry out and plead my case, but obeyed straightaway, glad to be out of the room and away from Ezekiel. I knew what Zachary thought he saw and realized I would have to come up with something exceedingly plausible in order to counter the story he was about to tell Abigail and Evelyn. But I was in the right here. Both the Heavenly Father and Holy Mother Wisdom knew it, too. Ezekiel was dangerous, and somehow I would have to convince the elders of that before someone got hurt.

Unfortunately, catastrophe would hit sooner than I realized.

12. UNIMAGINABLE

The interview was short. Abigail and Evelyn sat across the table from me. "Are you and Brother Ezekiel close?" Abigail asked right off.

"Of course not!" I said with such conviction Evelyn smiled. I explained that Mr. Aldridge had asked me to search the room for loot from the bank robberies, recalling too late that I had been sworn to secrecy.

"That isn't Mr. Aldridge's responsibility," Evelyn said. "Why didn't either of you come to me?"

"I didn't think you would allow it," I said honestly.

Abigail paused, probably pondering whether or not to punish me for insolence. "Did you find anything?" she finally asked.

"Nothing certain. I didn't have time. But I did discover something suspicious," I said, in a half-whisper. "When I lifted Ezekiel's boots from the floor of his cabinet, they were too heavy, and when I dropped them, there was something hanging out of the heavier one. It was brown, but didn't look like a wool stocking."

"And when Brother Ezekiel entered the room, what did he do?" Evelyn asked.

"He pushed me aside and tossed the boots back into the cabinet."

"Were they muddy or dirty?" Abigail asked.

That threw me. I did not understand why she would want to know that now. "Yes, but they would be, wouldn't they?"

"Why?"

"Because he spent his time—" I stopped right there. I should not have known where Ezekiel spent his nights, and admitting to it now might drag both Sarah and Elizabeth into the fray. "He's on the road for long periods of time. I wouldn't expect them to be clean."

"He hasn't been on the road for nearly two months, Sister Lucy. Why would they still be soiled? I think someone would've noticed by now if his boots were dirty."

"Not if he bought new ones while he was on the road. I mean, ones for travel." I was beginning to make no sense. "Perhaps Zachary would know why they were dirty better than I."

Abigail glanced at Evelyn, and they both stood up.

"Maybe we should visit Brother Zachary and have him check out these boots," Evelyn said.

But they were not finished. Without discharging me, Evelyn proceeded with the lecture. "I believe the liaisons between you and Mr. Aldridge are improper, Sister Lucy," Evelyn began. "In the future, Mr. Aldridge is to come to Brother Thomas or me and give us reason for you two to convene. I regard your meetings with this outsider as imprudent and foolish. They shed a bad light on the temperate and purposeful nature of the Community. If in our opinion his need isn't significant, you and he won't speak to each other at all. Sins of the flesh are evil, and I'll do everything to keep them from occurring during my watch."

Needless to say, Ezekiel had had plenty of time to empty and clean his boots. I believe Abigail and Evelyn realized that. They sent me off with the warning that I was to avoid the members' dwelling and Ezekiel. That was not a problem. I did not want to run into the brother again that day. When I got back to the trustees' house, I asked Eli to send Ezekiel on another trip.

Eli looked surprised. "What's the problem?" he asked.

I was not sure how to answer. Should I tell him about the way Ezekiel bothered me? Should I tell him about Sarah's problem with Ezekiel? "He's a troublemaker. I was cleaning his room, and he came in and threatened me," I finally said.

"Did you tell the eldress? I'm certain the elders will take care of that."

"They already know, but I don't think they understand the problem."

"Really?"

"He grabbed me and tore my dress, but Zachary made it sound like I was the one making trouble."

"I'm sure it'll all come out in the end. If I find a need for someone to make a delivery, I'll certainly send him. But you should go to Eldress Evelyn. She'll know you had nothing to do with it."

"I'm not so sure of that," I said under my breath.

As for my discussion with Mr. Aldridge, I was definitely upset I could not participate in the investigation. What would he think when he came around expecting to hear what I had discovered about Ezekiel? He would have to learn that the silly girl, unable to keep her mind off her brothers, would no longer be able to help with the investigation without special permission from an elder. Surely he would not understand. He did not see me in a romantic light. I had long given up on the idea that I was stunning, like Sarah, and though I was smart, intelligence was not a particularly valued trait in a woman. But he did not come around. Not only would permission be unnecessary for me to talk to Mr. Aldridge, but he seemed to have lost interest in the investigation and me. Events in the Community, however, would force me to think less about Mr. Aldridge's bank robbery and send me to examine a puzzling incident much closer to home.

Something occurred not three weeks after my tangle with
Ezekiel. One morning, still dark because autumn had chased
away the sun, I got up with the others, changed into my work
clothes, and went to the dressing area to wash my face in a bowl
of cold water Elizabeth had pumped and brought up. When I
found my way back to the room to slip into my shoes, I noticed
for the first time Sarah had already pulled her bed together and
left. This did not usually happen. I turned to find Elizabeth, but
she too was already gone.

For a split second, I thought maybe they had wandered out
together the night before without me. There was no sense of
jealousy on my part. Having felt very tired, I was glad I was allowed to get a full night's sleep. Nonetheless, a bit of worry that
they had not returned began to creep into my mind. Then I realized the bowl of water was in the dressing room, and Elizabeth would have had to rise to fetch it. The two girls were probably just more prompt than I was, and I would see them at
breakfast.

I should have concluded something was afoot when I
stumbled down the stairs. There was an unusual bustle of activity as I passed by Evelyn's office. Peg entered without knocking,
and Elder Thomas emerged. I figured the scowl on Thomas's
face was due to the hour of the morning and did not stop to
greet him. I went directly to the trustees' house to begin balancing the books. I could get a lot done if I worked until breakfast,
still three hours away. An hour or so later, I was still engrossed
in the numbers when Eli entered my office.

"Good morning, Sister Lucy. You look busy. I just got word
they've asked Brother Leonard to fill in as the elder brother in
your dwelling."

"Oh? Is Damien sick?"

"No. Gone. He absconded last night, or so Brother Leonard tells me. I'll need you up front in the shop today because Brother Leonard will be gone for at least a few weeks."

I was still in shock with the first sentence: that Damien had suddenly left. He just did not seem the type to leave without telling anyone.

"I'm surprised he'd do that," I said.

"Brother Leonard?"

"No. Damien. His father's a pastor, and he's always acted like the Community came first."

"I guess when love arrives there's nothing to stop it. I sure hope I don't get hit with that bug," he said, rubbing his eyes.

"Really? He met someone?"

Eli just looked at me. "But of course you heard. How could you not? Brother Damien ran off with Sister Sarah."

My heart must have stopped. I could not hear it above the pounding in my ears. But my hands were frozen, making me unable to put my pen down.

"I'm sorry to shock you with such news. Maybe you should go talk to Eldress Evelyn. I'm positive she wants to speak with you about it," Eli said, a sincere, almost pained, expression on his face. "But do you think you could return after breakfast and help out in the shop? I'm not certain I can handle everything on my own."

Without replying, I got up, donned my cape, and headed back to the dwelling. The sun was rising, but a thick mist still pervaded the fields. I longed to feel the warm rays of sunny re-assurance, but a fog was more befitting the weight I felt in my heart.

Peg came out of Evelyn's office and ran into me. Taking my arm, she turned me toward the main hallway saying, "Oh dear, Sister Lucy. Let me tell Eldress Evelyn you're here, and then we can get some tea until the eldress finishes with her interview."

I sat in the kitchen for about ten minutes, letting Peg fret over me. I had taken just one sip of my tea when Evelyn appeared and asked me to follow her back to her office. She was stern, and I hoped her manner did not have to do with something I had done.

"Please sit down, Sister Lucy," she said as she closed the door.

"I just heard what happened," I said. "Eli told me, and I was shocked. Please say it's just a rumor."

She gazed at me with a look of astonishment. "I was just going to ask you what you knew."

"I know nothing. I rose this morning and noticed neither Sarah nor Elizabeth was dressing. I supposed they were out late and never returned." The instant the words were out of my mouth, I knew I had made a mistake. "I mean early."

Although Evelyn had heard my assumption loud and clear, she put it away for later. "So you'd heard Sarah's run away with Brother Damien?"

"That's what I was told."

"And you were aware Sister Sarah and Brother Damien were having some sort of relationship."

"No. I didn't know. I guessed she was enamored with him. But he wasn't the only one."

"Pardon?"

"She bragged about meeting others," I said, feeling somewhat empty after the words escaped my mouth. Sarah's clandestine activities had been a secret for so long, growing into a part of me, concealed in my depths. Was I betraying her? Somehow I knew I was not.

"How could she meet others? There'd be many witnesses. There's little opportunity for a sister to meet with a brother without the others noticing or without our assigning them a purpose for being together."

My lips quivered. I did not want to tattle further. But Sarah was in trouble, and I needed help to find her. "She'd sometimes go out at night."

Evelyn squirmed as if she did not want to know about it. "And who went with her?" she finally asked. "You? Sister Elizabeth?"

"I'm not sure she took anyone," I said, trying to skirt the issue. "She told me she was meeting boys. How do you know she left with Damien?"

"Brother Damien," she corrected.

I thought this formality rather trivial in light of the circumstances, but I always had trouble adopting the habit of calling my friends and family by the title sister or brother. If I were to stay, I would have to work at that because the others seemed to have it down pat.

"Sister Elizabeth found a note written by Sister Sarah on Sarah's bed this morning," Evelyn said, handing me the piece of paper.

I read it in the gray light.

Dearest Sister Lucy,

I'm so hapy. Me and Brother Damien have decided to elope. We will take a train to Albany where we will live but I'm sure I'm sorry that I will never see you agin.

Love Sister Sarah.

"Where did you find this?" I asked, my heart racing.

"I told you. Sister Elizabeth discovered it on Sister Sarah's bed. I find it difficult to believe you didn't know Sister Sarah was leaving when you went gallivanting around with her after hours."

"I didn't say I was out with her, Evelyn. To tell you the truth, Sarah often kept secrets from me. She thought I would tell on her."

"You should have told on her, Sister. Now you can see the consequences of your inaction."

"I'm still not sure what the consequences are."

"What do you mean?"

"This note was addressed to me. Elizabeth had no business reading it. Wasn't it folded?"

"Sister Elizabeth's in charge of the care of those in your room. Of course, she would've read the note. It was her business to know."

"Then ask Elizabeth. Maybe she knew Damien and Sarah were meeting," I said loudly, my voice high.

"Everyone knows you two are very close. How would Sister Elizabeth know things you didn't?"

"Because we were no longer close. You humiliated us about trying to keep warm that winter, and Sarah told me she could no longer trust me. You made it sound so sinful, and it wasn't. She was never the same after that. I suppose she turned to Elizabeth for companionship."

Evelyn stood up and began to pace. "One of the brothers found a piece of cloth on the hay in the barn. He thinks she was meeting Brother Damien there. You say you knew nothing about it? I find that hard to believe."

"I would've been appalled by such activity." I said, choking on my tears and listening to the silence as Evelyn tried to compose herself. "It's sinful. But how could I see it any other way? I've been here more than half my life. At least Sarah knew she wanted to remain with the world's people. I have no experience in making that kind of choice. How do we know she really went with him?" I asked, thinking of how Mr. Aldridge would conduct himself. "Have we searched all the buildings?"

"What are you saying, Sister?"

"Have you found a similar note from Damien? I mean Brother Damien? Maybe we should search his things."

"She told us she went off with him in the note. He isn't here, and his clothes are missing. Isn't that enough?"

"But she didn't write that note. Maybe Damien did, but these words aren't hers."

Evelyn was so astonished by my revelation, she forgot to ask me how I might know. I excused myself when she did not say anything and joined the others at breakfast. As I picked at my food, I thought about what I had inadvertently told Evelyn and, after she came to her senses, what she still could ask me about our evening jaunts. Obviously, I was not out of the woods. But I did not ponder the consequences for long. Instead, I thought about poor Sarah and could eat nothing more.

I had to get word to Mr. Aldridge but did not know how. Later that afternoon, I talked Eli into letting me leave the shop and take a ride into town with Jeremiah, who planned to make a delivery to Mr. Barnard. I knew if I waited, word would get out I was not to talk to Mr. Aldridge without permission.

"But you need a chaperone, Sister Lucy," Eli said. "Who will chaperone you?"

"I'll go get someone. You just stop Jeremiah from making that delivery. He'll see my chaperone and me at the carriage house in fifteen minutes."

"You'll get us all into trouble one of these days, Sister Lucy. Hurry back. Dinner's at eight."

"That gives me plenty of time. It'll be dark by eight, so Jeremiah will want to get back too."

Jeremiah pulled up the wagon to the general store and came around to help me down. Then he gave a hand to Georgia who waved him off.

"Thank you, Brother, but I wish to stay right here and watch the people go by."

He handed me a crate to help carry inside. Luckily, the object of my search, Mr. Aldridge, was just coming out the door.

"Hello, Miss Hammond," he said, removing his hat. "What brings you to town this afternoon?"

Jeremiah stood behind me, still holding his heavy box. I turned to him and said, "That's all right, Brother. Georgia's here. You can take care of business with Mr. Barnard while I have a word with Mr. Aldridge."

He hesitated a little longer, most likely pondering the advisability of leaving me alone, and finally walked inside. "You'll bring that box with you?" he asked.

"Yes, but in a minute," I said before turning back to the man who always managed to fluster me. "Mr. Aldridge, the last time I saw you, you wanted me to search for a bank robber, but I haven't had anyone around to report my findings to."

"I'm sorry. I thought you'd need more time. Did you discover anything?"

"Nothing specific, though I do have a person in mind. I just have no evidence for you to hold him."

"That would be necessary."

"And I'm not sure if he actually committed the crimes or if I just thoroughly loathe him."

"Ah. We'll have to keep looking, then."

"But there's been another turn of events that might also point to your bank robber."

"Yes?"

"Damien's left. I thought you should know in case you wanted to go after him."

"I know where he's probably headed. I don't really see the urgency right now," Mr. Aldridge said. "Maybe I can ask Mr. Dixon to search his room for evidence."

"I believe he would've taken it all with him. Money can come in handy when you're going to the city to wed."

"What do you mean?"

"He supposedly ran away to Albany with Sarah. They're to be married there."

"Someone told you this?"

"Yes. The note," I said, suddenly realizing it would have been stupid for Sarah to tell me where they were going, especially because Albany was so close by.

"What note?"

"Sister Sarah wrote me a note, but Elizabeth gave it to Evelyn before I could read it," I said, inadvertently dropping back into my old habit of leaving the off titles and making no sense at all. "I don't think she wrote it. Maybe Damien did."

"I find it difficult to believe Mr. Rathburn would write that, because he wouldn't have told anyone where he was headed— particularly if he were an accomplished bank robber," Mr. Aldridge said. "Are you telling me you don't think I should go to Albany to search for them?"

"I guess I'm telling you that. Of course, Thomas will try to hire you to search for them. Sarah was indentured to the Community. She wasn't supposed to leave until she was eighteen." I hesitated, realizing I was off the subject. He must have thought I was stupid. "But that's beside the point."

"The point being?"

"That you should go after Damien—"

"Though not in Albany."

"That you should find Damien, because then you'll find Sarah."

"And why do I need to find Sarah?"

Jeremiah suddenly came out and took the last crate from my hands. "Get up on the wagon, Sister Lucy," he said, his voice flat. "We have to leave to get back by dinner." Then he walked back into the store.

"To make sure she's all right," I said.

Mr. Aldridge turned me around and helped me up into the back of the wagon. "I'm sure the two of them will be very happy, Miss Hammond. I believe she's old enough to make up her own mind where she'll want to spend the rest of her life."

Jeremiah came out the door again and circled the wagon to climb up into his seat.

I grabbed Mr. Aldridge's hand. "Because I fear she has been kidnapped or worse," I said, the wagon beginning to move. I let go. "She didn't write that note, Mr. Aldridge, and if Damien Rathburn didn't write it either, then who did and why?"

13. The Return

Mr. Aldridge did indeed return to the Community, but the search for Sister Sarah was not the reason—at least at first. Autumn was fading like its fallen leaves, and the harvest was in progress. The Community had to move on. I saw him a few weeks after my plea in front of Barnard's General Store. It was Sunday, and our meeting had already begun.

Robert stood and repeated his prayer for the souls of Damien and Sarah. "We're here today to pray once again for the souls of Brother Damien and Sister Sarah, who left Zion a few weeks ago. Our losses, however, teach us an important lesson. Brother Damien, whose strong soul rejoiced in the gifts from heaven, must resist the evil lures of the world and try to regain his strength with our prayers. Sister Sarah will have to build on his resolve to realize she's left Paradise. She was truly one with the spirit. The Heavenly Father and Holy Mother Wisdom blessed her with many gifts during past meetings, and hopefully these gifts will keep her strong enough to resist outside temptations. Now, let us sing in one voice for news that God keeps them safe so they are free to return if they decide to."

As we rose to sing, I noticed Mr. Aldridge among the visitors, but I no longer felt the giddiness about his presence I had only weeks earlier. He was still busy trying to catch his bank robber, and I had somehow lost interest in helping him.

I loved the hymn we sang. It reminded me of joy and the harvest, and I continued to hum it throughout breakfast and

159

later when a group of us grabbed baskets and climbed ladders in order to collect the first ripe apples.

Mr. Aldridge approached and informed my partner, Georgia, she was wanted in the members' dwelling. Without delay, she handed him her empty basket and made her way out of the orchard. I suppose she was not enthusiastic about standing there, waiting for me to fill another.

I smiled. "Well, Mr. Aldridge, what made you decide to join us today? I didn't see you at breakfast this morning."

"Mr. Tyler's call to help at today's service was quite moving. I've heard there's a shortage of strong arms."

"Oh? From whom?" I asked, carefully stepping down a rung.

He strode forward and took hold of my ladder. "There's talk in town the Community's hurting. Probably just a temporary phenomenon. As for breakfast, I had a meeting with Mr. Dixon on the investigation."

"I see. And is the elders' dining room nice?" I asked, handing him a full basket of apples.

"I probably would have experienced better company in the big dining room. The food was excellent, however. I'm not used to such abundance, living in the hotel."

The peel of the dinner bell broke the spell.

"It's time for dinner, Mr. Aldridge. I really must go and help. I'm sure you'll want to sit with Thomas."

"There isn't a seat next to you?"

I must have blushed. "I'm not sure the elders would agree you should sit next to me. You'd be surrounded by women, since the women sit at their own table," I said, smiling. "Seriously, Mr. Aldridge, we probably shouldn't even be talking now. There's a rule that in the future, you must ask permission to consult with me. I shouldn't have approached you at Barnard's. I'd already been informed I was being too forward."

"I didn't think you were being forward at all. You're helping me investigate some strange happenings that have occurred here over the last few years."

I thought about Ezekiel and realized the detective did not understand how strange things actually were. "You also can't sit with me now because I won't be sitting. I'm serving all of you."

We stopped at the cart to deliver our baskets, and I let him go on ahead. Served at long tables set up in the warm sun outside the kitchen, the early dinner proceeded smoothly. I was handed a pitcher and poured apple juice for all the men. I could feel the eyes on me whenever I stood near Thomas, who sat next to Mr. Aldridge, and Mr. Aldridge was nice enough not to talk or acknowledge my presence when I was near. I appreciated that. It felt good to be outside, warming my back in the sun and inhaling the special smell of dried grass. I was grateful for the change of scenery, still yearning to be outdoors in the garden each day.

But it would not last. I would not see Mr. Aldridge again until the new year. I had heard he returned to Springfield for the Christmas holidays. I did not exactly desire his presence but longed to push him to continue the search for Sarah and Damien. Then one day after the beginning of the year, Evelyn called me into her office.

"I thought you might want to know that Mr. Aldridge sent a note to Elder Thomas, telling him he visited Albany before Christmas."

I was flabbergasted, speechless—almost. "Well? What did he learn?"

"He said he couldn't locate them, that they probably hadn't stayed in the city because no one seems to have recognized them by their description at all. Now that doesn't mean they weren't there somewhere. They could have stayed at a farm around Albany, even though Mr. Aldridge checked into the backgrounds of both, and neither has close relatives in that part of New York."

"Because they didn't go there," I said. "And now we've lost them entirely."

"You don't believe that's what Mr. Aldridge is telling us, do you?"

"I don't think Damien or Sarah would've told us where they were going. I assume Sarah would've felt you'd be inclined to go after her."

"She's underage, yes, but we don't usually hunt down the young people. It's a waste of money."

"I'm not sure she was aware of that. I certainly wasn't."

Evelyn glared at me. "You've always had a unique perspective of events here, dear Sister," she said. "But I thought you should know what Mr. Aldridge did so you wouldn't pester him further."

"Has he returned?" I asked, easily ignoring her provocation because his presence would more than make up for it.

"I don't know. I didn't ask Brother Thomas if he saw any indication of that. I assume if he were here, he would've come directly to the Community, but I may be mistaken. Either way, the rules about conversations between you and any outsider remain the same."

"I understand," I said, turning to leave. While I had succeeded in hiding my excitement from Evelyn, my step down the hallway was much lighter when I headed to the dining room for lunch.

Not a fortnight later, more information arrived. There had been a storm that week that deposited a couple of feet of fluffy snow on the fields and walkways. Kicking at the mounds that had blown onto the shoveled path, I was returning to the dwelling after working all day in the trustees' house. I loved it when the

162

snow was light and fresh. For at least a few days, the glorious blanket of white cleansed everything—the muddy fields, the broken trees, the dirty hay. It was not the oppressive ice that smothered tree branches in February or the heavy, wet snow that often ravaged the landscape in the early spring. But the downy snow of January cosseted my surroundings, mirroring the impeccability of the dry odorless air.

It was late afternoon, yet an hour before dinner. The sun was well below the tree line, but it still lit the sky in the vagueness that reminded me of that short period between vigilance and sleep where thoughts become surreal and disjointed. I noticed the wagon parked in front of the carriage house and even saw a figure circle it to untie the horses. Though I could not see him clearly, I assumed it was Jeremiah, who would have been there to stable the animals and pull the wagon into the carriage house. I heard the click of heels on the icy walk behind me and finally turned around to see another figure approach.

"Sister Lucy, what a glorious evening. Shouldn't you be at work or helping in the kitchen?"

"Damien," was all I could manage.

"You look like you've seen a ghost, Sister. I realize Elder Thomas must be angry with me, but I didn't think he'd declare my death to everyone."

"Where's Sarah? Did she come with you?"

"What do you mean? I haven't seen her yet. I've only just arrived," he said easily. "If I appear nervous, it's because I must meet with Elder Thomas and beg his forgiveness. Do you happen to know his mood?"

"But she went with you, didn't she? You must know where she's staying."

"That's ridiculous, Sister. Look, we can play games later. Would Elder Thomas and Eldress Evelyn be in their dining room now? I'll talk to them as soon as they're free. I'll take my things to the boys' room first. Do you know if there's still a bed for me? Who's taken my place?" With that he turned off, following the path that led around the dwelling to the boys' entrance. "Talk to you later, Sister, or at the next meeting. I have a lot to tell everyone," he called back.

I hurried on to the door, my stomach roiling, but no longer from hunger. I did not go to the dining room but leapt up the stairs. When I got to my empty room, I pulled out a sheet of paper and began to write Mr. Aldridge a letter. I did not know how to get it to him or find out where he was, but scribbling my ideas on paper was a start. An hour later, I wiped the tears from my eyes, curled up under the quilt, and fell asleep.

The next morning the heavy heart remained, but I was definitely hungry. Anxious to get something to tide me over until breakfast, I skipped down the two flights to the kitchen. Peg, busy organizing breakfast, greeted me.

"Where were you last night, Sister? Did you get dinner?"

"No. I wasn't well. Is there something for me before I go to work? My stomach's much improved."

"You'd better not eat anything harsh. I'll toast some bread for you. Sit down. I'm brewing tea." She nestled beside me and filled me in on what she knew. "Did you see Brother Damien was back?"

"Yes. He informed me he knew nothing about Sarah."

"Eldress Evelyn told me she and Elder Thomas sat down with him in the elder's office."

"Do you know what was said?"

"Yes. He admitted he and Sister Sarah had been out together on occasion, but he said he never thought to elope with her."

"Elizabeth wasn't in this meeting, was she?" I asked.

"What are you talking about, Sister? What's Sister Elizabeth got to do with this?"

"Never mind. My short illness has made it difficult for me to concentrate. Go on."

"Brother Damien couldn't handle the deception. Guilt heavy upon him, he went home to talk to his father, the well-known preacher in Hudson. After spending a few months in his father's church and even sermonizing, he came to the realization he belonged here. He asked if he could return."

"Is that it? Weren't they concerned about Sarah?"

"I suppose, but what could they get out of him if he said he hadn't seen Sister Sarah or didn't know anything at all about the elopement?"

"So what'll he do here?"

"Elder Thomas told him he could only come back if he returned to his old job as elder brother for a year. Brother Leonard will be allowed to move back to the trustees' house as before. That should make you happy, Sister Lucy."

I sighed, "How will they find out about Sarah now?"

"I believe they've called for Mr. Aldridge this morning and will meet in Elder Thomas's office after breakfast."

"Really? Mr. Aldridge is back?"

"I suppose. It'd be difficult to have him here if he weren't close by," she said, picking up my cup and plate. "I can see your stomach's much better. Maybe you should run along to work before we both get into trouble."

I was indeed much better. I collected my cape and hat at the girls' door and faced the blustering winds outside.

I dallied at breakfast, hoping to catch a glimpse of Mr. Aldridge. It had been months since I had seen him, and I feared he had forgotten me. As I placed my dirty dishes on the lift, I heard Evelyn's approach.

"Your presence is requested in Elder Thomas's office, Sister."

"Is he here?" I asked without thinking.

165

"Yes, Brother Damien's returned, and he and Brother Thomas would like you to be present. One word of advice, though. I expect you to sit demurely in the corner and not contribute to the conversation. Do you think you can do that?" she asked. We marched toward the transept. "Be forewarned, too, Sister Elizabeth has talked to both Brother Thomas and me. She claims you and Sister Sarah went out in the evenings to meet young men. You might be required to defend yourself."

I could feel all the air push out of my chest. I tried to hide my sudden concern from Evelyn, fearing any reaction would only confirm my guilt.

Without warning, she took my hand and squeezed it. "I know this will be difficult for you, Sister. I realize you fear something has happened to Sister Sarah more than any possible punishment, but please be strong. The men need to know we women are strong."

I was confused. What did she mean? How was I to appear strong when I felt I was being attacked from all sides? Was she reassuring me that in spite of my part in the episode, I would not be punished unduly? Or did she know something worse about Sarah's fate?

When she opened the door, Mr. Aldridge sat on the edge of Thomas's desk facing Damien, who was seated across from Thomas.

Mr. Aldridge stood up when I entered and gazed directly into my eyes. "Miss Hammond," he said, bowing his head.

Evelyn directed me to a chair in the corner.

"We're grateful Mr. Aldridge here has agreed to join us," Thomas said. "Unfortunately the weather has turned foul, making his travel more treacherous. Perhaps we can have Sister Peg prepare something for him to dine on later. Sister Evelyn, will you make sure she's done so?"

"I've already dined, Mr. Dixon," Aldridge assured him.

"Jeremiah sent word you could use my services?"

"Yes. You've met Brother Damien, I suppose."

"Met but haven't been introduced," Aldridge said, putting out his hand. "Hello, Mr. Rathburn. To tell you the truth, I'm very surprised to see you here."

"So you also think I ran off with Sister Sarah? Word has spread far, I see."

"And Miss Bishop has returned with you?"

"No," Thomas said. "Brother Damien tells us he never left with Sister Sarah. Evidently the timing of her disappearance was coincidental to his trip home."

Mr. Aldridge sat back down on the edge of the desk. "To Hudson?"

"Yes, sir. You seem well informed about the comings and goings of the Believers in this community."

"If I were, I'd have known right away you weren't headed to Albany," Mr. Aldridge said, turning to Thomas. "You said you had a note, Mr. Dixon."

"Yes. It's in my drawer. It was addressed to Sister Sarah's best friend, Sister Lucy."

Mr. Aldridge turned to acknowledge me but again spoke to Thomas. "Have you all come to an agreement about the author of this letter, or is there still a question?"

"You know about that?" Evelyn asked.

"I have heard about that, yes. But it was through rumor."

"Sister Lucy claims the letter wasn't written by Sister Sarah," Evelyn said.

"I see," he said, turning back to Damien. "How's your father, Mr. Rathburn? I heard he was ill."

"He's recovered sufficiently, though I don't see how you could know that unless you were investigating me."

"We've had a series of bank robberies over the past few years, Mr. Rathburn. It was necessary for me to keep an eye on you. I hope you didn't find that too inconvenient."

"So you knew he was in Hudson?" I asked.

"I'd like to interview Miss Hammond, if you don't mind."

"Would you like us to dismiss Brother Damien?" Evelyn asked.

"I'd prefer to listen to her explanation about the note alone, if that's all right with you. I'm afraid she might hold her tongue if her elders are present."

"There's nothing she'd say we haven't already heard," Thomas said.

"Really? I was under the impression there's been an issue raised by this other young woman, Miss Wilcox. You yourself were telling me, Mr. Dixon, about this complaint by Miss Wilcox against Miss Hammond. I'd think that revelation might make Miss Hammond hold back on incidents she may have witnessed."

"A young sister doesn't meet with . . ." Evelyn began.

"A person of the opposite sex? I assure you such an interrogation is not only common but necessary, Miss Clark. I'll treat the interview with the utmost professionalism."

"This is preposterous!" she said under her breath.

"This is a possible case of homicide, Miss Clark. It's unfortunate this community is involved, but it is, and as such, will have to deal with the laws of the outside world until it's solved. Perhaps you'd like me to involve a judge. He'll be in the area next month. But if you're in any way concerned with the safety of not only Miss Bishop but all the sisters living in your community, I suggest you help me find out what happened to Miss Bishop."

I braced myself for the battle. I knew my eldress was not going to give up easily. She did not seem to trust any of her charges, and I was appalled she would think we were so bad. But then, had I given her reason to trust me? Had I obeyed the rules? I thought about my escapades with Sarah and had to wipe the tears from my eyes. But Evelyn had no right to believe we girls were interested in boys. I certainly did not break the rules to be with the boys. I had no feelings of longing at all for my brothers and did not understand now why she would imprison me for what I had done.

Of course, the time would come when I would understand what responsibility for others meant. But I had a lot more to learn about the dangers of our escapades—and I would discover many of them all too soon.

14. Surprise Arrest

Crossing the main hallway, I was reminded of the times I actually feared going to Evelyn's office. I watched my feet as we approached the doorway.

"You may use my office. I ask that you keep the door open, however. I'm sure no one will hear you," Evelyn said as she accompanied us to the room.

I sat down across her desk from Mr. Aldridge, and we waited until the sound of her footsteps faded before we began. He handed me the note.

"Sarah didn't write this note," I said.

"That's what I understand. Tell me about it."

"There are errors in it Sarah wouldn't have made."

"But I've been told she wasn't a model student."

"Then you didn't talk to Jerome. He thinks she's wonderful."

"I don't believe he praised her ability to learn, Miss Hammond. He did have good things to say about *your* intelligence, however."

"I don't think Jerome would've known Sarah could write because spelling and grammar aren't really taught to the sisters well, and he doesn't assign papers because he doesn't expect much out of us. Many of my sisters have failed to learn the basics. But Sarah went to school outside the Community and learned to write and spell very well. Her handwriting's superb. She even taught me how to form my letters so my writing would be more legible—something I needed to use as a trustee."

"Do you have any samples of her handwriting?"

"I'm not sure I do. Let me think about that."

"Anything you could find would help, even if it's a practice sheet where she corrected your writing," he said, pausing. "What do *you* think happened to Miss Bishop? Has anyone asked you that?"

"So Damien's telling the truth?" I asked, it suddenly sinking in that they believed him. "She never went with him?"

"Mr. Rathburn says he went home. I verify that. I had him watched, hoping we'd find Miss Bishop there. Unfortunately, if he was with Miss Bishop, he didn't take her to Hudson," he said. "So you *did* believe she could have run off with Mr. Rathburn?"

"Well. They did seem to like each other."

"Did she tell you that?"

"I don't remember her doing so. They gazed at each other at the union meetings."

"Union meetings?"

"Meetings where we could talk to the boys as long as they were across the room."

"Is that all?"

"And she spoke of meeting him outside at night. I'm not sure she ever did. She never did when—" I stopped, my face turning hot.

"Yes?"

"Never mind. That has nothing to do with this."

"When you went out together at night?"

I looked up at him.

"I was present when Miss Wilcox told Mr. Dixon and Miss Clark you and Miss Bishop would go out at night to meet the boys."

"I assure you we didn't go out to meet boys," I said, unable to breathe.

"And how would Miss Wilcox know all of the details unless she was present with you? I'm confident her vivid descriptions weren't lost on your elders, Miss Hammond. Did you two ever see Mr. Rathburn on these occasions?"

"No," I said, beginning to trust him. "We only saw Ezekiel on one of them."

"Mr. Parker? What was he doing?"

"He was camping. That's yet another story you should hear. Sarah spoke of telling Damien she was going to meet him, but that was only because Elizabeth pressed her. I believe it was Elizabeth who wanted to see Damien, because she kept urging Sarah to go find him, and Sarah only bragged about being with him to upset Elizabeth."

"Ah. And how many times did you go out with her?"

"Once. I mean twice, but not really with her. I went out looking for her one night on my own."

"Did you find her?"

"Yes, she went swimming in the pond."

"At night?"

My face must have turned blood red. "We were out at night, yes."

"Was she alone?"

I paused, realizing this might negate everything I had told him thus far. "No. But I couldn't see who she was with. I got tangled in something hanging from a tree."

"What was it?"

"Her gown," I confessed, only getting deeper into details I did not want to divulge.

"I understand."

"You see, while she only wore her gown out, I wore my boots and work dress," I said, making sure I did not reveal I wore nothing underneath. I do not know why I continued with the story. It sounded like I was tattling on Sarah, when all I wanted to do was make sure he knew I was chaste and ladylike.

"And this other person swimming with her was male?" he asked, seeming to ignore my incoherent ramblings.

"I believe so, though I never found his clothes. I thought I heard Edgar coming down the trail and had to get out of there."

"Edgar?"

"He's a man I saw when I was in the kitchen," I said, tears filling my eyes. "Don't ask me about him. I'm afraid I sound like a fool."

"Not at all," he said gently. "You've been a great help. Is this when you saw Mr. Parker?"

"No that's when I got out of there. The next time I went with both Sarah and Elizabeth. We hiked up to the shrine and then came down. Sarah and Elizabeth noticed the campfire through the trees and went over to talk to Ezekiel. I didn't go all the way. I didn't want to see Ezekiel."

"But you listened?"

"That doesn't shed a good light on me, but yes. When Elizabeth insisted Sarah ask, Ezekiel said he'd seen Damien out earlier, but he didn't know where he was."

"Is it usual for a brother to have so much freedom while a sister doesn't?"

"No. But Ezekiel travels a lot for the trustees. He delivers goods and makes sales all over the area, so I suppose he doesn't want to be told what to do when he's on his own so much. He hasn't committed, either, because he isn't sure he wants to be in the Community."

"Yes, I saw he traveled by the documents you provided."

"There's more. Elizabeth left the campsite that night and returned to the dwelling."

"She left Sarah alone?"

"Yes, because she wanted to meet boys, I suppose, and Sarah

didn't care if we met any boys."

"I see."

"And I think Ezekiel attacked Sarah because he pulled her away from the fire and she complained. I yelled out to scare him because he didn't know I was there, and then I ran back to the dwelling."

"Did Sarah return?"

"Yes, but she had bruises on her arms."

"So Sarah only went out twice that you know of?"

"No. She went out more than that. She talked about going out and meeting people. Once she came back with hay in her hair. The hay gave her a rash, and she had to go to the infirmary for a cream."

"Where did the hay come from?"

"Probably the barn. She didn't say."

"I see," he said. "Did she ever mention any other boys or young men?"

"Not that I can think of. She did mention Seth several times. That was probably because she thought I liked Seth."

"Do you?"

"What?"

"Do you like Mr. Deming?"

"Oh, no. Seth's very devoted to the Heavenly Father. I was going to tell you she didn't usually mention any specific boy. The boys, however, often talked about her. I know most of them thought she was beautiful."

"You've given me so much information, I'll have to think about it."

"Oh, but there's more. You told me to check Ezekiel's room. Don't you remember?"

"Ah, yes. You reported you didn't find anything."

"I didn't, but maybe you should know that all wasn't normal. There was a boot full of something that fell onto the floor. It was heavy and had a piece of cloth sticking out of it."

"What was it?"

"I've no idea. Ezekiel walked in at just that moment. He threatened me and pushed me down onto his bed."

"I didn't want you to be in danger."

"I might have been in danger had not Zachary thrown the door open just in time. Of course, the elders blamed me. I'm not sure what he thought I was doing, but he didn't deal with Ezekiel as an attacker."

"Did they go back and look in the boot?"

"Yes, but the pair had been polished, and there was nothing inside of either. I only wanted to tell you so you wouldn't think ill of me. You might hear things from the elders that make me sound despicable."

"But I sent you to investigate Ezekiel and realize you wanted very much to protect your friend, Miss Bishop. I'll believe nothing they say. I promise."

"And thank you for checking on Damien. I now know you were helping me find Sarah all along."

It was then Evelyn appeared in the office doorway. Neither of us had heard her approach.

"I believe you have enough information to keep your investigation going, Mr. Aldridge," she said coolly. "I trust it won't be necessary to involve Sister Lucy again, but if it does, you'll continue to speak first with either myself or Elder Thomas."

I am not sure if my confessions to Mr. Aldridge comforted me. I certainly was not out of the woods with the elders, so there was little relief from the tensions it caused. But for the first time, I had a confidante. Mr. Aldridge knew so much about my adventures and did not seem to be shocked. Thus, no matter what happened between the elders and me, I felt he would be there to defend me.

The investigation was not over yet, however. Indeed, it was just beginning. Life would go on as it always had—I would have kitchen duty in February and even into the beginning of March. But finding Sarah would always be on my mind. What I did not know was my search would be over in a matter of weeks. Finding the answers to my questions would send me into a spiral of darkness.

Still giddy the next day, I went up to my room after breakfast to put together my freshly laundered bed. But instead of rushing, as Brother Leonard's return from the boy's dwelling assured my workload would ease, I stared out the window at the icy field. Elizabeth suddenly entered the room.

"What are you doing here, Sister Lucy? I'm sure you have chores to do."

"Yes. I'll have to get back to the trustees' house. I like the view from here. Do you mind if I switch with Valerie and sleep in Sarah's old bed?"

"I don't think that would be convenient."

I turned to face her. "I already asked Evelyn, and she said it would be all right." I swung back to look out the window again. "What do you think happened to her, Elizabeth?"

"She probably just ran away. You knew how she was. She wanted to go."

"That isn't true. She would've told me if she weren't happy."

"I can't believe you aren't upset with her. She tried to get you into trouble—tried to get both of us to go out with her on her nightly escapades."

"But she didn't tell Evelyn."

"That would have made trouble for *her.*"

"And *you* did," I said.

"Eldress Evelyn wanted to know who could give her more information about Sister Sarah."

"I never told on you. And anyway, I think you told on her before that. Sarah thought I was spying on her, but I believe it was you."

"I was never close to her. I went out with you two to make sure you did nothing stupid. You were ruining the reputation of the Community. But now I see the Heavenly Father himself exacted punishment on Sister Sarah," she said, taking off again.

I had no idea what she meant but shuddered in response. I pulled the folded sheets off the bed and flipped the mattress over. Out flew a piece of paper onto the floor. I sat down to read it in the light from the window, but never got a chance. There were more footsteps ascending the stairs. I pocketed the paper and quickly remade the bed.

"Brother Russell," I said later that afternoon. "I need to go into town."

"Did you obtain Eldress Evelyn's permission?" Russell asked. "Before he went to Harvard Community, Brother Jeremiah told me I had to get permission to take you."

"She only objects to Mr. Aldridge seeking my company to help with the investigation, not my doing business in town."

"What kind of business?"

"Mr. Barnard has a problem with his account. You're going into town today, aren't you?"

"Will Brother Eli verify what you are saying?"

"I have no idea. I haven't spoken with him about it because the accounts are my responsibility."

"Do you have someone willing to go with you?"

"Yes. I'll get her. Wait here."

I was not sure what I would do once I got into town—how I would approach Mr. Aldridge after I failed to tell Russell I was seeking him. What if Mr. Aldridge came out of the general store just as we were going in? Would Russell let me talk to him? And

177

then there was the note. I felt for it in my pocket. The note itself was not Sarah's handwriting either. Whose was it?

I returned in fifteen minutes, dragging Georgia by the hand. "Slow down, Sister," she said. "He won't leave without you. I hope the weather holds. Another storm might do me in. Do you have your mittens, Sister Lucy?"

Russell glared at me when he climbed onto the wagon. "Are you sure you're warm enough, Sister Georgia? I'd hate to see you take ill with a cough because of the cold."

"I'm fine, Brother. I've survived much worse over the many winters of my life."

When we arrived in front of Barnard's, I noticed there was no one about. "I must go to the bank and check the records there first," I said.

Russell took a box from the back but stopped short when he heard my announcement. "You didn't tell me you had business at the bank. Perhaps Sister Georgia should accompany you."

My heart pounded. The Community rarely had a need to deal with the bank, and I wondered if he would investigate my lie. "Yes, I'll help her down. Please finish your work here. We can handle it."

Georgia had not planned to get down and began to argue with me.

"Please, Sister, I really *do* need to get something to the bank. Russell won't let me go there if you don't come with me."

"Why are you always so busy? Are you going in search of your beau?"

"Shhhhh. He isn't my beau, Georgia. We're looking for Sarah, and I've found a clue."

Finally crossing the busy road together, we walked into the bank. A man stood behind a long counter, and a short line of people waited to speak with him. I turned to leave, but Georgia stopped me.

"There's a man over there. Talk to him."

The well-dressed gentleman sat at a desk in an alcove with an arched portico. He leaned back, the quill of his pen at his lips.

"Excuse me, sir," I said, almost inaudibly.

He sat up suddenly, as if I had surprised him.

"I wonder if you know how I might find Mr. Aldridge," I said.

Without standing up, the stout gentleman leaned to one side. "Wilmot, will you please get Daniel for this young lady?"

The clerk walked down a short passageway to his right and disappeared.

Mr. Aldridge followed the clerk into the lobby. "I'm surprised to see you both out in this weather."

"Mr. Aldridge, I've found something that disturbs me," I said, trying to speed up the interview before Russell had time to get suspicious. "This note isn't from Sarah, but it concerns her. The writer's threatening to tell the elders she's meeting boys at night."

"The writer doesn't say who he or she is?"

"No. But it makes me fear for Sarah's safety even more."

"Where did you find this?"

"I was making her bed—my bed now. It must have been caught in the webbing. I can't believe I didn't see it before now."

"Ah. I'll look into this. What do you think the writer wanted from her? What could Miss Bishop possibly give this person?"

"She had no possessions," Georgia offered. "She was indentured to the Community. All her possessions were turned over to her new guardians."

I didn't counter what Georgia said, feeling Sarah's stash was irrelevant; minor trinkets owned by a farmer's wife.

"This note is very interesting indeed. Let me look into it."

I was happy I had found a clue but disappointed he did not want to use more of my services in the investigation. Was there nothing more I could do to help?

Needless to say, Mr. Aldridge did not ask me to accompany him on any more of the search. Nearly a week passed before I saw him again, and he had not come to see me.

One evening, I returned to the dwelling from the trustees' house, tired after a difficult day. We had been selling seeds to a new market in New York and were excited about a possible relationship with our most recent customers.

"These orders are great, Sister Lucy," said Eli, shuffling through the order sheets. "They come at a good time for the whole Community. Sending Brother Ezekiel there was a good idea. I'll put the shop to work on them immediately."

"Wait a minute, Brother Eli," said Leonard, entering the office with another man. "This is Brother Eugene from Enfield. He has a problem with our foraging for customers beyond our area."

"I'm sure you weren't aware of it, but we at Enfield have been working with these customers for more than two years," said the visitor. "It does no good to either Community if we overlap our areas. We seem to be creating new markets at the expense of ourselves."

Leonard looked at his map again. "You're correct, Brother. They are indeed your customers. Sister Lucy, will you gather the orders for Brother Eugene? The Enfield Community will fill the orders themselves. We apologize for the inconvenience of your trip, Brother. Perhaps you'd like to dine with us and let us find you a bed in the dwelling so you can return to Enfield refreshed in the morning."

The whole episode made me tired. As the stars twinkled in the black sky, I trudged through a foot of new snow, hoping to eat and go directly to bed. Unfortunately it was Friday night, and Elizabeth and Damien would expect me to attend the union meeting.

The wind was icy, and I had forgotten my scarf. Thinking it would be smart to cut through the brick dwelling, I entered the kitchen and greeted some of my friends there. They asked me to stay for tea, but knowing they were busy feeding the North Family, I headed up the stairs to the first floor where I could exit closest to my dwelling. Just as I got to the transept, I heard it. Someone was struggling to make it down the stairs. There was yelling, as more than one person chased someone back up to the second floor. Caught, the perpetrator of the fight made little effort to take the steps on his own, now dragging his feet and letting his toes thump against each tread. I winced, imagining Brother Gordon's discomfort at watching someone mar his beautiful carpentry. The trio reached the last few steps when I realized Mr. Aldridge and Zachary fought to control a prisoner between them.

"*You* told him, Sister! That damn nose of yours is going to get you into trouble. As soon as I'm released, and liberty will be mine, I'll be back for you."

Mr. Aldridge pulled him toward Zachary's office.

"It's because of you Sister Sarah's in trouble, you meddlesome cur," Ezekiel said as Mr. Aldridge yanked him through the office door. "Watch out for Edgar. Don't think he'll let you get away with this."

Five minutes later, Mr. Aldridge emerged with his prisoner, now calmed, his arms and legs tied.

"Excuse me, Miss Hammond. This man seems to be a bank robber. I'll accompany him to Springfield and return as soon as he's been delivered to the proper authorities."

"Sister Lucy's the one who got me arrested," Ezekiel said, pulling away from Mr. Aldridge and lunging at me.

He did not make it far, because his feet were bound, but I backed away just the same.

"Come now. Miss Hammond had nothing to do with this. Next you'll be telling everyone you've taken up the ways of your Heavenly Father."

I stood frozen. Mr. Aldridge dragged Ezekiel out the dwelling door. His reassuring words still ringing in my ears, I wondered if Mr. Aldridge did indeed plan to return now that he had captured his bank robber.

15. Treasure

The end of February brought a slight thaw. Robert lamented there might be no more hard freezes and that they had squandered any opportunity to harvest the ice. We all prayed at Sunday meeting we would get another chance to collect the slabs, which would be needed during the hot summer months ahead.

Lavonia assured us there would be another freeze. "The last of winter almost never arrives in February," she said.

The boys' school term was just about over. Having helped Jerome correct papers, I'd had reason to consult with him more than once since my final year of schooling the previous June. I had not looked forward to the end of classes, but juggling school and work kept me very busy. I enjoyed learning, even though most of my sisters and brethren agreed women needed to learn a trade because busy hands were more important to the survival of the Community than a lofty mind. The brethren, however, were encouraged to continue their schooling for another year.

"Good morning, Brother," I said one morning. "I've brought you the papers I corrected. Are there any more?" I looked across at Jerome who stood in front of the window, his hands clasped behind his back.

"Just put them on my desk, please," he said. "I don't have anything more for you right now."

I walked up beside him. "Do you miss her?"

"You mean Sarah Bishop? Yes, a bit. I miss her energy. Has

that detective of yours found anything out about where she went?"

"Not that I'm aware of. He's been in Springfield for two weeks now. I don't know where he is or even if he's coming back."

"It isn't really his job to hunt for her, you know," Jerome said. "He works for the bank and, in the eyes of his employers, he's finished this job. I doubt he'll ever come back. Do you know what prompted him to arrest Brother Ezekiel?"

"Thomas told me the note I gave Mr. Aldridge was the proof he needed."

"Note? What note? I never heard about another note."

"He threatened to tell the elders about Sarah's nightly assignations if she didn't pay him."

"With what? Was she able to pay him?" he asked.

"I have no idea. I believe Mr. Aldridge compared the handwriting to that of some hold-up notes, and they matched."

"Does he plan to investigate further?"

"I don't know. As I said, Mr. Aldridge hasn't returned."

"I don't think we'll ever find Sister Sarah without him," he said.

"No. I fear not."

"It looks like we'll have to have our skating party next weekend," he said, perking up. "You'll join us, won't you?"

"I'm afraid I have kitchen duty. I'll certainly watch you all amusing yourselves from the window."

He smiled. "It'll be fun if the ice holds. Certainly it won't get warm enough to make the ice dangerous." He went silent again, but I could tell my news bothered him.

His hands shook, and he crossed his arms in order to hide them. It made me wonder if he worried Ezekiel might disclose something about him too.

"Good luck with the skating party, Jerome. I'll pray for a

freeze so the ice will be good and hard."

He did not respond.

I began to hear more about the party. I was glad the children were excited about it and looked forward to it too, even though I still did not think Peg would let me go. A wet snow followed, making the chance for a party more unlikely. I started kitchen duty and found myself glad to keep busy. Baking Wednesdays always reminded me of Sarah, but this one proceeded slowly. There were mainly younger girls in the kitchen with me. Most did not know how to bake, and I had trouble getting them to use their muscles for kneading. With too few loaves ready for the following week, I worked well into the night, trying to produce more.

Suddenly, Peg walked in. "Oh, Sister Lucy, are you still up?" she asked.

"Yes. I have to let this bread rise and bake it before I go to bed. I'm afraid we couldn't accomplish as much as we desired this evening. A few more loaves will help," I said, placing some dough in a pan and covering it with a cloth.

"Have you heard anything more about Brother Ezekiel? What did they find for evidence against him?"

"It was the note."

"The note about Sister Sarah's elopement?"

"No. I found a note from Ezekiel to Sarah. Evidently, it was the same handwriting as that on a note he used in one of the bank robberies."

"You mean she was seeing Brother Ezekiel too? That must make all of them."

"All of whom?"

"All the brothers must have met with Sister Sarah at one time or another. Oh, and I heard Brother Damien may be leaving again," Peg said, sitting across the table from me and pouring us both some tea.

"Not again," I said. "Where's he going?"

"I don't know. I heard him talking. Elder Thomas was trying to convince him to take a position as elder at Enfield."

"I sure wish I knew how he fits in to all this mystery. I'm certain the talk about Sarah's involvement is an exaggeration. No one's missing, are they? I mean, if she ran off with one of them, why are they all still here?"

"Because she ran off with someone outside the Community. That's what I think. You yourself said she'd mentioned having a beau before she came to us."

"But she never wrote or talked to anyone on the outside—at least not that I remember. It's odd she and her beau didn't wait until she was eighteen and free to go. As it is, the ministry still has the right to go after them." I got up to check the dough but determined it was not yet ready. "And why the note? Why would anyone write a note about Damien and Sarah if she ran off with another? Who else knew about it?"

"Are you certain she didn't write it?"

"I'm positive . . ." I said. "Almost."

At the end of the week, Peg sent me to the barn to collect some squash we had stored there. Suddenly, Jeremiah entered.

"Hello, Sister Lucy. I'm here to take a load over to Barnard's. Is everything ready? Do you want to come?"

My arms full, I looked up surprised. "You'll have to ask Eli to go with you. I have kitchen duty. You were at Harvard, weren't you? When did you get back?"

"Late last night. Elder Henry is much better."

"How did it feel to be an elder? Are you sure you want to come back?"

"It wasn't so bad. It was quiet. I'm not sure I'm cut out to be an elder, though. I missed Dakota and Mamie. Brother Russell took good care of them, but horses are sensitive when their caretaker disappears. Brother Russell said Mamie nipped at him."

"Did you hear all the news about what happened here?"

"I was here when Sister Sarah ran off with Brother Damien and when Brother Damien returned without her. What did you determine from talking with him? Is he guilty?"

"He evidently didn't elope with her after all. Damien just went home to his family. But that's not all."

"Isn't that enough?"

"Do you recall Ezekiel?"

"Not well. I didn't associate with him much. He was kind of a weasel, if I remember him right."

"He was arrested as a bank robber."

"Oh, yeah. That Aldridge fellow was looking for an outlaw in these parts. Did you get him arrested or did Aldridge do it?"

"Well, both. I gave Mr. Aldridge a note from Ezekiel, and Mr. Aldridge discovered the handwriting matched one of the bank robber's notes."

"So now the elders don't mind if you speak with Aldridge directly?"

"They still mind, but it doesn't matter. Mr. Aldridge took Ezekiel to Springfield nearly three weeks ago and hasn't returned."

"Are you sure you don't want to help me deliver a load to town?"

"No. I have kitchen duty."

"By the way. What did the note from Ezekiel say?"

"He threatened to tell the elders about Sarah's adventures if she didn't pay him."

"Really?" asked Jeremiah, picking up a crate. "That doesn't sound like a murderer. If he wanted to kill her, he would've threatened something more than telling the elders. And I don't think she would've cared if he did tell the elders. I believe they already knew."

But I am not sure I heard his final comments. Had I been stupid? Of course Sarah could pay him. Why had I disregarded her mother's jewelry? Sarah could sell the jewelry to pay for Ezekiel's silence. More notably, if Sarah had run away, she would've taken everything from the hiding place, even if there had been no jewelry left there. What remained at the shrine would tell me if she had left on her own.

That evening I prayed Mr. Aldridge would show up so we could go to the shrine and find Sarah's treasure. I trusted no one else. But he did not return. After hours lying awake, I decided to go myself.

While there had been a thaw, the night was still cold. I slipped into my dress and cape and took a scarf and mittens too. In the garden shed, I found a spade, just in case I could not locate the shovel Sarah used that night in early fall when she, Elizabeth and I visited the shrine. From under the oak, I stopped and stared at the road and the path beyond. Did I have the courage to go through the woods by myself? I had no choice. At least Ezekiel could not accost me now, but of course, I feared Edgar as much as I did Ezekiel.

The clouds began to clear, revealing moonlight to guide me. Crossing the road, I trudged up the snow-covered slope toward the trail. The moonlight off the thin layer of snow made the path stand out, and I tramped on, fearing if I stopped, my heart would give out.

About a third of the way up, I did stop once. An owl, deep in the darkness to my right, hooted and then attacked something in the snow. My knees began to give way. Determined to get to the top, I willed myself on.

I reached the shrine winded and tried to make out the pool

and altar through my frosty breath. Surprisingly, the top of the hill had little snow at all. Stopping to rest only a second, I heard a commotion. There were voices, low, but not in a whisper—two men, I believe, digging in the pool. I waited behind the last branches and watched as they dug up mounds of dirt at the wrong end of it. Who were they? Were they looking for Sarah's treasure? Did they have Sarah?

A third man emerged from the shadow and howled at the moon. I stood frozen and watched. He wore a cap over his head so I could not make out his hair color. He looked in my direction and laughed, revealing darkness where there should have been teeth, and hair seemed to grow out of one side of his face. His twisted features made my heart stop. Had he seen me? Was this Edgar? I stepped back farther into the thick branches of the tree.

Suddenly, the digging man tossed the shovel to the side. "Let's go. I can't stand it in this holy asylum one more minute. What do you say we call it a night? I do believe the brother has put one over on us. I'll see him hanged. I swear, I'll make sure we have a front row space at the gallows when his blessed body dangles at the end of a rope."

The other man cackled and then followed his friends down the other side of the hill. Dropping my spade, I waited for at least five minutes. I was beginning to feel the chill through my clothes and knew I had to hurry or freeze. Crossing the clearing, I picked up the shovel the man had flung away and marched to the spot in the pool Sarah had pointed out to Elizabeth and me. One of the tiles was chipped on one corner. That surprised me, because it was not chipped the last time the three of us had been there. Too impatient to look for the crowbar to pry the tiles open, I dug at them with my nails until they bled. I was able to remove them one at a time. What I found, however, was not what I expected. Under a thin layer of dirt, I discovered one brown bag after another of heavy coins and currency. There were four in all. Mr. Aldridge would want these, but they were too heavy to carry down the hill. I dug until the mud was up to my elbows but was relieved to find nothing else. Sarah must have removed her treasure before she left. That meant she was still alive. But then how did Ezekiel know about the hiding place in order to bury his loot? Had he removed the items or was it already empty?

I looked around. There did not seem to be anywhere I could conceal the bags. I decided to take them over to the tree where Sarah had buried her shovel and crowbar, knowing the two men had already discovered the shovel, and dig another hole beside a massive rock just a few feet away. The hole was not very deep, but I was able to cover the mound with leaves and snow so few could tell something had recently been buried there. Then I went back to the brush under the first tree to conceal the shovel. It was then I saw something. I lifted what looked like a gown from under the pile of branches. A brooch pinned to the collar twinkled in the moonlight. It was Sarah's mother's dress. Even in the dark, I recognized the cut of the neck. Beneath it lay a couple of books and a small doll. These were Sarah's things. I had been wrong. Evidently, Sarah never took her treasure with her. My heart ached.

I would have stood there longer, but the clouds had managed to slip in front of the moon, preparing to drop another several inches of snow. I covered up my discovery, replaced the tiles in the pool, and started back down the hill, this time with little light at all. But I did not worry about that. Nor did I feel concern about what I would do to clean up the mud on my cape and the sleeves of my dress before the others discovered it. I only reflected on the loss of my friend.

I arrived late for the Sunday meeting and quickly sneaked into the last row, trying hard not to disturb the prayer Robert offered. I looked over at the visitors' seats and was disappointed Mr. Aldridge had not returned.

"Amen," I said, repeating along with my brothers and sisters.

"As you've discovered, the sun doesn't quite indicate what it really feels like outside," Robert said. "It only warms the surface each day. The night freezes it over again until it's downright slippery. We can be like that too, brothers and sisters. Sometimes we don't feel our Father's gifts deep inside. But we need to let him know we do feel. We need to let him know he's penetrating our skin. Only when we experience his love deep inside can we melt the cold that has overtaken us."

"Amen," I said again, taking the hymnal from the seat next to me.

Continuing to stare at the visitors' benches, I absently opened the little booklet. But it did not contain hymns. Ladies' underwear peeked out at me when I pulled back the cover. This was the same advertising pamphlet Sarah had shown me that night winters ago. How did it get here? Why did someone not see it and pick it up? I turned the page. In the margin next to a picture of a corset with lacy frills framing a woman's ample bosom, someone had penned a message:

Darling Seth, I want to see you again. Meet me at the barn tonight at eleven o'clock. We can talk about our trip soon. Love Sarah.

Needless to say, I was astonished. The notation was blatant in its meaning. I feared the handwriting was indeed Sarah's. Was she also meeting Seth? I could not believe he was a party to meeting with Sarah after hours, but here was a note in Sarah's own handwriting. I closed the booklet. The outside looked just like a hymnal. Had no one else opened it up over the last months, or maybe even years?

191

I would have to get it to Mr. Aldridge. But, of course, I could not. Mr. Aldridge probably was not going to return, and if I gave the booklet to one of the elders, he or she might jump to a conclusion and banish Seth without listening to his side of the story. I did not know what to do and decided to hold onto the booklet and tell no one.

Robert stood up and again began to speak. "Let's pray the cold weather remains so the children can have a wonderful skating party this Friday. Winter's a difficult season, but children seem to know how to have fun with the cold and often annoying snow. Let's also pray the cold remains for the ice harvest shortly after that party. We all know how difficult it is to actually fill the icehouse every year. It's a monumental task to remove ice from the pond, carry it down the hill, and prepare the layers in the barn itself. But when we have a short winter season, the job becomes almost impossible. This week will be winter's last gasp. Let's all go out and close the door to a difficult year when the outside infiltrated our midst and brought corruption to the heart of the Hancock Community. We're children of our Father and Mother, of our Savior. Let's all go finish off our winter chores and clear the way for spring, for rebirth in this Zion we've worked so hard to create."

Monday progressed without any mention of my being out at night. I wore my work dress and cape to the trustees' house, stealing out of the dwelling without notice.

"What happened to your dress?" Eli asked when he saw me at my desk.

"I slipped on an icy spot on the walk over," I said. "I'm afraid I'll have a sore backside tomorrow."

I realized what I had said the second the words were out of my mouth, but of course, he did not seem to be aware the dirt was not on the backside of my cape but only on the front and up the sleeves of my dress. I must have fallen very awkwardly indeed to have dirtied myself that way.

Fortunately, by breakfast, the whole Community was celebrating another surprise. The temperatures had plummeted in the last few hours, and the ice was beginning to harden again. On top of that, it was snowing. This time it was a dry snow that would be easy to clear so the children could enjoy their party on Friday. I took breakfast time to wash out my dress and cape and hung the dress to dry in the closet. I wore my Sunday outfit back to the trustees' house, under my still-damp cape, of course, so Elizabeth and Evelyn did not have reason to stop and question me. Hopefully, my work dress would be dry by dinnertime.

Over the next few days, my thoughts about my last trip to the shrine continued to play out in my mind. I still could not figure out how Ezekiel found Sarah's hiding place. Had she told him? Had he beaten her until she revealed it? Had he watched us when we went up there that night to check on her things? All I knew was somehow he must have known she would not return to steal his bank money. Did he in fact murder her in order to pocket her little treasure?

16. Sinking the Header

It was wonderful the children had the opportunity to play. My mind had toyed with the idea of my gliding over the slippery surface the evening before as I cleaned the kitchen and finished the bread to be served at breakfast the following morning.

Jerome told me it would take all morning to scrape the ice. Jeremiah would have the horses out at dawn, harnessing Dakota and Mamie to a scraper that looked like a long dustpan. I did not get to watch him because I was busy in the kitchen with Peg, but I had seen them out there in years past.

I am positive some of the children watched, however. In the other bedroom, I could hear the commotion of the girls at the window. I do not know how they knew Jeremiah and the horses were up there. With the window closed, I could barely hear the jangle of their gear.

Ambrose assembled some skates of different styles for the new children. I let one of the young boys, Randolph, borrow mine, since my skates were too big for most of the young girls. I looked for Randolph in the afternoon, hoping to see if my skates helped him stay on his feet at all. I did not see him, however. Perhaps the sleds interested him more.

The whole party began as a snowball fight. Although he would never admit it, I believe I saw Jerome instigate it before sneaking away to play with a toboggan. The fight lasted for hours as strongholds were erected and fortified with enough armaments to last the day.

But alas, I was too busy and unable to continue to watch either the battle or the skating exhibition. I did observe a group of elders out there once. I wanted to see if they planned to sled down the hill too, but Peg called me back. Already having stirred the pudding, I had to return to the oven and pour it over the hot drippings.

"You look pale, Sister," Peg said as I closed the oven door. "Maybe you should go to bed right after dinner. The girls and I can clean off the tables."

"I *do* have the sniffles, and my head aches slightly," I said. "But I'm sure it's nothing serious."

I inquired about the fun as I served dinner. The partygoers explained everyone had a good time and that no one was hurt except for Jerome, who had managed to twist his ankle when he crashed into a tree—and the sled, of course, which needed a thorough mending.

Oddly, that was all I heard about the party that day. I heard nothing about anything else afoot except talk about the weather among the senior members as I filled their pitchers during the earlier sitting.

"I saw buds on the bushes yesterday," Lucas said.

"That was probably from the warm days we had last week, Lucas," I said, filling his glass so he would not have to pour it himself.

"No. These were new. I think it's going to warm up again. Wouldn't that be nice? Spring's here."

"It can't be spring already, Brother," Timothy said. "The young men haven't harvested the ice, and the icehouse is almost empty. What'll we do in June when the ice runs low?"

"The moon's full, and because of the party, Brother Jeremiah cleared it already," said Lucas. "I'll stake my bet they'll do it tonight. We've harvested it in the dark before, remember? I think it was ten or fifteen years ago Brother Harrison had the young men harvest at night because it had been such a warm winter. The thaw would make quick work of the thin layer of ice on the pond."

"Isn't that dangerous?" I asked before crossing over to the women's table.

"Oh, it was thick enough to stand on," Timothy said. "Just not solid so the slabs would last. I think we ran out in August that year, but we were able to borrow some from Canterbury. They had an ice storm in April and collected more than enough. Of course, transporting that much ice can be difficult."

One of the sisters stood up, prayer book in hand, and the room went silent.

Thus, after helping serve the children at the second sitting, I went to bed, still wanting to stay up and hear the beginning of the harvest. But my head pounded and my throat hurt after a long day. I could not keep my eyes open. I was asleep soon after my head hit the pillow.

It must have been two or three in the morning when a shout outside roused me. The window beside my bed was shut and the sound muffled, but when I turned onto my back to listen further, I could hear the ruckus clearly. There were people somewhere behind the dwelling. My mind still clouded, I did not even think of the possible nighttime harvest. My first thoughts were of Edgar and my fears someone had left a door unlocked. Sitting up, I became aware of the full moon peeking in at the top of the window. I finally reflected on dinner and talk of a possible ice harvest before the weather turned warm again. Pulling my quilt around my shoulders, I crossed over to the window seat to watch.

The pane was frosty, but after wiping it, I was able to see the string of lanterns someone had affixed to a line that ran over the pond. There were several men, dressed in wool caps and gloves, dashing about over the road that glowed in the moon's radiance. I did not know why they had to run. They had hours, after all, and the precision it took for the horses and men to guide the marker over the surface would surely take time. Even if they had made progress beyond marking the ice, the sawing and square removal was also a slow job. Failing to see a wagon up there with them, I did not understand what the commotion was about.

But I could hear voices—shouting. I slid the window open a crack to see if I could learn what was going on. Had someone fallen into the icy water? I suppose that could be a problem when cutting the surface into tiny islands.

"Get the toboggan up here at once," someone said.

"Do you need anything to hook the horses up?"

"Brother Robert, move the light over here. I just about have it," a voice in the distance called out.

"Watch out. Don't harm the body."

My heart stopped. What could possibly be going on?

"Is it she? Can you tell by the dress?"

"This is definitely a cloth we use to make nightgowns. It certainly looks like her. I'm cutting some strands of hair. Mr. Tyler, who are you sending to the doctor's office to positively identify this body?"

"Look here under the lantern. These are definitely blond."

I am not certain I heard all of the last line. I was already out the bedroom door and on the stairs. There are always pairs of boots lined up along the wall of the boys' entry, and coats hung on the pegs. But I did not think of stopping. I darted down the boys' hall so fast, no one could have stopped me even if they had tried. When I was out the door, I kept running—past the shed, under the shadow of the oak tree, and across the road without looking, without thinking. I only wanted to be with her before someone took her away.

I did not see him descend from the pond. I do not know who saw me trudge through the foot-deep snow on that side of the hill, but there was someone in my way. I slowed and started to break sideways to pass him, but guessing my move, he zigzagged into my path. There was a hint of my legs tiring, though I tried hard to ignore it. I saw the opening beside him and took aim in that direction, but he stretched out his arm to catch me before I could slip by. I fought and scratched my challenger, but to no avail. He held fast.

"I have her," he yelled up to the men at the pond. "I'll take her back down."

It was then I recognized the voice of Mr. Aldridge and, for the first time, was able to let my muscles relax. That was a mistake. Relaxation made me suffer the icy cold that bit right through my perspiration-soaked gown. As for my feet, I could not feel them at all. Looking at my face, Mr. Aldridge guessed I was not going to make it down the hill easily.

"I want to see her," I yelled, still wheezing. "I want to see Sarah!"

"Later," he said, taking off his coat and wrapping it around my shoulders.

I turned to start down the hill, but my knees buckled. He picked me up and carried me to the kitchen. I can only remember watching the frosty air emanating from his mouth and nose and a dark stream of blood oozing from a gash on his cheek. Later, I learned I clung to his neck, even after he put me down on the stool in the kitchen. Sister Peg had to pry my fingers loose.

"What's happened?" Peg asked him softly.

"Heat some water. I'll work on her feet. She needs hot tea. Quickly."

"No. I'll work on her legs and feet," Peg said, gently taking over. "You can fix the tea, please."

Mr. Aldridge understood immediately but made no move to fill the kettle. I could see he wanted to say something but looked down at my face and changed his mind. "Has anyone gone to retrieve your eldress, Miss Clark?" he finally asked, grabbing the kettle.

"I'll go," said someone in the doorway. I could not see who was there.

Evelyn arrived shortly afterward. Mr. Aldridge helped me drink some tea and then handed her a couple of hot compresses he had made.

She put them on my bare legs and then stood, turning to face him. "I believe it's time for you to go out and help the others. Sister Peg and I can take care of Sister Lucy. We appreciate your help, but—"

"But I'm getting too close? Is that what you were about to say, Miss Clark? You'd rather have a sister die than be seen or touched by a man?"

"Mr. Aldridge, I won't have you speak to me that way in this house."

"I can't have been the first to speak it. My concerns are for the welfare of a young woman who's clearly traumatized by tonight's events," he said, staring directly into the eldress' eyes. But he paused for only a few seconds. "I'm sorry if I've overstepped my bounds and shall leave immediately, satisfied she'll receive the care she obviously needs."

I watched him spin around and walk to the door. He did not look back, though I knew his face must have been visibly angered by the tone Evelyn used. She returned to work on my legs, even though he had walked out into the cold without his topcoat, which was still wrapped around my shoulders. I wanted to cry out, to call to him and give it back to him before he froze, but I could not. I only recollect watching the flicker of

Peg's candle on the table and nestling deeper into the folds of his coat.

I do not remember anything about what happened after that. I do not even recall how I got to a bed. Peg would later tell me what she and others actually witnessed that night, most of them not realizing the men had discovered Sarah's body. I have knitted these stories together and am now able to relate what happened in the weeks after they found my Sarah.

"You should have been in the infirmary for a few days, but Eldress Evelyn wouldn't have it," Peg explained. "In the morning, the others awoke to the news of Sarah, but you didn't. Sister Elizabeth felt your forehead and found you had a blistering fever. You eventually roused but didn't say much. Mostly groaned. We feared moving you to the infirmary in the cold would make you worse, so we had the nurse come to us. Elder Thomas carried you to the extra room that belonged to Brother Abel before he died."

"Did the nurse know what was wrong?" I asked.

"She said you were very ill and weren't to get out of bed. She seemed so concerned, she suggested we bring in a doctor from Albany. Eldress Evelyn doesn't normally have a male doctor examine female patients, but in this case, it was obvious you needed help. Dr. Hayworth examined you, with the eldress present of course, and explained you had symptoms of pneumonia. He told us to watch you day and night, use compresses to keep the fever down, and have you inhale steam to keep your lungs as clear as possible."

"Did I cough?"

"You coughed until there was blood coming up, and you talked gibberish," Peg said.

"What kind of gibberish?"

"You spoke with Mr. Aldridge a few times, even though he

wasn't there."

"I didn't say anything to worry Evelyn, did I?"

"Eldress Evelyn frets when one talks about the Heavenly Father," she said, laughing. "She thinks once you mention a man's name, you're going to run off and leave us. But you said nothing about finding him handsome or about love. You only talked about clues to Sister Sarah's possible murder."

My stomach still churned at the reference to her plight.

"You mentioned Edgar and how he messed up the kitchen. That worried the eldress more than Mr. Aldridge did. I hope you're over that nonsense about Edgar."

I said nothing.

"But your conversation with Sister Sarah was what took the cake. I was there. She was trying to feed you. You turned away from Sister Evelyn and began to speak to Sister Sarah like she was there with us all. I saw the eldress' face go white. I believe she realized right then the possibility we were going to lose you."

"She was there, you know."

"Sister Sarah?"

"Yes. I really did talk to her."

"Did she say you needed to get well and stay here?"

"No. She just smiled, held my hand, and sang softly to me. Her hand was warm and soft like it always was, and her bright hair glowed in the shaded light of the lamp. She was happy, Peg. I could tell she was happier than she'd been here."

"Did she talk about the night she was killed?"

"No. She never mentioned it at all. Neither of us did. I wish we'd discussed it so we could arrest her murderer."

"After a week," Peg continued, "I listened in on a meeting between Mr. Aldridge and Elder Thomas."

"He stayed away a week?"

"Good Lord, no. I've heard Mr. Aldridge was with Elder

Thomas every day. The two looked over the crime scene and poured over possibilities until late every evening. Even though I didn't hear him talk about you, I'm sure he did ask each day. But whenever members ambled through the hallway, they'd lower their voices to a whisper. Eldress Evelyn didn't speak of him either. She wasn't with them because, of course, she was helping me care for you."

"Why didn't she speak of Mr. Aldridge?"

"I believe it's because of their argument the night he brought you in from the pond. The night they found Sister Sarah. He made it clear he thought she was acting silly when she wouldn't let him touch you—that she was making a mistake placing the church rules over your health."

"I suppose I remember something about that, though it's hazy. His coat," I suddenly said. "He left without his coat."

"Don't worry. Elder Thomas returned it to him the next day. He offered to have them remove the blood and sew it up, but Mr. Aldridge refused their offer."

"Why was there blood?"

"You drew blood with your fingernails," she said. "You fought him off when you tried to get to Sister Sarah. He'll have a little scar under his eye, thanks to you. You also ripped his coat. I'm sure he's had someone sew it up for him by now."

Peg got up and poured us both tea. I glanced over at the chairs that had been pushed back from the bread table. I couldn't distinguish which one I sat in that night but had the urge to get up and touch one of them.

"As I was saying, Mr. Aldridge walked into Elder Thomas's office that night fit to be tied. I was in there and so was Eldress Evelyn. We'd been discussing your treatment and how to get your fever under control when Mr. Aldridge marched in. He slammed his hat on the table and demanded an update. Eldress Evelyn's face went white. She immediately stood and walked out, telling Elder Thomas she didn't want to leave you alone for very long. But I stayed."

"What have you heard, Mr. Aldridge?" Elder Thomas asked soothingly. "We were just talking about Sister Lucy's health."

"And there has been little improvement, am I right?"

"The doctor informed us she might go on like this for weeks. I'm not sure there's cause for more alarm—yet," Elder Thomas said softly.

"Perhaps she needs more reason to get better."

"Such as . . ."

"I believe she needs to know she must help me find Miss Bishop's killer. I'm supposed to be talking to Seth Deming because of that notation Miss Hammond found."

"But I was never able to get the hymnal to Mr. Aldridge. How did he know about Seth?"

"Evidently Eldress Evelyn found it among your things. She didn't want Mr. Aldridge to see it, but Elder Thomas knew Mr. Aldridge would need the information."

"Brother Seth moved to Niskeyuna a few days ago to become the ministry elder," Elder Thomas said. "Certainly you don't expect Sister Lucy to accompany you there."

"Mr. Deming trusts Miss Hammond. They were close when they were growing up here. I believe Miss Hammond could get him to open up about his relationship with the victim. In addition, I suppose looking forward to the trip might make her condition improve. Give her a reason to get well."

"Are you saying she's lost the will to live here, Mr. Aldridge?"

"Yes!" Mr. Aldridge said, pounding his fist on the table. "That's exactly what I'm saying. The complexity of your rules and regulations got in the way of everything she did. She needed to follow the mandates but somehow got tangled in them every time she tried to help me find Miss Bishop. If you want her to get well and be a productive member of this Community, she has to have a choice. Imprisoning members and trying to block what's happening outside

of this Community doesn't work. You know that. You're losing members because you're choking them."

"I suppose Sister Evelyn should be in on this discussion. I feel as though we're speaking about our practices behind her back," Elder Thomas said.

"We climbed the stairs. The two men stood on the landing. I went in to fetch Eldress Evelyn. She put a bowl of soup, your favorite soup, down on the sideboard and followed me out of the room."

"She won't eat. I fear she'll starve," Eldress Evelyn said, wiping her hands on an apron. "Perhaps we should call Doctor Hayworth again."

"Mr. Aldridge here suggests you tell Sister Lucy she's needed to accompany him to Albany to question Brother Seth," Elder Thomas said.

"I won't lie to her," the eldress said.

"I don't intend for you to tell her a lie, Miss Clark," Mr. Aldridge said firmly. "She's needed to investigate the murder of one of your indentures. I must have her healthy soon so we can talk to Mr. Deming."

"I'll never agree to that," she said. "I don't believe her presence is necessary. I'd never let a child loose in the wilds with a man your age."

"I'd hardly call her a child, Miss Clark. She's a talented detective who helped me capture a man much more dangerous to herself than me. I'm not sure you realize she was nearly violated by him when he surprised her in his room."

"Which occurred because you asked her to rummage around the room alone. I refuse to allow you to get your hands on one of my charges. Why don't we have all the single young men from town come in here and pick out who they want?"

"I put my hand on the eldress' arm and told her I didn't think this bickering was helping you."

"*Our sister's very ill and needs help,*" I said. "*I can't see why we should sacrifice her life because of our principles. She's been raised under our care, and I'm positive she'll remember what we've taught her. Of all the young women, Sister Lucy's the most indoctrinated. She always reminds the others how to act. That, and she's already experienced in dealing with the outside world. She's a trustee and very popular with the other members. Both Brother Eli and Brother Leonard have come daily to ask about her. The plant in her room came from Brother Benjamin. It's also very important to realize if we lose her to the outside, we're losing one woman. If she doesn't recover because we haven't tried everything possible, we'll lose male members, something we can't afford to do. I can vouch for that.*"

"Evelyn looked up at me and then at Mr. Aldridge," Peg said.

"*I apologize for insinuating you have other motives for being with Sister Lucy, Mr. Aldridge,*" Eldress Evelyn finally said. "*I'll try to tell her about the trip. We'd all better pray it works.*"

"With that, she walked back into the room and shut the door behind her. Hours later, I arrived with your dinner and watched her try to get you to eat once more. You pushed her away time and again. She finally put the food down and pulled your chin toward her."

"*Sister Lucy, you'll never get well if you don't eat. The doctor's concerned about your lack of appetite. He suggests you go to a hospital. Brother Thomas and I mentioned this to Mr. Aldridge this morning, and he's very upset. He tells me he hopes you're better because he must be off soon to arrest Elder Seth and knew you wished to be a part of the investigative team. He refuses to go to Niskeyuna to interview Elder Seth without you.*"

"I was shocked by the eldress' bold-faced lie but even more surprised by your reaction. For the first time, I saw a remarkable progress in your recovery. You looked straight at her and talked."

"*Seth isn't guilty of killing Sarah,*" you said softly. "*I didn't give Mr. Aldridge some evidence I found because I was afraid he'd think*

Seth was guilty."

"I noticed Eldress Evelyn didn't bridle at the fact you failed to use any titles."

"Then you have to eat and get well so you can help Mr. Aldridge with the investigation. You must go with Mr. Aldridge to Niskeyuna and make sure the interview's handled properly."

"Did I get better then?" I finally asked.

"Yes, but not right away. I handed Eldress Evelyn a dish of stew, and you actually took a bite, then two. You were able to get out of bed on your own in a few weeks."

Even though I was still weak, it was wonderful to feel better. But there remained much ahead I had to do. First of all, there was Sarah's funeral, which occurred as soon as the ground thawed enough to allow it. Then I had to get back to thinking about the case. I would need to speak with Mr. Aldridge about what he uncovered concerning the cause of death and why he thought Seth was guilty. He had to convince me Seth was somehow involved, because I felt he was definitely innocent. And then I thought about Ezekiel's bags of money, the ones he must have buried in Sarah's hiding place. Were they still where I had hidden them? What did all of these things mean? When would I get to share my discovery with Mr. Aldridge?

17. PRINCIPAL SUSPECT

As the train pulled up, I stood there beside Mr. Aldridge, trying to take everything in. But there was too much to absorb all at once. The sound of the whistle pierced the frosty late-spring air, and the tangle of men and women on the small platform leaned forward to be the first to spot the cloud of smoke and steam cloaking the engine. When the train finally came to a rest, Mr. Aldridge stepped up first, took my small bag from me, and then reached down to pull me up. He treated me as if I were a fragile doll. He did not need to. I found I had become much stronger in the last week. When we were seated, me by the window, the train jerked forward.

"How long does it take?" I asked.

"About an hour and a half if the tracks are clear. But they might stop along the way because the mountains are steep."

"Have you made this journey before?"

"Yes. This train travels all the way from Boston to the Hudson River. I have taken it to both ends."

I watched as we moved away from the station. We rounded a wide bend and chugged by newly ploughed fields. Before long the trees, their branches thick and tangled, began to cross in front of the view.

Mr. Aldridge was reading. I looked up at the luggage rack, and realizing that someone had left a magazine, stood up and pulled it down. Turning it over, I found *The American Journal of Science* and was disappointed. Afraid that Mr. Aldridge might

207

consider me mindless, I opened it anyway and began reading the story of a woman who had to be cut open to remove a tumor the size of my hand. The rhythm of the tracks soon made me think about that morning.

Evelyn had let me sleep while the others got up to go to work, but I had awakened with them, too wound-up to doze. With Evelyn's help, I donned my Sunday dress. Still concerned about my strength, she tied my hair back. Then we strolled downstairs to have a breakfast Peg had made especially for me.

"Aren't you excited, Sister Lucy?" Peg asked, spooning some oatmeal into my bowl. "Be sure and use some cream on that. You'll need it to stay warm."

"I'm both excited and worried. I want to help Seth but am not sure I can convince Mr. Aldridge Seth wasn't involved in Sarah's death."

"Elder Seth will have to convince Mr. Aldridge, Sister," said Evelyn. "You aren't responsible for him, nor is Elder Seth incapable of speaking about Sister Sarah."

"But—"

"I assume you didn't tell Elder Seth about the hymnal, since you tried to keep it from both Brother Thomas and me."

"I believe Mr. Aldridge told Seth. I'm not sure. Was Seth upset when he was told we were coming?"

"No one spoke with him directly, so we aren't sure. He and Brother Thomas have exchanged letters, but Seth wasn't there so we were unable to watch for a reaction. Remember, Sister, to call him by his title. It's a sign of respect you too often ignore."

The next thing I knew, we were outside. I could see my breath, but did not feel the frosty air at all. I carried my cloak over my arm.

Making me slip the cape around my shoulders, Evelyn placed my bag in the carriage Jeremiah had brought around. "You really must think to take care of yourself," she said. "I'll have to tell Mr. Aldridge your mind's always in the clouds and that you need to be treated like a child."

I turned to her. "Please don't," I said, trying to hide my agitation. "I'll stay warm. I promise."

She did not mention the matter again when Jeremiah pulled up in the wagon or when Mr. Aldridge approached with his bag and papers.

"Good morning, Miss Hammond, Miss Clark," he said, helping me up beside Jeremiah.

It was the first time I had been up front in the wagon. Then he slid in beside me just as Peg came running out with a package.

"This is something to eat on the train, Mr. Aldridge. Be sure Sister Lucy eats. And some hot tea along the way would be good for her strength."

"I'll make sure she gets something," he said as the carriage started rolling.

I waved to them, hoping they would go back inside out of the cold. Then I purposefully returned my thoughts to Seth and calmed down. I looked forward to seeing my friend again, wanting to make sure he was content in his new home.

"I saw you at the burial," Mr. Aldridge said, suddenly interrupting my meditation and thankfully saving me from the next article on hospital hygiene. "But I didn't get to speak with you."

I suddenly realized I was actually on the train and had not been paying enough attention. "I know. It was pretty difficult. I'm not sure I thought about the perpetrator at all at the time. I only thought of what it would be like to have Sarah back again."

"Ah. It was a good thing I was there to do the detecting then."

I smiled. "And was there anything odd about the funeral?" I

recalled the cold wind and the approach of clouds, swept by an April storm—not wanting her placed in the ground, still frosty and cold. I tried not to imagine what it would be like to lie there in the frozen earth, to awaken in the dark, airless box, but my mind kept wandering back to the site.

Calvin had dug the grave. I heard he complained the ground was still frozen and that it took much effort to dig that deep. But he persevered, knowing how important it was to get her coffin out of sight and realizing the whole Community needed to move on to planting and raising baby animals. They had not postponed it so I could attend the actual burial but had instead waited for the ground to thaw. That was perhaps ironic, since they had also cut through the ice to get her out of her first grave—the pond.

That ice-covered mass—it reminded me of the ice harvest that was supposed to happen that night. They had harvested some of the ice, but not much a week after discovering her body. No one had the heart to do it. Jeremiah mentioned traveling up to Willow Pond about a mile north of us and seeing if it could yield some of the precious ice. He suggested fixing the toboggan so it could be pulled back along the road. I am not sure if that was where they got enough ice to fill the barn or even if they succeeded in satisfying its gaping interior. When I was well enough to care about it, no one mentioned they still worried about finding ice for the summer.

"Did you notice anyone at the burial who shouldn't have been there?" I asked.

"There were a couple of men from town, an Albert Brewster and an Edward Avery. I guess they weren't really from town, but drifters who had been seen at Barnard's. I questioned them, and they acted funny."

"I wonder if they were the same men I saw at the shrine."

"You mean the men who dug a hole by the fountain? I

received your note several weeks ago and went there to investigate as you asked. I guess you mentioned the strangers in the note."

"Was anyone there?"

"No. But the tiles of the pool were misarranged and damaged. I reported that to Mr. Dixon. He explained animals looking for food probably foraged in that area. There was still a foot of snow on the ground, so I could look for nothing more at the time. A few weeks later, Mr. Dixon and I hiked up together. This time I found the money you said you'd buried. It seemed to be Mr. Parker's stash. There's been no verification, but the amount's about the same. Mr. Dixon found the shovel, and I finally believed your note telling me people had been up there."

"What did you do with Mr. Brewster and Mr. Avery?"

"I incarcerated them for a while in town and turned them over to the judge, but they couldn't be held any longer. There was no evidence against them."

"Did you find out if they knew Ezekiel?"

"No. They wouldn't talk about it. It's quite possible, however, that they were involved in the theft itself. There was only one gunman in the Springfield bank robbery, but they might have helped Mr. Parker escape the scene. It's just as likely Mr. Parker met them on the road and stopped to drink with them, inadvertently bragging about what he had pulled off. I'm not sure we'll ever know. If Mr. Parker has talked to officials at his jail, I haven't heard about it. He would've been the leader. You'd know that if you'd spoken to the other two. He was definitely wilier then they were and very capable of other crimes committed around your Community."

"What about Sarah's things? Did you find Sarah's jewelry?"

"Mr. Dixon located the old list that came with Miss Bishop when she arrived four years ago. There were pieces of jewelry and other items missing from the wagon when its contents were sold two years ago, but we never found anything. Mr. Dixon thought they were stolen by someone in the Community. Then he saw the few items around the spiritual pool that had been discarded. He now believes Sarah herself had been stealing from the wagon, and somehow Mr. Parker had seen her bury the jewelry. The brother probably pilfered her stash and sold items of any value. I'm not sure we'll ever know more."

I did not tell Mr. Aldridge Seth knew about the wagon, because I was not sure Seth was aware of the hiding place at the shrine. It was just another piece of evidence against Seth I would quietly ask Seth about when we were alone together.

The journey nearly half over, the train stopped and most of us disembarked to look at the next valley through the trees, the leaves now coming out, resplendent in the subtle colors that suffuse the branches just before the buds burst forth. A man gave us each a cup of tea, and Mr. Aldridge and I broke out Peg's feast of bread and cheese.

"This is quite a meal for you, Mr. Aldridge, isn't it? Does the hotel serve such tasty food?"

"I'm no longer living in the hotel, Miss Hammond. When I returned from Springfield, I had no place to stay, so Mr. and Mrs. Osborne took me in. I do chores for them in return for a bed and wonderful home-cooked meals. Can't you see how much weight I've put on?"

I laughed. "No, Mr. Aldridge, but you do look healthy. Don't you usually stay at the hotel?"

"I don't have the same employer now, Miss Hammond. Mr. and Mrs. Osborne hired me."

I was surprised. "You're no longer a detective? Then why are you still helping us find out what happened to Sarah?"

"Sit down on this rock, Miss Hammond. When I took Mr. Parker back to Springfield, my job was done. They assigned me to another case in Shrewsbury, but I told them I hadn't concluded my work here. When I explained that a sister at Hancock was missing, they understandably told me it wasn't their business. I could either go to Shrewsbury and keep my job or resign. I'd already promised everyone here I'd help find Miss Bishop, so I quit to finish this job. Since it's now a murder case, I'll have to see that through too."

"I'm glad you came back," I said. "I had the feeling you might not be able to do so."

He smiled. "I thought I might have been foolish for quitting my other position until that night. If I hadn't stopped you, you probably would've ended up in the pond too. That would have caused even greater tragedy for the Community. I'm glad I returned to help."

"How did you know about Sarah? Who told you to come?"

"I'd returned from Springfield a week earlier and ran into Mr. Osborne at Barnard's store soon afterward. Mr. Barnard told Mr. Osborne of my plight, and Mr. Osborne invited me to dinner, where he and his wife asked me to stay and help with the planting. I sent word to Mr. Dixon I was there if he found any clues to Miss Bishop's whereabouts. I'd begin the investigation again as soon as Mr. Osborne and I had finished mending a stone fence that had given way in numerous places during a heavy snowstorm in January. We'd just sat down to supper that evening when one of the young men from the Community came to the door with a message from Mr. Dixon that someone had seen something strange in the ice while skating that afternoon."

"I remember the party. I recall some commotion but wasn't sure it had to do with protecting a part of the ice that was weak or what. I was too busy to investigate further, and until now, hadn't even thought about it again."

"One of the children said he'd seen a face in the ice. At first the skaters thought it was just an anomaly. The teacher guessed the ice had formed over a rock or something that just looked like a face, but evidently he mentioned it to one of the brothers, and word got back to Mr. Dixon. He had some of the boys shovel the snow closer to the edge where the ice became darker. Jeremiah and some of the other men picked at the ice until they could feel some kind of cloth. That's when Mr. Dixon decided to send for me."

"They knew it was Sarah?"

"They suspected it was Miss Bishop," he said. "After examining the object of concern with one lantern, and being unable to make out much in the dark, we decided to string up more lanterns and cut around the body with the same equipment they usually use for the ice harvest. It took quite a while. I was descending the hill to make sure a wagon was being prepared to carry her to town when you came running up."

I looked down, embarrassed. "You thought I was being silly, I suppose."

"I thought you were concerned. When I saw you were barefoot, I picked you up. I'm sure Miss Clark would have died had she seen me do it."

I stood up and looked at his face. "And I gave you that scar."

"Yes. I suppose it shows."

"I'm sorry. I didn't mean to resist. I didn't even realize it was you," I said, continuing to stare at him. "Actually, it looks pretty good. It gives you character."

"I don't blame you. If I had to receive such a reward for my work, I'm glad it came from someone I care about."

That was when the whistle blew. We walked back to the train. This time I did not need any help up the steps. Peg's treats and the tea had renewed my strength.

"Tell me about the notation I discovered. The one from Sarah," I said.

"The one to Mr. Deming?" Mr. Aldridge asked after the train was moving again. "What do you want to know? I compared it to the handwriting on some of her assignments Jerome had kept. You were right. Miss Bishop probably wrote the new note."

"Do you think Seth murdered her?"

"I won't know that until we question him. Your elders and I agreed not to tell anyone else about the contents of that message, so he'll only learn what it says from us. Did you tell anyone else?"

"No. I guess I was afraid what the others would think of him."

"Then we'll see how he reacts to the news."

"But what do *you* think? Do you believe he might have been involved?"

"When it comes to passions, anyone could have killed Miss Bishop. But to tell you the truth, Miss Bishop's ties to Mr. Parker appear more intriguing."

"What do you mean?"

"You yourself saw Miss Bishop with Mr. Parker one night."

"She didn't want to be there."

"But you don't know what happened after you ran. Did she look unduly frightened before he pulled her away from the light of the campfire?"

I thought about it. "I'm not sure."

"And what about Mr. Parker knowing where her treasure was buried?"

"You said he could have observed her there on numerous occasions."

"Or he could have helped her steal and bury the items," Mr. Aldridge said, returning to his book.

"But I saw Seth do that too."

"What do you mean?" he asked, looking up. "You saw Mr. Deming steal from the wagon?"

"Yes. I mean Seth brought her a diary from the wagon once. I was surprised he'd do it because I thought it was stealing, but she laughed it off. Sarah told me no one would be interested in a diary. She also said she had other items retrieved from the wagon in addition to that, but that may have been later. I don't remember exactly," I said, my head hurting.

"Did she tell you Mr. Deming stole all of it?" he asked, seemingly lost in concentration.

I thought a minute. "I'm not sure. I don't think she mentioned anyone else, but maybe Sarah didn't say he did the *whole* job either. She told me she'd probably want it all, because she'd need it when she was free to leave."

Somehow telling the story made me feel better. Perhaps I had misconstrued what she was saying and thought she and Seth were together in this crime when she was not even talking about him specifically. Had she written the notation with the intention of making me jealous and just never shown it to me? Could Sarah have been that cruel? For the first time, I actually saw Seth as an innocent victim, too, and crossed my fingers.

We did not talk again until we boarded the ferry to cross the Hudson River to Albany. I had never been on a boat before and was a little apprehensive at first, but I settled down when I saw the city buildings on the other side. Mr. Aldridge took me out on the deck to watch but quickly made me go back inside out of the biting wind, and we again sat down to talk.

"Mr. Deming isn't totally above suspicion here. As you said, he *did* help her steal at least one item. And here in the notation, she's asking him to meet her again, implying she'd met him at night before."

My heart sank.

"But I have no evidence of a motive for his killing her other than her rejecting her, and she seems to have done the same to almost every other brother in your community."

"She often mentioned him," I confessed. "But I always thought she did it because she wanted to make me jealous."

"Were you jealous?"

"I don't think so. I was a child who sewed on his buttons. I only wanted her to leave him alone. He had a lot of promise."

"It sounds as if you care for him."

"I do care for him, but I don't dream of running off with him. He treated me like a younger sister," I said, thinking of my brother, Willie.

Sarah probably would have destroyed Willie, too.

"How could you go around with someone you thought was going to destroy your friends?"

I looked at him. "Because she was my friend, my sister. She was my sun and moon. How can I explain that to you and make you understand? Without her, I would've been dead inside. I'd continue to worship like everyone else, not knowing what living was."

"Thinking you were happy? Isn't happiness a state of mind? I mean, if you knew nothing about the outside world, wouldn't your upcoming decision be easier?"

"I suppose I might be content, but how long does contentment last? I wouldn't really be making a decision to stay, would I? Yes. How could it be a commitment if I didn't have something to compare the Community to?"

"Sounds like you aren't sure you want to stay with them."

"I now know committing to the Heavenly Father is a sacrifice that shouldn't be taken lightly. If I choose to stay, I'll have made the decision knowing full well what I'm committing to. Only then will the Heavenly Father and Holy Mother Wisdom realize how much I care for them," I said, looking at him. "I honestly don't know what I'll elect to do. But I have a period of time left before I have to make that decision."

Mr. Aldridge returned to his reading, and twenty minutes later, the whistle sounded. We were approaching the dock. My heart fluttered in anticipation. Everything that had happened so far was new and exciting. Hopefully our investigation would not undermine my confidence in Seth. If I was wrong about my favorite brother, who else could I have misjudged?

18. A SIMPLE GIFT

As the ship pulled slowly up to the dock, I saw Seth in the distance. He was standing on the pier, waiting for us. I could not make out his face but immediately recognized his tall figure and stance. He wore spectacles now, though I could not see them until we were closer, but his hair was still dark and short. It was the wide smile and gleam of straight teeth that were so familiar and unchanging.

"He's there. I saw him, Mr. Aldridge," I said, almost giddy. "Is this Albany? How close is Niskeyuna?"

"Not far," Mr. Aldridge said, smiling. "I'll ask him if he can show us the main street of town before we head out."

Seth evidently had seen me, too, because he took my bag from Mr. Aldridge and gave me a big bear hug as we stepped onto the pier. The two men walked faster than I did because I had to study all the brand new images around me.

"Do you need anything, Sister Lucy?" Seth asked, spinning around to urge me to walk faster. "Did you get something to eat?"

"Yes, I'm fine," I said.

Mr. Aldridge helped me up onto the front of the wagon.

We did indeed take a trip through downtown Albany before heading off into the country. I was amazed at how many buildings there were compared to the little towns around Hancock.

219

"Do you send trustees out to do business here or do you go yourself?"

"Our Community isn't as big as yours, so I sometimes do the business myself. Most of the time, however, we have enough trustees. How are sales at Hancock?"

"I suppose the efforts are going smoothly. I was sick for some time and wasn't allowed to ask about my work. I can't wait to get back to it. Even though Eli and Leonard were advised not to say anything negative, I know they must need me."

"I heard you were very ill. I hope we don't make you work too hard here. You must relax. This should be a holiday for you."

"I'll sit back and let you and Mr. Aldridge talk first. If Mr. Aldridge gets something wrong, I'll interrupt."

"You make him sound like your deputy, Sister Lucy. I'm not sure Mr. Aldridge will agree to that."

"Miss Hammond's a first-rate detective. She can take over whenever she likes, Mr. Deming."

Niskeyuna was indeed smaller than Hancock. The dwellings were similar to my dwelling, but the view offered no modern brick ones.

"Eldress Evelyn made me promise not to keep you here more than a day or two," Seth said. "We have a few hours before dinner. My counterpart, Sister Miriam, will be happy to show you to your bed so you can stow your bag. You'll be sharing with three other members, but they'll probably be out working this afternoon. I can show you, Mr. Aldridge, to a private room off the men's hallway. Do you feel like talking before dinner? If so, we can all meet in my office when you're ready."

Miriam was younger than I expected, though I believe not so young as Seth. Her shiny auburn hair was swept back into a bun, and a million tiny freckles dusted her nose and cheeks.

"Did I hear Elder Seth mention you're a trustee?" she asked. "Such a lofty position for one so young."

I smiled. "We were short of members, and they needed someone to learn the job. You seem young for a ministry elder."

"Sometimes I feel I am. I don't know how the lead ministry chooses us."

"Aren't Father Elizur and Mother Hanna here?"

"No. They live at the New Lebanon Community. Brother Seth and I meet with them occasionally, but they're often on the road visiting the other Communities. I don't think they're at New Lebanon now," Miriam said, showing me to a dressing table so I could rinse the soot from the train off of my face. "Dry yourself off and follow me downstairs to Brother Seth's office. We're living in the dwelling until the offices are renovated at a new ministry building." She hesitated. "Are you sure you're strong enough? Brother Seth mentioned you'd been ill."

"I'm fine but anxious for the interviews to be concluded so I can see more of the Community here."

"I hope the interviews are over soon, too. I wanted to show you something tomorrow after breakfast. On Sunday, I believe you'll want to stay and see how Brother Seth conducts the meeting before you must catch the ferry home. Hopefully you won't run out of energy. Brother Seth wants me to make sure you aren't overtaxed."

Seth's office wasn't as small as Thomas's or Evelyn's but certainly messier.

"You'll have to excuse me while I move these papers onto the other table, Sister Lucy. Sister Miriam and I are trying to make sure Mother Ann's rules are transcribed into a book that can be sent to all the Communities. The different ministries keep changing our goals. Oftentimes, I believe, they're venturing too far from what Mother Ann envisioned for us."

"You mean like our having to become vegetarians when I first came to Hancock?"

"Yes and even the scheme to build shrines. Who knows who comes up with these ideas? I guess the elders suppose we always need something new to stimulate our faith or we'll all get bored and leave. I don't believe that. Maybe if Mother Ann's sayings were written down in a prayer book, we could search back to what she did when there were apostasies among her own believers."

"That looks like quite a feat, Mr. Deming."

"Yes, Mr. Aldridge. It'll probably take years and years. But I have the time. Now, please sit down. I'll get Sister Miriam to find us some tea before she joins us. You don't mind if she attends, do you Mr. Aldridge?"

"Not at all," he said.

Seth strolled to the door to summon help.

"Maybe you can begin by telling us how well you knew Miss Bishop," Mr. Aldridge said when we were settled again.

"I knew Sister Sarah when she was indentured to the Community nearly four and a half years ago. She was friendly and asked for all types of favors from the brothers."

"Nothing from the sisters?"

"I suppose she did, but I don't know much about the interactions between sisters. I was more aware of what happened with the boys and young men because I worked with them, and they often talked about the sisters—though that is frowned upon for obvious reasons."

"What favors did she ask of you specifically?" Mr. Aldridge asked.

"She asked me to raid the wagon that carried her bequest to the Community. There were a few items in the wagon that would be of little value when sold. I believe I once retrieved a doll for her and a diary. I felt guilty about the doll, which might have

222

fetched a few dollars, but not the diary."

"That was all? Did any of the other brothers mention looting the wagon?"

"Maybe it came up. I don't really remember. Most of the talk was of a more vulgar nature than salvaging items from a wagon," Seth said, eyeing me as if to ask me to take a walk.

I was not about to leave and must have looked determined. Mr. Aldridge saved him. He left the questions about nightly visits for later.

"What else did you do for Miss Bishop?" he asked Seth.

"I helped her with homework on occasion. She'd borrow my assignments and copy them, I believe. I'm not proud of what I did, Mr. Aldridge. I didn't do her work to gain any special favor. It was more my inability to turn her down. She had a way of asking that made her seem so helpless. It was difficult for me, and probably for most of the other young men, to come up with a reason *not* to help her."

"So when she asked you to come out with her at night, you couldn't refuse," Mr. Aldridge said.

Miriam interrupted, pouring some tea for each of us before sitting down. She had also brought some buns to go with the tea. I was glad, because I was beginning to get hungry.

"I'd probably have gone out at night had I been asked, Mr. Aldridge. As I wasn't, it's a relief to tell you I never did."

"I have a message here in Miss Bishop's handwriting, asking you to meet her."

Seth watched as Mr. Aldridge opened the hymnal. "Sister Camilla's booklet," he said. "I thought Sister Sarah had disposed of it. I know the brothers would like this back. Where did you find it? You know I always wondered why she'd never invited me."

"She didn't ask you because she knew I would've killed her," I said, interrupting him.

Mr. Aldridge ignored my outburst. "Why would you wonder? You must have heard others mention meeting her after dark."

Seth seemed uncomfortable. "Yes. It was sort of the talk of the shops. Some of the other brothers boasted about it. Their tales often seemed exaggerated, so I didn't think there was cause for concern."

"What about Ezekiel?" I asked.

"What do you mean, Sister?"

"Did Ezekiel brag about going out at night?"

"Ezekiel didn't work in the shops. He remained on the road. I never heard him say anything."

"Did Miss Bishop ever ask you to do anything more than pilfer small items from the wagon?" Mr. Aldridge asked.

"No. Nor did I hear that any of the brothers were asked. If they'd done anything for her, though, they probably wouldn't have said anything."

Mr. Aldridge finally handed the hymnal to Seth, and Seth smiled after he read it. "At least I'm normal," he said. "That said, these nocturnal meetings are probably what led to her murder. I haven't heard of such a thing happening any other time in the Community."

"A murder?"

"No. Murder is rare, but there have been one or two of those. It wasn't usual for any of us to be out at night. We always worked hard and were very tired. It's beyond my imagination that some of the things the brothers said they did were actually true."

"I went out with her, Seth," I said. "And Elizabeth did, too. Sarah didn't seem interested in the boys. I mean, she admitted meeting them or running into them on occasion, but never really acted like she wanted to when she was with me. It was Elizabeth who wanted to meet with them."

"Oh? Did you meet any boys out at night, Sister Lucy?"

"No. I mean yes, sort of. Sarah and Elizabeth ran into Ezekiel when I was with them. He was camping in the woods. I hid behind a branch because I thought the campfire belonged to . . ."

"To whom?" Mr. Aldridge asked, seemingly fascinated.

"Edgar?" Seth asked. "But when you saw it was only Brother Ezekiel, why didn't you join him too?"

"I didn't trust him. Ezekiel could be mean. Elizabeth left when Sarah made it clear she wasn't planning to meet Damien. Then Ezekiel asked for me. That was when I ran. I wanted to stay because I thought Sarah was in danger, but I didn't. Luckily, Sarah showed up the next morning with nothing more than bruises."

"So you think Brother Ezekiel had something to do with Sister Sarah's death?" Seth asked.

"I don't know," Mr. Aldridge said. "If anyone had a motive, he did."

"What motive?"

"Evidently, Miss Bishop had a large stash of her family's items buried up at the shrine. Miss Hammond discovered thugs who seemed to know the vicinity of Miss Bishop's burial site. They tried to dig them up but couldn't locate the exact spot."

"What does this have to do with Brother Ezekiel?"

"There's no proof they're connected with Mr. Parker," Aldridge said. "But if he didn't tell them about his buried cash, how were they aware of the shrine without knowing where to dig? I questioned them and wasn't able to establish the association."

"Just that like them, Brother Ezekiel was a thief who liked items of value. I understand, Mr. Aldridge. I didn't know Brother Ezekiel well enough to make a comment about him."

"What about other possibilities?" Miriam suddenly asked. "Maybe you, Brother Seth, should write down all the names of the brothers who talked of meeting with Sister Sarah."

"But that doesn't mean they actually did, Sister. Boys often brag of events that never occur."

"But at least it'd show other possibilities," she said.

"There are numerous possibilities. That's the problem," Mr. Aldridge said. "There's a dearth of proof for any of them." He paused. "Who knew about the treasure buried at the shrine, Miss Hammond?"

"I did, though I couldn't tell you there was anything of value. Sarah didn't confide in me about that. I saw some clothes. Oh, and she mentioned jewelry, but I didn't see any, except the pin on the dress I recovered."

"That pin was worth nearly a hundred dollars, Miss Hammond," Mr. Aldridge said. "Perhaps that's why this is such a puzzle. Mr. Parker would have taken the pin along with the jewelry that disappeared. I believe he, of all people, would've known its value."

"Elizabeth saw the site. I don't know how many times Elizabeth went out with Sarah, but it must not have been that many, because she was as surprised as I was Sarah didn't meet with the brothers. Other than that, no one I knew was aware of the hiding place. Sarah didn't mention she'd shown the spot to any of the boys."

"Did you ever check that diary, Mr. Aldridge?" Seth asked.

"You mean the one discarded by Mr. Parker at the site? Yes. It wasn't her diary but a family member's—maybe her mother's. The handwriting didn't match that of anyone in the Community. I'm not sure it's the same one you recovered for her though."

By the time someone came around to ask us to join the others for dinner, I was relieved the conference was ending. It did not seem like we were getting anywhere with this questioning, and I was beginning to tire. After dinner, I went upstairs to splash water on my face and to lie down for only a few minutes.

I did not get up until morning when the sun shone directly through the window over my head.

The other beds were empty and made up just as I had found them the evening before. Miriam came in and asked me if I wanted to come down for breakfast and I accepted. Most of the others had already eaten, but a few people remained in the dining room.

"Don't you have an elders' dining room?" I asked.

"We used to, but Brother Seth felt he could influence the members better if we ate with them."

"What about the rule we don't speak during the meal?"

"We have that on Sundays, but not most days. Brother Seth doesn't think Mother Ann intended us to have that rule."

"And you don't question him?"

"Vigorously. I win on occasion too. He just shows me some of the passages from which we're creating the book of prayer. I believe he's correct here. We both feel the key to teaching Believer doctrine is to demonstrate Mother Ann's strengths, just as she did. We can't tell the rest of the family what to do if they never see us do it, can we?"

"Where are Seth and Mr. Aldridge now? Shouldn't we take part in the investigation?"

"I'm sure we don't need to be with them all the time. Brother Seth could see you trust Mr. Aldridge and has been more open with the detective than he was before. I'm not certain either of them wants you to hear about some of the sinful events that took place while Sister Sarah was in the Community. How could you face your brothers and sisters if you knew how they sometimes embarrassed themselves?"

"Do you believe Seth had anything to do with the sinful events?"

"No. And I don't believe Mr. Aldridge thinks so either. While they talk about the details, I thought you might like to take a ride with me. I have an errand to do this morning, and Brother Seth thought you'd enjoy seeing more of New York. Are you strong enough?"

"Yes. I'd love to accompany you. I don't think I want to hear what my brothers have done anyway. It'd be difficult to face them again."

Miriam took a couple of apples from the kitchen before we left. She thought it might be fun to sit beside the road in a meadow surrounded by wildflowers and knew of just the place. The sun was warm on our shoulders. We got down from the wagon and trudged through the long grasses and blooms to a spot atop a small hill. In the valley below, houses sparsely speckled vast fields of sprouting crops.

Miriam pointed out where she grew up, a dot near a small copse of oak trees. "My father owned that farm until I was sixteen. Then he and my mother and two brothers decided they'd move out west to start over. I heard from relatives they were killed by Indians in western Iowa."

"I don't know where my parents, brothers and sisters are," I said. "They went west too, but I've never heard from them again."

"There. Now I've frightened you. I should have realized the story of my parents' demise would."

"How could you know my past was similar to yours? I'm not sure I want to know of their deaths. That would be difficult."

"Well maybe we should move on. I have to deliver these pies to a family who has just welcomed a new baby into the world."

We proceeded on our journey, neither of us saying another word about our pasts. The warm sun made me lazy, but I felt better when the horses pulled us through an arbor or tangle of evergreen branches heavy with needles that filtered the light. As the wagon emerged from the thicket, I spotted the small farmhouse off to the right.

"You're turning the horses in here," I said. "Is this it? What a lovely farm."

"Yes. It looks like they're all home."

"Who's that man? Is he the owner and new father?"

"Yes, that's Mr. Hammond, William Hammond. Brother Seth thought you might want to meet him. He used to be a member when I was growing up but left the Community to marry a sister before he committed. His wife, Deborah, roomed with me."

"How strange you'd know someone with the same name as my brother. Willie had bright red hair, and his face and lips would turn pink when he worked out in the fields. This man doesn't have red hair."

"I believe he's wearing a straw hat to prevent having the sun in his face, Sister Lucy."

I did not make a move but watched. The man stood up to see who approached. He pulled a kerchief from his pocket and began to wave at Miriam.

"Get down and talk to him, Sister Lucy. I'll take the pies inside to Deborah."

I slowly stepped down from the cart. Suddenly feeling like a small child needing to hide behind the folds of my mother's skirt, I did not know what to say.

"Mighty hot," he said, nodding to me and removing his hat to wipe his forehead on his sleeve. Bright red hair lay flat against the top of his head. He bent down to pull some weeds out of his garden.

"Willie?" I mumbled.

He stood up again, his pink lips beginning to turn up into a smile. "Lucy," he said as I ran into his arms. He was unable to extricate himself from my grip for quite a while. Then he held me back and examined me. "My God, you're beautiful. You were so scrawny when we left you at Hancock. They must have fed you there as much as they did me," he laughed, rubbing his belly.

We spent the whole afternoon at the Hammond house. I played with his toddler and held the new baby.

"You know, Lucy, Willie's heard from Martha," Deborah said, busily chopping vegetables. "Has anyone else in the family contacted you?"

Martha was the younger of my two older sisters.

"No. Where is she?"

"She was at Tyringham until recently when she moved on to Sabbath Day Lake in Maine because there was an opening for a cook."

"Tyringham? But that's very close to Hancock. Why didn't someone tell me?"

Deborah bit her lip. "I don't know what the rules are at Hancock, but until this last year when Elder Seth came, we at Niskeyuna weren't allowed to contact family on the outside. I guess he waited too long to talk to you and Martha and then thought you'd probably moved on."

"Is Martha still in Maine?"

"Yes. She signed the covenant shortly after Willie and I decided to leave Niskeyuna. He was disappointed he couldn't travel there for the ceremony."

I still did not understand why Willie had been dropped off so close by. Of all of my brothers, it would be Willie with his strong arms and farming experience that would be most valuable to my father when they got to their new farm.

"Paul was supposed to come here, but remember, he was only six," Willie said. "He cried so much, they gave him back. We'd been staying in Albany with Mother's sister, Aunt Eloise, to get more supplies. They offered the elders Constance next, but the Community insisted they get a boy who'd eventually be able to help out in the fields. Seeing how miserable Paul looked, I talked Father into leaving me. There just wasn't enough money to feed us all. Where they went from here, I haven't heard."

"Did Martha hear from anyone?"

"No. Father still owes Aunt Eloise money, and she hasn't received a letter either. If you want to talk of Shaker settlements between here and Ohio, there have been many started, but few have carried on. Often surviving members were shuttled to other Communities, but none of those remain either. If Constance and Paul are still alive, they're probably living out west and aren't residing with other Believers."

I didn't want to think about that. It sounded so hopeless. Instead I concentrated on appreciating and enjoying what little family I had left. And that I did, promising to make the trip again as soon as I could get away. I figured as a trustee, I would eventually be able to gain more freedom. Then I would return and visit my niece and nephew.

I was exhausted when the wagon pulled up to Niskeyuna.

Mr. Aldridge saw my face and helped me down. "Perhaps we shouldn't have let you two go off for so long."

"Oh no," I said, tempted to find Seth and give him a big hug. "Miriam took me to see my brother and his family. Seth thought it was just too much of a coincidence another Hammond and former Believer lived around here. I have family," I said. "And I cried when I had to leave them again."

"We're boarding the ferry for home tomorrow," Mr. Aldridge said.

"What have you learned?"

"Quite a bit. Don't look so worried. I am not arresting Mr. Deming. I believe you were correct that he's innocent."

"Can we stay for the meeting?"

"Yes, if you're up to it."

"Miriam here can wake me up in time, I'm sure."

But then Mr. Aldridge surprised me. I'm not certain I hid my disappointment very well.

"I'll see you off at the station in Pittsfield. Someone from the Community is scheduled to pick us up so you'll certainly have a ride home. The train's headed to Springfield. I received a message that a judge has arrived in Springfield, and I have to be present for Mr. Parker's trial."

"But what about the investigation?"

"I'll return, Miss Hammond. You can count on that. I'll return as quickly as possible."

19. BETRAYAL

I was hardly back a week when the excitement of my return wore thin. It was not because I failed to do my jobs, made a mess in the kitchen, or sneaked out at night. But my offense became apparent when I was called to Evelyn's office one day. This time, I suspected nothing.

"Sister Elizabeth showed us something very troubling, Sister Lucy," she began, shaking her head. "I have no choice but to turn these items over to the authorities. You understand, don't you, Sister? I'm relieved Mr. Aldridge isn't here. He'd find it difficult to carry out the task of taking you to the jail in Pittsfield."

I froze, trying to understand what she was saying. Thomas walked in just as I pulled up a chair to catch myself before I landed on the floor. Evelyn took a kerchief out of her drawer and opened it, revealing two small pieces of jewelry, a ring and a pendant. I reached for the ring, but Thomas put out his hand to stop me.

"Sister Elizabeth found this jewelry in the baseboard next to your bed and brought the pieces to me immediately. She says she's seen them before. Sister Sarah told her they belonged to her mother."

"I've never seen them," I said, suspecting little would help save me from a trip to Pittsfield. "The only jewelry I found was a pin on a dress I discovered after Sarah's death."

"Where's that?" asked Thomas.

"Mr. Aldridge has it. I'd left it on top of Mount Sinai, and Mr. Aldridge retrieved it the night you and he went up there. Do you remember seeing it, Thomas? Mr. Aldridge said it was worth nearly one hundred dollars. If I'd wanted to steal from Sarah, I would've taken the pin."

"But perhaps you found these earlier, Sister Lucy, right after you killed Sister Sarah," the eldress said, looking directly into my eyes.

Without flinching, I said, "I couldn't have hidden these items, Evelyn. I haven't seen them and have no idea what they're worth." Then I pictured Elizabeth on her hands and knees, removing the items from the baseboard. "I didn't know there was a hiding place in the baseboard near my bed. Have you checked her story?"

Thomas and Evelyn both stood. "We can examine it now."

I followed them up the stairs. It was quiet. Most of the sisters were out at the shops. Lunch was not for another hour.

"Which bed's yours, Sister?" Evelyn asked.

I crossed to the window and crouched with them as the elder ran his hand along the rim. Pulling my bed out, Thomas continued until he got to the corner. Standing, both of us eyed the baseboard as it ran behind other beds.

Then he looked at me. "We'll have to call for Sister Elizabeth," he said. "Sister Lucy, I believe you should get back to work. This matter isn't over, but I assure you, we'll get to the bottom of it before the evening's out."

"Yes, sir," I said, walking quickly from the room. "Thank you, sir." I flew down the stairs, not wanting to be about when Elizabeth showed up.

I did not dare reflect on the problem until later that evening after dinner. I sat in the upstairs meeting room, trying to read. I was not alone. Two younger sisters sat together at the other end of the table, studying between giggles. All of a sudden, a shriek pushed up the boys' stairway just outside the door. It was long—like a moan only higher. I imagined it was Elizabeth, trying to explain where the jewels had been hidden.

Spring ran into summer and still no Mr. Aldridge. I suspected the trial he'd had to attend to would take a while, but not this long. Perhaps something else had taken him away. I jealously watched the other girls go to school while I sauntered to the trustees' house after breakfast each morning. I was too old to attend school now. I was supposed to be planning to commit to the Believer Community. In the meantime, I continued to have kitchen duty, and one Saturday, Peg wrangled me into helping clean the cupboards, something with which I was happy to oblige.

"You can start there at the top, Sister. I'm too old to get those higher ones, so I'm glad you volunteered."

I pulled over the stepladder Brother Gordon had kindly built for the kitchen and climbed up the four steps. "Are you keeping an inventory, Peg?"

"Yes, yes. Here's a sheet of paper. If anything up there looks suspect, please bring it down."

I finished that cupboard in half an hour and climbed down to heat up some water for tea.

"No time for that, Sister Lucy. Come in here. I'm trying to inventory one of the pantry cupboards and need some help."

I walked into the pantry and had her step aside. "You write. I'll check them, okay?"

The uppermost shelves contained items that were relatively new. I examined a couple of jars of apple butter preserved the previous fall. They were fine. There were some tins of sweets there too. Peg sometimes used them on cakes and cookies.

"Now I'll have to move those," Peg said, sighing. "Nobody's supposed to know where they are."

I smiled. "Just one to go with my tea, Peg?"

"Hand me the tin. I suppose we'll have to taste them to make sure they're fresh."

"What are these?" I asked when I bent down to look at the middle shelves.

"Those are medicines, things the doctors or nurses have given to us over the years to care for you sisters. I haven't thrown them out. From here down are the remedies I keep for times we don't need outside help. Nurse can provide us with more plasters if we get low. Those there are salts for baths on the third floor."

I began to remove the tinctures from the middle shelf and read them out to her. "What was this for?" I asked.

"That was for Sister Molly's cramps. Sister Molly moved to the other dwelling a few years ago now, but you never know when one of you will need it. Put it back. What's the next one?"

"This is ether," I said. "It doesn't look like there's much in it."

"Really? There was more the last time I checked. I guess it could have evaporated. Be sure the cap is tight."

"I read an article about this on the train."

"Hmm," Peg said, sounding preoccupied as she pulled the items off the bottom shelf.

"Yes. It was in a science journal. It said doctors are using ether as an anesthetic now. Just a few drops put patients to sleep so they don't feel pain when they're being cut open." I shivered and put it back.

"You shouldn't read stories like that, Sister. I hope it didn't have pictures in it. That kind of thing would give me night-mares."

"What did we use it for?"

"Let me see. A few years ago, Sister Elizabeth had that cold, remember? She was coughing up a storm. The ether seemed to calm the coughs so she could sleep."

"I remember. Sarah and I couldn't sleep because she was coughing so much. Sarah asked Evelyn to put her in another room. I didn't have the courage to say anything."

"She was very sick. We were worried it would turn into pneumonia, like you had. But the little tincture I made up for her did the trick. Once she could sleep without interruption, she got well quickly. I wish we had more of that. Remind me to ask the nurse for more."

The next day, I returned to the trustees' house to catch up on the accounts I had missed.

Eli entered to put a jar of fresh flowers on my desk. "Brother Leonard and I just want to show you how much we appreciate you, Sister Lucy," he said.

"That's very thoughtful, but I fear it means I have to do some extra work on the books. Did a fairy come in and mess up my cards?"

"It was an accident, Sister. You know how we had that summer shower yesterday? One of the brothers decided to clean up the floor before you came back and put some of your boxes outside the door. Alas, much of the ink on them has run. Someone will have to create new ones from the ledger."

"How many do you think?"

"Only thirty or forty."

"I guess I'll have to start that immediately. Do you have some blank sheets?"

"Aren't you going to inquire about the name of the culprit?" he asked.

"Not unless he has good handwriting and a head for numbers."

"I know it's been a while, but I don't think I ever asked how your trip went, Sister," Eli said.

Leonard entered with a handful of clean cards. "Yes, Sister, what did you find out?" Leonard asked.

"Mr. Aldridge didn't believe Seth was guilty of Sarah's murder. That was the main thing. He also gave me the names of two men who might have been involved in some of the bank robberies."

"Are they from around here?" Eli asked, his eyes wide open.

"I'm not sure where they're from, but they evidently visited the area quite often. Their names are . . ." I said, stopping to dip my pen into the ink. "Let me see, Mr. Aldridge mentioned an Albert Brewster." I looked up to see if there was a flicker of recognition in either set of eyes.

"Who was the other one?" Leonard asked, still scratching his head.

"It was Edward," I said, trying to think. "Edward Avery."

"I believe I know him," Eli said. "Isn't he Sister Elizabeth's brother?"

"Ed Avery, yes," Leonard agreed. "That's correct. He'd be about Brother Eli's height, rusty hair. He was kind of a bully, if I get my stories right."

"Elizabeth's last name is Wilcox. You must be teasing me."

"Wilcox is her father's name," Eli said. "You remember Ethan Wilcox, don't you, Sister Lucy? He moved to the Sabbath Day Lake settlement when Sister Elizabeth was seven or eight."

"She was eleven when I came here. I'd heard her father was a member, though."

"The mother's family name's Avery. Madeleine Avery's her mother. Not wanting to be a Believer herself, she left with the two boys before Brother Wilcox committed. Sister Elizabeth was really young when she left."

"And probably pretty upset her mother didn't take her along too," Leonard said.

"But the boys would still carry the name Wilcox, wouldn't they?"

"Not if the mother didn't want them to—if she somehow convinced them their father had tricked the family into joining," Leonard said.

"Anyway, Sister Lucy, we don't want to interrupt you anymore," Eli said, pulling on Leonard's sleeve. "You have too much work to do. It's just so interesting. What a coincidence Ed Avery might have helped Brother Ezekiel rob banks around here."

"Coincidence, yes," I said quietly.

I did not get much work done. My mind kept slipping back to Elizabeth's brother and how I could get word to Mr. Aldridge. Returning to the dwelling for lunch, I had wondered if I should not go back to the trustees' house that afternoon. There were a few things about the new information that intrigued me, and I wanted to find out more.

Elizabeth sat across from me at lunch. She did not say anything. Of course, we were not able to talk anyway. Our Community had not received a new directive from Seth or the lead ministry about silence during meals, so the reading of prayers and the singing of hymns during meals continued as before. I never realized how annoying they were.

But I do not think Elizabeth would have spoken to me anyway. For some reason, she must have decided I was no longer a friend. Perhaps her failure to have me jailed accounted for it. I tried to catch her eye a few times but did not succeed. After lunch, I watched her and some of the other sisters go upstairs to our room. I waited in the dining room until I saw them return and head for the girls' entrance that led down the path to the sewing shop. Then I ventured upstairs.

I had done it before. I'd investigated the items in Ezekiel's room, but now that I was up in the room alone, it felt strange to rummage through Elizabeth's things. I started with her cupboard, pulling out the drawers and slipping my hand under her clothing. I found her father's picture in one, but that was all. I then bent down to examine the bottom of the cabinet. In a box behind some books, I found a family Bible.

With great interest, I leafed through the first few pages. There on the third page the names of the family of Ethan Wilcox, who had married Madeleine Williams Avery in 1822, jumped out of me. Martin Williams Wilcox was christened in November of 1823 and Edward Jeffries Wilcox in early 1825. Elizabeth Avery Wilcox was born February 7, 1826, but there was no date for her christening. I wondered if Mr. Wilcox had trouble deciding on a new religion at that time, even though he waited until his daughter was three before he and his family chose to move into the Community. Had he forced his wife into joining? Had Madeleine Wilcox doubted the Believer faith even before entering?

I could not imagine the pain Mrs. Wilcox must have felt when her husband told her they would have to live apart. If that had happened to me, I would have died right there, thinking I did not please my husband. But then, that did not explain why Madeleine left her daughter. Was it because the young boys would better help her start a new life, while a young girl would be nothing more than a burden? That sort of thing must have been common, because it had also happened to me. Was Elizabeth as upset as I was when she lost her mother and brothers? Poor Elizabeth.

I did not return to the trustees' house at all that afternoon. Instead, as was my habit, I sat in the window seat, staring beyond the leafy oak and schoolhouse. Of course, I did not really see anything but tried to figure out what Mr. Aldridge would do if he were here. My stomach tightened at the thought of him. What if he never returned? Had he had an accident somewhere? I tried hard not to let the tears fall, but a few of them did, and I wiped them away with the back of my hand.

I wanted to search the records on members to see if I could find out anything more. I knew where they were kept. No one would stop me from entering now. I had seen the files in the chamber off the kitchen when I went to retrieve some boxes to transfer to the trustees' stockroom one afternoon. The files were stacked up in one corner and labeled by year and the first letter of the last name. I didn't investigate them further then, but could still see the dusty files in the back of my mind.

I did not want to go in there so close to dinnertime. If Peg did not notice, Elizabeth, who would have returned from the shop by now, certainly would. I decided to wait until later— until Elizabeth and the others were asleep.

Elizabeth was indeed back. She startled me as I rose from the window seat.

"What are you doing in here, Sister? I hope you worked today." She walked over to the cabinet and examined her things, including the box at the back of it. "How long have you been in here?"

"Just for a few minutes, Elizabeth. I was tired and thought I might rest before dinner." My stomach churned, and I was unsure I could eat anything.

"Well we'd better get to the dining room. Dinner's ready."

I followed her down the stairs, but did not sit near her. After the meal, I collected my book and went to the meeting room. I was unable to read. I listened to the whispers of some of the younger girls and the giggles of a couple of adolescent boys in the other corner. I should have been excited about the investigation, but was not. Instead, I felt cold. It was still the middle of summer so my gooseflesh was not caused by a brisk evening after the sun had set. The chill was the result of terror. Something told me I had to watch my back. Was Edgar about?

Would going down to the room beyond the kitchen lead me into more trouble than I could handle?

I changed into my nightgown, and someone blew out the chamber candle just after blackness filled the sky. I did not go to sleep, however. I lay there and listened to the frogs through the open window for at least a couple of hours before determining no one in the room was stirring. I donned my clothes, still modest about being discovered in my gown, even though Mr. Aldridge had already seen me dressed in it. My shoes under my arm, I tiptoed into the hallway and felt my way down the stairs.

At the bottom, I crept down the second flight to the kitchen and slipped into my shoes, something that I would not regret later. From the tinderbox on the wall near the mudroom door, I grabbed a candle and holder. Then I slowly opened the oven. By closing the oven each evening, we were assured of hot coals from which we could light candles in emergencies. Luckily, there were embers under the first layer of ash, and I was able to light mine. Then I slowly opened the creaky door to the large room beyond the kitchen. I did not let it shut, however, sliding an empty crate into the entry to keep it open. Once inside, I crept toward the near corner not fifteen feet from the door.

Passing the flame in front of the boxes, I read the labels in an attempt to find the year 1829. Elizabeth would have been three. The family may have entered the Community earlier, but this was a start. I tugged at the container I wanted but could not budge it. Setting the candle on the floor, I stepped over the other boxes blocking my way until I was right beside it. I pulled once more.

It was then I heard something. I froze, my heart racing. Was there a creak somewhere above me? What was up there? Was the noise coming from the staircase? I did not hear another sound but could not stop shaking. Then there was a bump behind me.

Again I froze. Was someone attempting to come in through the kitchen? I dared not look. But the scrape—I recognized that. The crate was being moved out of the doorway. I turned just in time to hear the door shut and feel a wind from the kitchen swoosh past my face and through my hair.

I did not see who had closed the door, but if I had forced my legs to step back over the boxes and make it to the doorway, I might have been able to observe the person exiting the kitchen. If I then ran to the stairs, I might have recognized the culprit trying to climb them. But that was not to be. I heard the distinctive click of the latch, dashing any hope of escape, even if I were able to clutch the doorknob.

I stood by the files and made no effort to move forward. Not only were my feet frozen to the floorboards, but I could see nothing at all. The wind that had whisked past my face had also put out my candle, making the vast windowless chamber pitch black.

20. Darkness

I don't know how long I stood there waiting for my eyes to adjust to the darkness. I heard no more noises and knew it would be hours before anyone rose. My best bet would be to sit and wait for help. But I did not. I was anxious to get out of there and discover who had locked the door. While many of the boxes stored in a chamber under our dwelling were dusty, most were not, and the area was otherwise spotless.

I knew if I could get out from among the boxes at my feet, there would be few obstacles to block the aisles between where I was and any of the doors. Grasping the lip of the top box, I lifted my foot to search for another patch of clear floor close by. Little by little, I made my way out until I could feel a wide area, most likely the main aisle down the center of the chamber.

I must not have stood far from the door to the kitchen, because the files rested along the same side. Fumbling around for a wall or shelf, I was able to determine where I was, and remembering there was a door to the outside under the boys' entrance, I began to creep, pretending I was on the first floor of the dwelling heading for Thomas's office. Just before the first floor transept leading to the elder's office, I hesitated. I would have to find another aisle that veered to the left, and eventually, the exit. The first passageway was narrower. I was not sure if it was the correct one. If not, I would just have to try each aisle until I found it.

Hanging onto shelves on both sides, I inched my way down

the corridor until I came to the wall. Dead end. I had to retrace my steps and do the same down the next.

At the end of the third aisle, I suddenly ran into something furry! Stifling a scream, I backed away, knocking items off the shelf. The animal followed, brushing my arms with its fur. My heart leapt. I did not know where to go to lose it. It clung to my shoulder and swung wildly one way and then another. At the entrance to that corridor, I stopped. There was no place to go to get rid of it, and I was forced to face my assailant. I tugged at the longish strands, tangled in the knot of my neckerchief. Instead of dropping it to the floor though, I held it up, gently feeling it with my other hand. The fur did not cover the whole creature. A few inches down, my hand came upon something hard and slightly rough. My eyes had adjusted well enough, allowing me to see the disgusting thing when I put it near my face. The hairless part hung sideways as I clung to the fur. I could just make out some dark spots—no, they were holes. I shifted the item so the holes were like a pair of eyes.

"*Oh my God,*" I said in a raspy whisper. "This is Edgar!"

I put the head to my nose and inhaled. Someone had created a mask out of some flour and salt concoction. Edgar was a façade. For the first time, I began to think about solving the mystery once more. Dropping the mask, I made my way back down the passage and found a large pair of trousers and a wool shirt. Both were stiff with dirt. Who had used them?

It was then I heard a click. The door must have been an aisle or two farther along my path. Someone was coming. I ran from my spot in order find my rescuer. The door opened just as I rounded the corner. I shaded my eyes but could not miss the figure in the doorway. He stood there, a black silhouette against the dark-gray field, moonlight twinkling under his arms and through his legs.

Suddenly, I realized the figure may not have been my savior.

245

More likely, it was one of the nighttime marauders I had seen before. Using the scant moonlight to glance around me, I intended to bolt, trying to make it back to the kitchen door. Of course, my analysis of the situation did not go beyond my realization that no one at the locked door would hear me, let alone save me. Instead, I looked up. Thomas's room was just above my head. I filled my lungs for the shrillest scream I could manage, but the ghost in the doorway stepped forward and cupped his hand over my mouth. I bit and chewed and kicked, but he held fast, dragging me out the door toward the road.

We were behind the schoolhouse when he finally threw me down. I wanted to spit, to remove the taste of his filthy hands.

"You keep that mouth shut, girl, and maybe we won't harm you."

"Which one are you?" I asked, more angry than frightened.

"I told you to keep it shut," he said. "I'm just going to tie your hands so you can't scratch me. Then we're going to take a little trip up the hill."

"Are you Brewster or Avery?" I asked.

He smiled, revealing a couple of gaps where there were no longer teeth, "You're the smarty they said you was."

Hoisting me up by the armpits, he shoved me forward—in the direction of the pond.

"What do you need me for?" I asked.

"You shut that mouth of yours, or I'll have to tie it shut," he said, pushing me harder.

I had to concentrate on keeping my feet because I am positive he would have kicked me had I fallen. I was relieved when he urged me past the pond and onto the trail to the shrine. Several times along the path, I contemplated veering off into the trees, but my curiosity about why I was being taken to the shrine got the better of me. Of course, that was foolish. I should have fled and made my way back to the dwelling. I was no longer afraid of Edgar or any outsider hiding out in the woods, because the one who held me now was an outsider. Could he even be Edgar? He certainly looked less sinister and nasty in person.

About a third of the way up the trail, he suddenly sat me down on a rock and took out a long band of cloth.

"You're lucky I don't tie your feet," he said.

"I won't run," I said. "I want to help you."

"I don't trust you, missy."

I stared at him in disbelief. Was he going to strangle me with the cloth right here? Would I never discover the truth about Sarah's murder? Would I never get to see Mr. Aldridge again?

But when the strip came down, he did not place it around my neck but over my mouth. I was relieved but terribly frustrated. With the cloth in place, I would be unable to ask questions or try to convince my assailant he had nothing to gain by hauling me along with him. More important, I would not be able to scream for help. Again we were up, making our way along the trail through the forest.

It seemed like an eternity before we pushed through the branches and saw the altar stone. Sitting atop it like Sarah had done so long ago, another man suddenly hopped off and approached us.

"Did she give you trouble, Albert?"

"Naw. She would if she could, though."

"Now, darling," the new man said in a sweet voice. "You're going to have to show us where you put that money."

I tried to move my head to indicate I needed the gag removed.

"No, no. You just walk over to the correct tile."

I looked at the pool, now dug up in several spots, including a hole where Sarah had hidden her family trinkets and from which I had plucked the cash. I moved my head from side to side.

The young man from the fountain finally pulled down the gag.

"You found it before," I said. "You've already dug in the spot."

He slapped me hard, so hard I nearly lost my footing. "I know the cash is here," he said, louder than before.

"C'mon Ed," Albert said. "She don't know anything. Let's just kill her and get it over with."

"She knows. Where did you put the cash?" he asked again.

I glared at him. "The detective has the cash. He dug it up himself in early spring."

"You liar," he said, winding up to hit me again.

All of a sudden he stopped. I listened to the crunch of drying grass. Someone was coming up the path.

A wide smile crossed Ed's face. "I hear you're scared to death of our friend," he said.

I turned to see Edgar saunter in. I did not cringe or shake. Growling, Edgar ran toward me.

"Take off that ridiculous costume, Elizabeth," I said.

Edgar stopped right in front of me. "Untie her," she said, her voice slightly muffled behind the mask.

"We were just having some fun, Lizzy," Albert said. "She was real scared when I mentioned what we planned to do with her."

"Ed, I told you not to bring him this time. He gives me chills," Elizabeth said, turning me around to untie the knots. "What did you tell them, Lucy?"

"I told them Mr. Aldridge had the cash."

"Just the cash? What about the rest of Sarah's things?"

"I only saw a pin on one of the dresses and the jewelry you told Evelyn I'd found."

"That wasn't Sarah's jewelry. Those were worthless baubles my mother left for me."

"Maybe Sarah took her things," I said.

"No. Sarah died here, remember?"

"She could have moved them before she was murdered."

"I doubt it. There wasn't time . . ."

"What do you mean?" I asked.

"Time between when she showed them to me and when she disappeared."

"But she could have taken time immediately after she disappeared," I said. "Someone could have murdered her later."

"I don't think so. Are you sure the detective didn't take Sarah's things? He could have, you know."

"If he did, he didn't tell me. What about Ezekiel? He obviously knew where her stuff was."

"Where could he have put it?" Elizabeth asked, pulling off her mask. "I suggest we go after your detective. Maybe I should send the boys to Springfield."

"Mr. Aldridge doesn't have it. He would've told me if he did. Ezekiel used Sarah's burrow for his cash. There was nothing else in there when I came up here before they found her body. Ezekiel must have taken out the jewelry when he discovered the spot. Who showed him?"

"Don't just stand there. Try outside the pool," Elizabeth said to the men. "We have only an hour or two before the others get up."

"Why are you doing this, Elizabeth?" I asked.

The two men pushed branches aside and started to dig by the tree line.

Elizabeth smiled. "You were always a goody-goody, Lucy. You never got into trouble because Evelyn liked you so much."

My brows must have shot up at that one. I felt I was always in trouble. "Surely you don't think Evelyn likes me. She always reprimands me for this or that."

We both sat down on the trunk of a tree that had come down the winter before.

"Sarah thought you were too naive, you know," Elizabeth said, removing the costume and tugging at her skirt. "She figured out you believed everything the elders told you."

"She didn't think that. We were friends."

"You should have heard the complaints. She'd talk about you in the sewing shop, and we'd all get a big laugh out of it."

"What did she say?"

"Just that you were always so serious. She'd imitate you in that overly sweet voice of yours as you begged Evelyn for forgiveness."

"Evelyn liked Sarah."

Elizabeth snorted. "Evelyn didn't trust Sarah. The eldress would try to be fair, but she knew Sarah wasn't interested in becoming a Believer—would never commit. You always said you were going to sign the covenant, though. You weren't serious, but Evelyn believed you. That's why you got the trustee job. Sarah wanted that job so badly, but they gave it to you because they liked you so much."

"What does this do for you?" I asked, turning to look at her directly.

"What?"

"Trying to destroy Sarah's relationship with me. I don't believe you, and Sarah isn't here to back you up. What can you possibly gain?"

"The truth."

"Oh yes. If Evelyn liked me so much, why didn't she like you equally? You were always going to commit. You worked hard to achieve that, and now you're a full member."

"I guess it won't hurt to tell you, but there was a reason I was the elder sister for so long, even after I signed the covenant."

I let her first comment pass without questioning the inference. Why would it not hurt to tell me now? "Because they thought you liked children?" I asked.

Elizabeth laughed, "No. Nobody wants the job of elder brother or sister. Most only have to do it a year or two. I'm still there. Evelyn makes me do it."

"Why?" I asked, placing my hand on her shoulder.

She shrugged it away. "Because of my mother. She wanted to join the group too, but Evelyn said right off she wasn't devout enough. Normally, my brothers and I would've continued to live with her until we were six. The elders feel a parent is better equipped to teach the child about doctrine. There are houses for families that want to join. The children stay with their mother or father if they have one. The elders prefer that. But Evelyn took us away from her."

"Your mother got the boys back when she left. What happened with you?"

"She got the boys back because she stole them first. When Evelyn discovered what she was doing, she hid me in the dwelling."

"Why didn't you leave when you got the opportunity?"

"My mother never came back for me. She couldn't. Evelyn made up some story about her being an unfit mother, and the court wouldn't allow it. My mother was afraid if she came back for me, the court would side with my father and the Community. She'd lose the boys again."

I felt so sad for Elizabeth I nearly forgot to keep my guard up. "I'm sorry, Elizabeth. If I'd known . . ."

"You would've done what? Been nicer? Confided in me about your fear of Edgar? I knew about it, yes," Elizabeth said. "Ezekiel told us about the night he tried to scare you in the kitchen. It was hilarious. The elders didn't talk about it, but Ezekiel loved to tell that story. You came downstairs when he was playing a trick on Peg. He said you just stood there, out of your mind with fright. You really believed it. You really thought he was Edgar."

"But he damaged the kitchen. Poor Peg had to clean it up."

"It only needed a little cleaning. You're always so dramatic, Lucy."

I thought about her being in bed the night someone raided the kitchen. She did not seem to have been involved in Ezekiel's joke. "When did you find out?"

"He bragged about it. He showed me what you did after Sarah disappeared," she said. "You were funny, Lucy. You really were."

Panting, Albert approached us. "It ain't here, Lizzy. We're never going to figure out where it is."

"I'll have to see if Aldridge has them then," Elizabeth said, pushing herself up. "We'll just have to find him and teach him a lesson."

"I get to do that, Lizzy," Albert said. "Let me get him with my shovel."

Elizabeth took my arm and pulled me toward the trail, "Come on, Lucy. I'm getting tired. Let's return to the dwelling so we can have breakfast."

"What about them?"

"They're working. They have to keep looking."

Hand in hand, we slowly descended the hill, both a mess. I did not pull away from her. I had decided to keep her talking so she did not have time to think about what she might have to do with me. But then I realized Elizabeth could not possibly allow me to go back to the dwelling. When I told everyone what she was up to, the elders would whisk her away to Pittsfield jail. I would have to distract her long enough to get within yelling distance or indeed run in that direction. Then I might be able to get away.

"I didn't know you needed the money, Elizabeth."

"You mean to tell me you wouldn't take it if you could have it? I don't believe that. Anyway, Sarah would've wanted me to share her fortune."

"Did you two go out that often?"

"Enough to see she had quite a stash."

"I thought you wanted to meet boys."

"When did I say that?" she asked, smiling.

"When you got angry with her because she hadn't planned to meet Damien the night you discovered Ezekiel's campsite."

"Ah, Damien. He's difficult to describe, pretending to be so pious and then skipping off when he has doubts. Ezekiel said he thought Damien was a woman—not able to make up his mind."

"Did you like him?" I asked. "Did Sarah make it hard for him to like you?"

"Sarah was like that. Did you notice? Who did you like? Seth?"

"I don't think Seth fell for her appeal."

"Neither did Damien. He just couldn't be a Believer when Sarah kept making him think about other things."

I wanted to ask Elizabeth if that was the reason she had set him up for Sarah's murder, but did not. She had not yet admitted to the murder, and I was too afraid of what she had in store for me. "Why did you keep the name Wilcox when your brothers chose Avery?"

"Because that was what I was signed up as."

"Would you change your name to your mother's if you left the Community?" I asked.

"Maybe. I'm not sure. I'm angry with my father. He moved away without so much as a good-bye. I kind of know what my mother must have felt when he decided to join this place."

"I thought you might have been closer to your father."

"I don't know what closer is. He worked hard to move up in the ranks and succeeded. That's all he really wanted."

"And your mother did more?" I asked.

"Not really. She was too scared to come get me. I think if she really wanted to see me grow up, she would've come."

"But your brother came. Didn't your mother ask him to?"

"I doubt she knows about this. He came to me after he overheard Ezekiel talk about a treasure trove buried at the Community. Edward didn't know the area like I do. He wanted me to help him find it."

"But you knew where it was."

"You didn't expect me to tell him everything, did you? He and Albert might come back when I wasn't there and steal everything. I had to make sure I would get it first. Then I would pay them what they deserved."

"That was smart," I said.

The forest thinned around us.

"I thought so too," she said. "Here's the pond. We need to wash up before we get there. Why not here?"

I looked down at the dwelling and beyond. A thin glowing streak lit the horizon, the stars fading into a slate sky. The dwelling windows were still black. I could hear the jangle of what I thought were restless cows, their udders full, and had the urge to run toward the barn. But I could not pick up my feet to run. I did not step near the edge of the water but stood back while Elizabeth pulled out a cloth and began to wipe her face and arms with it. Then she reached into her pocket and removed a small bottle, pouring liquid onto the cloth.

"This is good stuff for cleaning," she said. "Come here, and I'll give you some."

"What is it?" I asked, knowing full well what she must have had in that bottle.

I backed up and turned to run down the hill. She was up in a flash, grabbing my arm and pulling me back. Her hand came around from behind and plastered the fabric to my face, but I was strong, ripping the cloth from her. We struggled. Each time I was nearly free, she would turn me around so I was heading back up the hill. I tried to scream and yell, but the effort interrupted my concentration. I pulled away with all my might. The exertion and the fumes caused me to lose my balance. She let go. I plunged into the eerily deep pond without a lungful of oxygen and unable to determine the direction of the surface. The darkness cloaked me like a pen in ink. That is all I remember.

21. Rescued

I had no idea what had happened. But when I opened my eyes, I could see pink ribbons encroaching on the expanse of slate sky. The chill was sudden. The gooseflesh crawled up and down my arms. Then I heard the screams and cries not ten feet away from my head. It was Elizabeth, struggling to pull herself free of a man's grip.

I wiped my eyes and looked again. The man was wet, the sleeves of his shirt and his vest clinging to his body. Elizabeth struggled, swinging her arms until she hit him in the face, causing his hair to fly back and sending a shower of droplets in all directions.

"I can take her," said another man, approaching from below.

"No. I've got her, Dixon," Elizabeth's assailant said. "She'll need to be taken to town."

"Unhand her, Aldridge. I can't tolerate you, a male and outsider, touching any Believer that way."

"Sorry, Dixon, but I outrank you on this. Elizabeth Wilcox, I hereby arrest you for the murder of Sarah Bishop and the attempted murder of Lucy Hammond."

"What about you?" Elizabeth asked. "You have the jewelry. Did you tell that to the elders? Technically, the jewelry belongs to the Community, but you've pocketed it yourself."

"Are you sure?" Thomas asked. "Are you sure Sister Elizabeth murdered Sister Sarah?"

"Yes. I'm sure. I'll explain the story when we're finished

here," he said, tying Elizabeth's wrists. "Her accomplices must be up the hill. I guess we can go after them later. This young lady's the mastermind."

Mr. Aldridge handed Elizabeth to Thomas and swung around to check on me, still lying flat on my back beside the pond. "Are you all right, Lucy?" he asked, kneeling down to help me sit up. "You had quite a bit of water in your lungs and stomach. You might still be sore, but at least we got the pond water out." He looked up. "Give me your coat, Dixon. She's cold. Someone's going to have to get her some help so she doesn't get sick again."

I managed to stand, confident I wouldn't let him carry me. "You're cold, too, Mr. Aldridge. Where's *your* coat?" I asked, my voice still raspy.

"Just down the hill a bit. I saw what happened and stripped it off before I raced up. Let me help you down."

"I'm fine," I said, pushing him away.

Later, I would regret that gesture. He had saved my life, and I failed to acknowledge it. Stubbornly, I insisted on making it back to the dwelling on my own. He continued to walk with me until we got to the kitchen door, where the others came to my aid.

"Oh my, Sister," said Peg, taking my arm. "You must go to your room right now and get out of those clothes."

"What's happened?" asked Evelyn, still in her nightwear. "How did you get so wet, Sister Lucy?"

I just stared at her, unable to say a word. Thomas came in behind me and walked Evelyn toward the stairs. Mr. Aldridge was no longer with him. I looked back and waited for the detective to follow him in, but Peg pulled me toward the stairway too, asking one of the girls to heat lots of water for tea.

I did not see Mr. Aldridge or Elizabeth again that evening, and when I inquired regarding their whereabouts the next day, I was told Mr. Aldridge had taken Elizabeth into town. I asked when he would return. No one seemed to know. I did not believe that, of course, but how was I going to implore them to give me the information without appearing to be overly interested?

I went back up to my bed where I remained for the next few days, questioning why I had failed to thank him or say good-bye. How could I live with myself, knowing I had been so ungrateful for all he had done for me? Why had the Heavenly Father brought him back to save me only to take him away again so quickly?

On the fourth day of my self-imposed exile, Peg came up and sat down on the edge of my bed. "You aren't going to miss any more of my meals, Sister Lucy, unless you can prove you're sick. Some kind of spiritual disease won't work. The body needs nourishment, and you're getting impossibly skinny."

"I'm not sure I want to get up, Peg. I just feel so tired."

"Quit your dramatizing, Sister. You weren't close enough to Sister Elizabeth to give her the satisfaction of killing you too. And if you're mourning the loss of Mr. Aldridge, then you'd better get over it. If he had intentions, he'd be here making sure you've recovered and not out gallivanting around Pittsfield displaying his prize arrest."

I smiled. Peg had a way of making my worries seem ludicrous.

"Now you just get up and come down to dinner at once. When you've finished eating, Eldress Evelyn wants to talk to you about your commitment ceremony."

"I'd almost forgotten about that. I was so busy. I hope she didn't think I planned to avoid signing the covenant," I said, slipping my dress over my head. I tugged at my nightgown, letting it drop to my ankles.

"She's counting on your committing, though I'm not sure if it's because she feels we're short of hands or because she can't wait for you to move to another dwelling," Peg said, standing up. "I have to go supervise the girls before they burn down the kitchen. We'll expect you for dinner when the bell rings."

The date was set. I would commit in late October when the harvest was finished. There would be a big celebration with testimonials for both the end of the season and my signing.

"I've heard from someone who's planning to be here for the ceremony," Evelyn said.

"Oh? Who's coming?"

"You'll see."

Was she talking about Seth? I thought it was Seth, but it could have been someone else. I hoped it might be Mr. Aldridge, whose return I awaited.

Summer grew lethargic as the date approached. The grains were already golden blades bowing in the breezes, and the smell of rotting fruit hung in the hot air. Of course, brothers and sisters in the Community were not sluggish. They scoured the trees for fruit, and the sisters spent long hours over a hot stove so that as much as possible could be preserved for the coming winter. Others gathered to thresh the grains, pick the vegetables, and dry the herbs. There was no time to sit at the pond and splash our feet or plan picnics. Maybe the children did, but not us. There was too much to do.

It was at this time Eli suddenly surprised me as I walked through the shop. "Oh, Sister Lucy. Come with me. I have something to show you," he said, excitedly. He rushed toward me, but suddenly stopped and returned to the counter where he removed and carefully lay down his spectacles.

"You have spectacles," I said. "They look so good I didn't notice them."

"Hah! You noticed. They make me look old. It's one step closer to retirement. You'll see. The Elders will come in here, look at my spectacles, and announce I have to be replaced."

"Why would they do that? Who would they replace you with? There's no one old enough to train."

"They'll probably replace me with a sister."

We split up. He took one flight of stairs to the second floor, and I took the women's, not more than twenty feet away. At the top of the stairs, we continued our conversation.

"Don't you want me to become a trustee?" I asked. "Is there a problem?"

"Yes, a big one," he said, already winded. Then he turned to go up another flight.

On the third floor, we both stopped to catch our breath.

"Well?" I asked.

"Thomas called Leonard and me into his office several days ago. He said he wanted us to make you a trustee at the signing celebration."

"Oh," I said, realizing the news was unexpectedly positive.

"You know what that means, don't you?"

"No—yes. It means I'll be a full-fledged trustee." Realizing how stupid that sounded, I must have cringed. Why hadn't I thought about this day before? "I assumed they were going to suggest I replace Elizabeth, so making me a trustee sounds like a delightful alternative."

"Yes, well. Trustees don't live in the brick dwelling, so we had to find you a place here."

"Is that a problem?"

"It was a problem, but Brother Leonard offered to move in with me, so there's no real problem now."

"There are only two rooms?"

"Yes, but they were meant to hold two people each, I guess. And if we find another female trustee, you'll have company too. Follow me."

We walked down a short hallway and turned at the only door. I pushed it open.

"There are all types of boxes along the walls. Surely Leonard didn't live in here."

"Yes. Brother Leonard said he'll miss his boxes. Without them, the room's quite big. It has a closet over here, and the window overlooks the fields. Brother Leonard said you'd want that because, on occasion, he sees you staring out the window in your office."

I walked over to the opening and looked out over the empty field. I thought of Sarah and Seth and missed them immediately. "Yes," I said. "It's wonderful. I can't wait to move in. Where do we dine?"

"In the brick dwelling, but the wood stove in the corner is good for brewing tea. I'm sure we can get a cabinet for your things, too. Brother Thomas will just have to relinquish one."

"I'm honored. You and Leonard are so thoughtful, Eli. My signing's just weeks away, but I can't wait. Maybe if we get back to work, the time will go faster."

"I guess that's a good idea. I hope Brother Leonard's in the shop. If not, no one is," he said, spinning around and walking to the top of the stairs.

"Watch your step, Eli. I'm afraid you'll miss a tread without your spectacles."

"I can see perfectly without them," he said, grasping the banister tightly.

Not a week later, Leonard came looking for me on the third floor. I had escaped from my office and navigated the steps to freedom. I was sitting in my new room, contemplating which box would have to be moved next to make room for a bed.

"You're here again, Sister. I wish you wouldn't wander so far up. Brother Eli and I are too old to make it up here more than a few times a day."

"Leonard, you're just who I wanted to see. Could you please take this box here down to the closet on the second floor?"

"But it's such a big box and it's full of books. I'm not sure I can do it alone."

"Then why are you here? Surely you don't want to make the trip down with empty hands. That would be such a waste. And, you aren't alone. I'll help you, though we'll have to break a rule to accomplish it. Which stairs do you think we should take, the men's or the women's?"

"I didn't come up here to carry things down. I came up here because a gentleman has requested your presence downstairs."

"Tell Mr. Osborne I'm busy preparing for my big day. He'll understand."

"No, no. It's Mr. Aldridge. I don't think he'll leave without speaking with you."

My heart fluttered. I let out an audible gasp and looked at Leonard standing in the doorway.

"Either you just burped or this is the final test for what you're going to do next week."

"Don't be ridiculous, Leonard. I've made up my mind. I wish Harriet would refrain from slipping cucumbers into the sandwiches."

"But when we all eat the same thing, no one suffers alone."

I followed him down the stairs without worrying how I looked but regretted it as soon as I walked into the room. He was standing at a window with his back to me. Leonard cleared his throat, and he turned around.

"Mr. Aldridge, you've been gone a long time," I said.

"Miss Hammond, yes, and I bring news. I was about to walk over to Dixon's office but thought I might pick you up along the way. That is, unless you'd rather not know the fruits of our investigation."

"Just let me get my cape. It's getting cooler. Pretty soon, we'll be seeing snow."

I sat down next to Evelyn and across from Thomas. Mr. Aldridge addressed the three of us. I could feel his stare and did not dare look up.

"Let me see," he began. "Maybe we should go back before Sarah's note and her disappearance. I had to collect evidence for Miss Wilcox's trial and traveled to Hudson for the verification."

"You did that recently?" I asked.

"In the last few weeks, yes. The trial's next month, but I believe we have all we need to put her behind bars for a long time. Evidently, Rathburn complained to Miss Bishop he wasn't happy here and even informed her when he planned to leave."

"But he sneaked away," I said. "If he'd told someone, we would've known right away the note wasn't true. Why did he sneak away?"

"I believe Mr. Dixon here can answer that better. Didn't Rathburn owe money or something to the Community?"

"Brother Damien had promised gifts to the Community when he entered," Thomas said. "We probably wouldn't have followed up had he stayed, but evidently he worried he hadn't kept up his end of the bargain and didn't want to confront any lawyers that might prevent him from leaving."

"That point aside, he'd informed Miss Bishop he was going to leave, and Miss Bishop shared the information with Miss Wilcox, who didn't tell the elders," Mr. Aldridge said. "Instead, Miss Wilcox used it to cover her own crime."

"But that doesn't explain why Elizabeth killed Sarah," I said. "Did she want Sarah's jewelry?"

"Perhaps, but not enough to kill her friend. More likely, that night by the pond, Miss Bishop informed Miss Wilcox that

Rathburn had asked her, Miss Bishop, to go with him and that she planned to accept his invitation. We believe Miss Wilcox killed Miss Bishop in a fit of rage and jealousy."

"Had he invited Sarah to go with him?" Evelyn asked.

"Rathburn claims he didn't ask Miss Bishop directly. He says he teased her about coming with him but never planned to take her. In fact, he was packed and on the road before bedtime. When I asked some of the boys in his charge, none had seen him that night."

"So Sister Sarah's murder had nothing to do with the jewelry," Thomas said.

"I suppose Miss Wilcox kept it in the back of her mind she could access the jewelry if she needed it to make an escape. But, of course, she didn't need to. No one questioned Miss Bishop's disappearance."

"Then it gets complicated," I said. "How does Ezekiel tie into the whole thing?"

"Miss Wilcox didn't worry about the money. As long as you, Miss Hammond, were happy here, you wouldn't steal anything, because personal wealth is neither a virtue nor a necessity within the Community. But remember, no one really saw Miss Bishop's jewelry. Did you see it, Miss Hammond?"

"No, but Elizabeth did."

"She saw a trinket or two maybe, but it was Miss Bishop who claimed it was there. You found one of those trinkets on the dress. Miss Wilcox maintains she saw the brooch, a locket, and a gold wedding band. Miss Bishop was wearing the band on her finger when her body was discovered in the pond. I suspect she wore the locket too. It's probably at the bottom of the pond."

"Ezekiel didn't take them?" I asked.

"Parker didn't find them. He knew of the hiding place and stashed his bank notes in the hole. He looked through Miss Bishop's treasure as he pulled them out but was probably disappointed to find nothing of value, discarding them in the woods. He apparently missed the pin you found."

"So how does that tie to Elizabeth?"

"On one of his trips, Parker stopped at a hotel. That night in a tavern he ran into a couple of men he recognized. He boasted to them about robbing some banks and hiding the loot at Hancock. Avery and Brewster knew how big the Hancock Community was. Avery had lived here as a boy, though not for very long. He went directly to his sister, Miss Wilcox, and enlisted her help. She told them to go to the shrine."

"But she didn't reveal the exact spot," I said. "Elizabeth didn't trust her brother. They were looking for the treasure on their own, based on the description Elizabeth had given them."

"Avery and Brewster climbed the hill to dig up the bank money, but you'd already found it and shifted it to another spot. Following your instructions, I hiked to the shrine and removed the money myself so there was nothing left to be found up there."

"But Elizabeth didn't know that. She, her brother, and Albert planned to go up to the shrine," I said. "The two men were to meet her at the top. Albert found me instead, but I don't understand why he came into the storage room that night."

"Brewster informed me Miss Wilcox told them both to meet her at the dwelling. Of course, Avery wasn't there because he still thought he could find the treasure first and take the whole thing before his sister arrived."

"Who locked the door from the kitchen?"

"That was Miss Wilcox. She saw you go into the room because she followed you downstairs. When Miss Wilcox ran into Brewster outside, she must have changed her mind about going directly to the shrine and told him to get you and take you to the top of the hill, too. To hide her identity, she returned to the storage area and dressed in the costume Ezekiel had created. If there was a problem, you might be able to help them find the money."

"So when they couldn't find any money or jewelry, and I identified her because I'd discovered the costume, she took me down to the pond and tried to kill me the same way she did Sarah. And she nearly did. The ether took away my energy, even though I tore the cloth from her hand. All I remember is falling into the water and not knowing which way was up. How did you know I was there?"

"I saw the fight from the road. Osborne asked me to deliver some eggs, and I happened to be passing through to get to town. I got down from my wagon and ran up the hill, though not soon enough to keep you from losing your balance."

"I was at the pump getting water for washing up when I heard a wagon and saw Mr. Aldridge running up the hill," Thomas said. "I knew something must be up, so I followed him. When I got closer, I could see Mr. Aldridge was already in the water, diving down to find you. He came up two or three times for more air, but thankfully didn't give up. Fortunately, he knew how to get the water from your lungs. You'd already taken in quite a bit. I didn't even think to apprehend Sister Elizabeth. I guess she didn't run because she figured Mr. Aldridge wouldn't be able to save you."

"She told me you'd fallen in on your own," Mr. Aldridge said. "But I'd already witnessed what she'd done."

I suddenly changed the subject. "I don't understand why I'm not needed to testify against Elizabeth or her brothers. Tell us about the trial. When is it?"

"I'll have to go back for the trial. I don't believe they'll need you to attend, Miss Hammond. At least, I took the liberty to tell them it would be difficult for you to go there. I concluded it would upset you too much to hear more about Miss Bishop. I hope I didn't overstep my bounds. Please tell me if you want to go there and testify."

"No. I'm not sure I could bear to be a witness against Elizabeth. She's a friend and sister, even though I have trouble understanding her."

"She's still in the Pittsfield jail. The details aren't important."

Maybe he didn't want to expand on Elizabeth's plight because of me, but my imagination would take over anyway. There was more to think about, though it would take a long time for me to be able to ponder the big step I was about to take in just a few weeks. But, of course, I would have to. Having already turned eighteen, I was determined to sign the covenant and live up to the expectations of my family, whom I loved and appreciated immensely after all we had been through together.

22. Impossible Choices

On Sunday, there was to be an announcement I would commit to the Community the following week. I was excited and scared. It was a big step, but I thought about my new bedroom in the trustee's house and knew I was ready. Of course, Mr. Aldridge's return stirred my emotions a little, but I knew the Sunday pronouncement would drive away any doubts I might still possess.

The autumn day was crisp. A strong breeze blew the leaves from the woods in our direction, and I watched them flit over the fields like butterflies, whimsical yet determined. The sun was out, spreading white light all around, light that carried little warmth but made my mind think it was warm nonetheless. Because I still lived in the dwelling, I took the same path I had taken so many times on my way to meeting with Sarah and had the urge to waddle like Jerome. But now I walked alone and, for the first time, noticed the icy breeze, making me long for the warmth of the meetinghouse.

Mr. Aldridge was there and nodded when I entered through the women's door. I had not told him about the event that was to take place the following week and reminded myself to invite him to the festivities after the meeting.

About halfway through, Robert announced I was to commit to the Community the following week, and I looked up to see Mr. Aldridge's face. If he was surprised, he did not show it. After the final hymn, I made a point of meeting him as he stepped out of the men's door. I would walk him back to the dwelling and invite him then.

"Good morning, Mr. Aldridge," I said, shading my eyes. "I'm so happy you came to the meeting. Did you enjoy it?"

The bright sun was straight up in the clear blue sky. Brisk winds had cleared a path for the rays.

"Yes, Lucy. I always enjoy it. Mr. Tyler's an excellent speaker."

"I'd like to invite you to the festivities next week. As you must already know, next Sunday I plan to sign papers committing my life to the church. After the meeting, we'll all gather in the dwelling for a party."

"I'm sorry," he said, turning to face me. "I won't be here. The Commonwealth of Massachusetts is starting a state police force in Worcester. I've been told I'd make a perfect candidate. I really should get on with my life, Lucy."

I stood there stunned, unable to say a word.

"You understand Mr. and Mrs. Osborne didn't intend to hire me long term," he continued. "With winter coming and the fences already mended, I'm not needed." Suddenly he took off his hat as we continued to walk slowly toward the brick dwelling. "I was hoping . . . I had no idea you were planning to stay on, or I would've asked sooner. I was wondering if you'd like to accompany me there. I'll have an income, and soon, a place to live."

"Mr. Aldridge, I can't leave here just like that," I said, unable to take in what he might be offering me. "This is my home. These people are my family. They need me. What would Eli and Leonard do without me?"

"I understand," he said, replacing the hat.

"You aren't staying for breakfast?"

"No. I have to get my things together. I plan to catch the two o'clock train tomorrow. I have some packing to do and shall ask Osborne if we can swing around here on the way to the station to say good-bye to the others," he said, failing to look directly at me. "Let me just say it's been a pleasure knowing you, Lucy Hammond. You make a very good detective."

Then he turned to leave. I could not move. I stood and watched as his cart turned onto the road toward New Lebanon. It slowly disappeared, but I waited until the last speck of dust had settled before walking on to the dwelling.

"Really, Lucy. You must let me look at your Sunday dress," Molly said.

Both Molly and Charity had settled comfortably into their lives as committed Believers. Molly had become an excellent seamstress, and Charity was in training under Harriet to become a cook if either Harriet or Peg needed to step down.

"I want to make sure it's in perfect shape for next week," Molly continued. "What's making you so melancholy all of a sudden? I saw the work that's been done on your room in the trustees' house and it's wonderful. The colors the brothers used are so bright and fresh. Sister Georgia sewed the curtain panels. You're going to love them."

Ignoring her, I crossed the room to the bed Sarah and I once shared and stared out the window.

"Well, if you don't feel like trying it on now, I guess we can do it tomorrow. Maybe you need a nap. Why don't you come get me in the other dwelling when you feel up to it?" she said, finally leaving me alone.

The sun crossed over the dwelling and now shone directly through the window, the rays splashing across the beds on that side of the room. I continued to sit, hugging my knees to my chest when Peg suddenly walked in.

"Why aren't you downstairs, Sister? You still have kitchen duty until next weekend."

I quickly wiped my face on my sleeve before looking up.

"You need a handkerchief, and I happen to have one right here," she said, sitting down beside me. "What are you studying that's so important?"

"I'm watching the sun sink behind the shrine."

"Who are you thinking about then?"

I swiveled to look at her. I was dying to tell her what was bothering me, but was not sure what she would do.

"I hear Mr. Aldridge is leaving tomorrow. Is that the problem?"

I couldn't stop them. The tears gushed forward with the force of a burst dam. She just sat there, not looking at me. Peg waited for the longest time while I tried to control the tears.

I blew my nose into her handkerchief, and we both laughed. "He asked me to go with him."

"What did you tell him?"

"I told him no. This is my home, and you're my family. How could I leave when you all need me so much?"

"I'm glad you decided to stay, dear Sister, but I hope you won't be so sad when he's gone."

"I'll try," I said, smiling through tears, beginning to well up once more.

"Have you prayed to Holy Mother Wisdom about your doubts? She might ease the pain of Mr. Aldridge's loss," Peg said, pausing to take my hand. "Or she might help you decide what your future should be. If you're meant to be here, you'll know. It's prideful to think you're indispensable. We're chosen to take on the role of creating God's garden. Perhaps Holy Mother's chosen you for another role."

That reminded me of Georgia's comments a few years ago. I would seek her advice now, but she had recently begun to forget things and sometimes even failed to recognize us.

"Georgia once told me we couldn't all be good at sewing or there'd be too many dresses," I said, trying to smile. "Do you

271

think that applies to membership too?"

"Very definitely. You pray to Holy Mother Wisdom. She'll help you decide. Splash your face and join us downstairs. Busy hands will keep you from worrying."

After dinner and cleanup, I went to the trustees' house to catch up on some of the accounts. I tried hard to concentrate on the numbers, but nothing seemed to make sense. Was I nervous about signing the papers? Why was I not enjoying it as much as the rest of the group? About an hour later, both Leonard and Eli urged me toward the stairs.

"You must go up and see your room. Though I did nothing more than clean it up, it's beautiful," Leonard said. "You'll love the colors."

It was indeed gorgeous. They had stained the walls yellow to contrast the green strip of wooden pegs and blue cabinet. My bed was under the window, and I walked over to sit on it. "It's beautiful. I heard Georgia designed the curtains."

"Too frilly for me," said Eli. "But something tells me you may not be entirely happy. Aren't you excited? Is it too much of a commitment for you to contemplate?"

"Oh, Eli, how can you say that? I've been preparing for this for almost my whole life. It's just that . . ."

"What's wrong?" Leonard asked.

"It's just you two need me so much, and I'm so grateful. You're the brothers I left behind when I got here."

The two men looked at each other.

"But . . ." Eli asked.

"It's nothing. It's just Mr. Aldridge asked me to go to Worcester with him when he leaves tomorrow."

"That's a problem," Eli said. "Did you tell him you'd think about it?"

"No. I told him no. How could I leave when there's so much

to do? You two can't possibly run this place all by yourselves."

"We did before you came," Leonard said. "If you must go, we'll make things work. After all, it's only work. You must be content with the rest of your life."

"Sister Lucy," Eli said. "Please don't use us as an excuse. You have to listen to your heart. Do you want to go with Mr. Aldridge, or do you want to spend the rest of your life here? Please don't commit if you really don't want to."

"I wish to do that more than anything. But I didn't think Mr. Aldridge would leave either."

"You'll forget him soon enough, Sister," Leonard said. "If he's just a passing phase, his memory will fade."

"Don't do that to her, Brother," Eli said. "She hasn't forgotten her family, and it's been years. I don't want her to go through that again. Have you prayed to the Heavenly Father? I pray to him for guidance whenever I feel conflicted. He always answers me. When I committed twenty-seven years ago now, I knew this is what I wanted to do."

"And he was only a lowly cheese-maker then," Leonard said.

"And you kept the stables when you signed up, if I remember correctly, Brother Leonard," Eli said.

"I want to stay here. You're my family, and I don't want to be without one again," I said. "Now you two let me get some work done."

That night I dreamt that morning had already come.

I was standing with the others when Mr. Osborne guided his wagon to the front of the dwelling. Mr. Aldridge stepped down, and we surrounded him to thank him for all he had done for the Community. But I could not get to him through the throng, nor did he look for me. I pushed and pushed, but something or someone kept pulling me back. Then he climbed onto the wagon, and the two men took off down the road. When the crowd thinned, I started to run after the wagon, yelling I had changed my mind, but it was moving away faster and I could not keep up.

I roused sometime after midnight and felt the chill in the air. Still groggy, I looked toward the window, expecting to see Sarah still sleeping in her bed. I did not stop to think I was already in Sarah's bed and that there was only the window in that direction. I lay back down, still confused, and slipped into another restless dream.

This time, the Sunday I was to make my commitment began with a windy rainstorm. I had forgotten my cape and was drenched when I arrived at the meetinghouse. No one was there. There was no fire in the stove, and the wind rattled the windows. I sat and waited, but still nobody entered through either door. Finally Robert sauntered in, gliding to the center of the chamber and removing a sheet of paper from his pocket. It was all wrinkled and dirty, like the assignment I had handed to Jerome years ago. The ministry elder gestured for me to sit down in the women's section and began to read every transgression I had committed over the years I had lived with this family.

"Sister Lucy stands accused of several crimes against Mother Ann's guiding principles as written down in Father Joseph Meacham's set of basic laws put into practice in 1795. Her sins are grave, irreversible, and many have yet to be confessed to her elders."

"But I—"

"Her thoughts about brothers, even trying to meet them after hours, her incorrect relationship with a sister, and while taking a picnic, removing her clothes in public to frolic with that sister, are all here on the record. In addition, she's fantasized about the outside and a man belonging to the world's people, meeting him without witnesses and letting him touch her. The actions I've listed constitute her inability to follow directives necessary for order in this Community."

I dropped my head, knowing all he said was true.

"And finally, the most egregious of all, her disregard for our Millennial Laws that state: If any follower of Mother Ann is aware of

any transgression, she's morally obliged to reveal it to her elders. If she fails to do so, she'll share the transgressor's guilt. While Sister Lucy may presently admit to being conscious of such acts as sexual liaisons, thievery, and murder, she chose to confide with an outsider rather than report such heinous acts to her family."

I attempted to open my mouth to set him straight, but nothing came out. I forced myself to listen as he read off the punishments I had not endured when I committed such ugly deeds.

"Finally," he loudly affirmed, his voice reverberating from the rafters of the empty chamber, "Until she's served the sentences called for, Sister Lucy Hammond won't be allowed to show her devotion to Mother Ann, the Holy Mother Wisdom, or indeed, the Heavenly Father himself by swearing her adherence to the laws of this Hancock Community in the year of our Heavenly Father, 1848." Then he crumpled the paper, letting it drop to the floor, and walked back out the men's door.

I just sat there, not knowing what to do. Where was I to go? How could I dedicate my life to a family that did not really want me?

Morning came all too soon. I got up with the others and helped with breakfast. After the meal, I slipped out to the dairy shop.

"Aren't you on kitchen duty, Sister Lucy?" asked Agnes. "You shouldn't be out here this morning. They'll get mad you aren't doing your own work."

I ignored her and pulled a chair up to the ten-gallon churn. Not a half hour later, I heard a wagon turn off the road into the Community. I listened but continued to agitate the cream by forcing the crank around in a never-ending circle. I could hear brothers and sisters take off in the direction of the cart but did not move. Even Agnes left her place at the molds.

Fifteen minutes later, my arms tired from cranking, I finally got up and went to the door. I could see the crowd in the distance but could not make out Mr. Aldridge. If I waited long enough, he and Mr. Osborne would take the same drive back out to the road, and I would see him then.

I returned to sit at the churn. The tears started again. I tried to hold them back, but they filled my eyes until I could see nothing. If I saw him, though, if Mr. Osborne drove him back down the drive, my heart would burst. I could not bear the thought of losing both him and Sarah.

Suddenly, through the blur of tears, I became aware of a feather, a downy one most likely from a chicken roosting in the neighboring coop, which had blown off the window sill above my head. It floated gently from side to side, capricious and natural. Agitated, I blew it and swung at it, trying to control its course. Instead, I stirred the air around it. It zigzagged up and down and all around.

"You're as flighty as down in a pillow fight," Peg had once told me.

Surprisingly, I realized for the first time that just as the feather fell to the floor, we do not all take the same path to heaven. Perhaps Holy Mother was telling me to follow my own course.

Getting to my feet, I scampered to the door and began sprinting down the road in the direction of the gathering. I would have to pass through them to get to the dwelling, but I did not care who saw me, tears staining my cheeks. The roar of excitement that filled the air minutes earlier suddenly became silent. I did not look up but continued to run down the slope to the kitchen door.

Mr. Aldridge would later tell me what occurred after I had fled into the dwelling. "Your family tricked us into waiting for you, Lucy," he said, smiling.

"Mr. Aldridge," Peg said. "I think Sister Lucy would like to say good-bye to you one more time."

"I have to get Daniel to the train station," Osborne said. "He'll miss his train if we wait much longer."

"I assure you Sister Lucy told me she wanted to give you a gift, Mr. Aldridge," Peg said. *"I'm certain that's why she ran into the dwelling, spinning like a top."* She paused, squirming.

"Don't you have something for Mr. Aldridge, too?" Eli suddenly asked, stepping forward and holding onto the reins of the team. *"We don't want to send you away with nothing, Mr. Aldridge."*

One of the horses suddenly reared his head, slobbering all over Eli's new spectacles.

Jeremiah walked up to the pair and relieved Eli who now held his glasses, trying to rub them off on his shirt. "I'm sure she'll only be a minute," Jeremiah said.

Peg entered the kitchen and quickly wrapped up some sweet buns. "Sister Lucy," she called. "I believe they're leaving in just a minute. Isn't there something you want to tell Mr. Aldridge?"

Evelyn walked over and stood at the bottom of the stairs. She could probably hear my footsteps as I tumbled back down the last flight. "Did you get your cape? Don't forget your cape."

"I have it," I said, winded from struggling with my bag. I stopped when I saw her. "I didn't know how to tell you. I can't stay."

"I figured that out days ago, Sister. I would've been surprised if you had." She pulled me close and kissed my tear-stained cheek. "You're welcome to come and visit again—you and Mr. Aldridge."

I circled my arms around her, my cape and bag weighing us both down.

"You'll miss the ride if you don't hurry," she said, most likely embarrassed by my uncharacteristic display of affection.

Peg went outside ahead of me and crossed over to the wagon. I watched her from the window in the mudroom. Mr. Osborne had managed to turn the horses around, despite Jeremiah's attempts to distract them.

"These are for the train," she said. "You can't go all the way

277

to Worchester without a snack." She almost had to run alongside. The horses, eager to go, had started forward.

Then I was out the door, nearly catching my bag on the door latch. Mr. Aldridge put his hand on Mr. Osborne's arm and told him to stop. Tears rolling down my cheeks, I turned and hugged Evelyn once more, handing the bag to Jeremiah who threw it onto the back of the wagon.

"I'm sorry," I said, wiping my tears from her face.

Then I turned to hug Peg, who patiently listened to my sniveling directly in her ear. Eli and Leonard stood at the foot of the wagon, waiting to help me up. I almost could not bear saying good-bye to them. I hugged them both at once. Then I looked up at Mr. Aldridge, who smiled and put out his hand. I grabbed it, and Eli hoisted me up beside him.

I watched them, my family, as Mr. Osborne swung the team onto the road in the direction of Pittsfield. No one turned to go back to work. I waved once more, trying to memorize each face, each building, before I could no longer make them out. I scanned the hill in front of the pond one more time, thinking about Sarah and what she might make of my decision. Then I looked forward, feeling Mr. Aldridge's arm around my waist and content with my resolve to brave my new life among the world's people.

ABOUT THE AUTHOR

Coralie Hughes Jensen has been fascinated since childhood by different cultures when her family explored their forebears as religious pioneers in the Pacific Northwest and Alaska. She saw firsthand how spiritual beliefs affect these cultures. Often traveling to far corners of the earth, she researches her stories by living with the residents and visiting their churches. While Coralie did not have to drive far for *Winter Harvest,* she did have to travel back in time. The author of three other books about life and spirituality, Coralie finally writes about something closer to home. A native of California, she, her husband and golden retriever live in Massachusetts.